Nowhere Near the Sea of Cortez

Nowhere Near the Sea of Cortez

Copyright © 2001 by Jim Harris

Willowgate Press
P. O. Box 6529
Holliston, MA 01746
http://www.willowgatepress.com

Printed in the United States of America

Cover design by *Desktop Miracles*

This is a work of fiction. Any resemblance to any person, living or dead, is strictly coincidental.

All rights reserved, including the right to reproduce this book, or portions thereof, in any form, without written permission except in the case of brief quotations embodied in critical articles or reviews.

ISBN: 1-930008-01-5

To

Brad Downs

In Memoriam

*My cousin, my friend, who died violently
During the writing of this novel, and
Regardless of his indiscretions,
Should have had more time
To make them up.*

Nowhere Near the Sea of Cortez

by

Jim Harris

Willowgate Press
Holliston, MA

Dorina pulled a handgun from her purse and shot a lawyer right between the eyes. He was running at her wearing only a stocking hat and an erection in the parking lot of a convenience store in Ormand Beach, Florida. Dorina had just gotten off work a little after eleven. She had opened her purse to take out the keys of her car. She took out her gun instead and fired and the Lawyer dropped like a rock. He was real close when she fired, his hands outstretched as if to grab her. Dorina walked around the body and back into the convenience store and had the guy inside call the police.

    They put Dorina in prison for what she did. The lawyer had friends in high places and they made it appear that it was Dorina's fault that the lawyer stripped naked and ran at her in that convenience store parking lot. She has been in prison for two years and will be getting out shortly. Dorina won an appeal of the original conviction of manslaughter. Her lawyer who made the appeal was Betsy Ann Brown. I read about it in the newspaper.

    I knew both Dorina and Betsy Ann Brown in the summer of 1969. I fell madly in love with Betsy that summer. I would never see her again. I grew up after that with Dorina and saw her one last time at my Grandfather's funeral back in 1975 and then haven't seen her since. It's so easy to lose track of people, it seems like.

    We all three, Dorina, Betsy, and I, grew up along the banks of the Wabash River in a little town called Darwin's Ferry. Wabash is a derivative of the Indian word for white. I always wanted to write a story about that summer of 1969 and had planned to work some apocalyptic irony into the fact that Wabash stood for white and Dorina was black and used to run around proudly proclaiming that, "My Daddy is as black as coal."

    But recently Dorina set me straight on this. On the telephone Dorina was ecstatic about my wanting to write a story about that summer of 1969. "You always said you wanted to be a writer," Dorina said on the phone. "But don't write about race," she said. "It won't sound *right."* But Dorina said it was all right to write about how she carried her dead baby brother around all summer long almost, trying to give it a decent burial. *"Why do you think nobody ever caught on about my carrying a dead baby around all summer?"* Dorina asked me. *"Stranger things have happened,"* I said. *"I suppose,"* Dorina said. Dorina even informed me that it was a green blanket that the dead baby was wrapped up in, not blue. Dorina says she laughs at the thought now. *"Poor Mama,"* she said. She also said it was more or less the truth when her Grandfather said, *"Nigger talk,"* Dorina blew up and slammed that dead baby into his face. *"I'd do it again,"* Dorina said on the phone.

  I got all choked up talking to Dorina on the phone. I had not talked to her in nearly fifteen years and she was in prison and we were talking about the summer of 1969. She said she was so glad I called because she had no idea where I was but that she loved me and thought of me all the time. I told her I thought of her all the time, too.

  She also told me her cellmate was a very nice woman who had killed three men. Dorina said her cellmate claims she killed two of the men in self-defense, but that she deliberately killed the third man. The man her cellmate killed so deliberately was her own father. "I killed him in the best way anybody can kill anyone," her cellmate told Dorina. I asked Dorina what that way was. "By ignoring him."

  "Don't ignore me anymore," Dorina told me on the phone. And I won't. I will be there when she gets out of prison December 14th, 1989. Dorina is in the Dwight Correctional Institution for Women in Dwight, Illinois. I will be there waiting for her.

  Dorina says when she gets out of prison the first thing she wants to see is the Wabash River and then she wants to sit on a front porch somewhere and talk about old times. She says she'll give Betsy a call and ask her to join us. "Great," I said.

  "You have that story ready, Jacob."

  "Okay," I said.

  What follows is that story.

A BLISTER

The historian had a blister on his foot. He had done too much walking lately. The weather had been nice and he was home again so he had walked all over town and down to the Wabash River and back. But now, as he sat on the front porch of his house at the end of a dead-end street, his feet hurt. The historian was an old man. He was bald and wore thick glasses and had a pretty good belly on him. He had not been home for a long time. He looked all around. He felt the splinters on the arm of the weathered porch swing he sat in. A strange feeling went through him suddenly. It was a feeling he once had all the time. He turned to see if his wife was sitting beside him like she always used to do on mornings like today. She wasn't, of course. She was dead.

Nothing else had changed. All things change but nothing had changed he believed as he sat with a blister on his foot staring at the empty street. Another incongruous thought popped into his head as he sat there in the porch swing, his feet propped up on several boxes: Perhaps he had spent a lifetime documenting and cataloging and objectifying change when nothing ever changes really. The thought made him smile. He sighed deeply and tried to relax. He had little need of fashionable thoughts now.

The boxes stacked on his porch were filled with books mostly. All sorts of books. Hardbacks, paperbacks, large, small books. Books so old the pages were yellow and brittle. Books with pages so disgustingly thin you could see through them.

Perhaps that is all the change there ever is, the historian mused, slipping back into a fashionable thought again, as he stared at his books: The pages it's written on.

He looked up as he heard someone pulling drapes shut somewhere. There would be an eclipse soon. The historian stared at the blister on his foot and his eyes glazed a bit. He believed he would die soon. His eyes went to the oak tree in his front yard and his thoughts went somewhere else, too.

"I am home again," he said, and the voice he heard was not

a familiar one. He folded his hands in his lap. Not a familiar one at all.

ECLIPSE

There was a dead child in the basement of the house across the street from where Jacob Belmo sat. He sat on the front porch of the house he lived in. Just down the street the sister of the dead child had her eyelids turned inside out. A handful of small children stood around her staring at her with looks of both delight and disgust. Her name was Dorina.

Dorina was ten years old, two years younger than Jacob, and had skin the same color as the inside of a Milky Way candy bar. Every time when she ate a Milky Way candy bar Dorina would break it in half and hold it up to her skin and look at this similarity in color.

When that eclipse happened all the children ran home and everybody in town pulled their drapes shut. Some people even locked their doors. Dorina walked down to the porch where Jacob sat.

The year was 1969 and the world was incandescent with all the wrong kinds of excitement, like some evil Mardi Gras, or so they said, but not so much so in the town Jacob and Dorina lived. In their town an eclipse was as terrifying and magical as it got. But the eclipse didn't scare Jacob. He wasn't frightened at all. His mother had told him what was going to happen and not to be afraid of it. So he wasn't. Dorina wasn't afraid of the eclipse either. Jacob told her not to look at it.

"I will if I want to," Dorina said, as she meticulously picked at a scab on her thigh. She wore a tattered and dirty blue dress and old black high-top tennis shoes that were several sizes too big for her. She picked at the scab on her thigh until blood oozed down her outstretched leg. She stopped a moment and squinted her eyes as she looked up at the eclipse.

"You'll go blind," Jacob said.

"No, I won't," Dorina said. She went back to picking at her

scab.

Soon that eclipse passed and gray clouds hurried into the sky and it began to rain. Dorina moved from the concrete steps to the wood railing around the edge of the porch so she wouldn't get wet. Jacob turned on a little radio that set beside him on the porch swing. They both watched it rain. It was a hot thick rain that made their lungs heavy. They both sat quiet for a moment. Then Dorina, her legs rocking back and forth as she straddled the railing, said what she always liked to say whenever she felt like it.

"My Daddy is as black as coal," she said.

MOTHBALLS AND LILACS

The historian was named Delancey J. McFadden. He got out of the porch swing and went inside. He pulled a white sheet off a chair in the living room and sat down. There was no television in his house. Or radio. Not even a newspaper. Delancey liked the emptiness of his house and planned to keep it this way. He had turned in on himself now at the end of his life, and was proud of it.

On the coffee table beside his chair was a photograph of his dead wife, Mildred. He picked it up and brushed the dust off of it and when he did so, his wife came alive for a moment and brought him a cup of tea. She kissed his cheek. She smelled, as she always did, of mothballs and lilacs. She had on a faded paisley dress and a thin white sweater. Her wrists were so thin you could see through them.

The eclipse came and a strange light filled the house suddenly. Delancey looked around and it hurt to move his eyes. He set the photograph back on the empty bookcase and leaned back in his rocker.

There was only one truly important thing left in this house Delancey planned to spend his last days in. It was in the den. It was a typewriter.

Tired all of a sudden, he eased his eyes closed. In his head Delancey's typewriter began to chatter. In his head he ripped the paper from the carriage, inserted a clean sheet and the typewriter began chattering again. With this strange mechanical litany going on in his head he began to doze.

Delancey dozed through the eclipse.

STAN MUSIAL

The town Jacob and Dorina lived in was situated on the Illinois side of the Wabash River. Where the town was located there wasn't a bridge to connect Illinois and Indiana but there was a Ferry. It was called Darwin's Ferry and it was used primarily to haul farmers and farm equipment back and forth between Illinois and Indiana.

One man operated Darwin's Ferry. His name was Malcolm Talbert but everyone called him the General. He was a rotund man who smoked cigars and wore overalls and a straw hat. He always had a pungent, sickly-sweet smell to him as if he didn't like to bathe all that much. His face was always a beet red from either too much sun or too much alcohol or a combination of the two. He was called the General because he had been one during the Second World War. Or so he said.

The ferryboat wasn't much to look at. It was flat and made of gray faded wood planks that looked very close to rotting away and the metal that held the planks together were coated with rust. It had the appearance of a gigantic old raft. It had been built back around the turn of the century. The General was the only operator of Darwin's Ferry and had been since he was a teenager.

"What about the time you spent as a General in World War Two?" Jacob asked him one time. "Who operated the Ferry then?"

The General stared down the Wabash and worked his cigar to the other side of his mouth. "I don't remember," he said. Then, taking his cigar out of his mouth and holding it up, said, "Stan Musial." He nodded.

"Who?" Jacob replied.

"Yep," said the General. "They brought in Stan Musial and he worked right here on Darwin's Ferry till the very day I got back from Berlin."

"He was a baseball player," Jacob said.

"Yep. Best big league hitter ever to play for St. Louis outside of Hornsby."

Jacob thought about this. "And he worked the Ferry when you were in the War?"

The General scowled. "Let me tell you something," he said, as he pulled Jacob up by the front of his shirt close enough for Jacob to smell his breath. It smelled like cigar smoke that had died.

"I saw Stan Musial one day in St. Louis and it was every bit a hundred and ten degrees in that damn Ball Park." He tapped his cigar ashes into the Wabash. "And that man went–it was a double-header–that man went four-for-four the first game and four-for-five the second game with three home runs and two triples. He only made one out all day long." He moved his cigar to the other side of his mouth. "And by God I'd bet every dime in my pocket that if that outfielder hadn't dove and caught that ball–" The General hesitated but still held Jacob firm. "If that fielder hadn't made the catch of his life, by God, ol' Stan the Man could have run around those bases twice and took a ten minute crap on home plate before they'd a'got that ball in." The General let go of Jacob.

He stared out across the Wabash. Jacob knew every inch of that ballpark in St. Louis. It was his favorite team. He stood there and tried to think of some place in that ballpark where that ball could have went. He couldn't.

"And he ran the Ferry when you were in the War?" Jacob said.

The General took a drag off his cigar, nodded very slowly and said, "Yep."

Jacob kept staring out across the Wabash and thought about what the General had just said, and for some odd reason, believed him.

LEONARD AND NETTIE

Just down from Darwin's Ferry around a bend in the Wabash River Jacob's grandfather lived in an old one-room shack. Jacob's grandmother lived back in town but they were more or less on the outs that summer. His grandfather was a professional fisherman. He put out big nets in the Wabash and sold the catfish, carp, and perch he caught in these nets.

Jacob's grandfather, also, as about everyone knew, was happily crazy. He had been this way ever since he fell out of a truck and split his head open. Before that he had been a very sane electrician during the Great Depression.

Back then there were a lot of people who wanted electricity in their homes and Jacob's grandfather would put it there for them. He would bring home as much as two hundred dollars a week and that was good money back then.

Then he fell out of a truck one of his boys was driving and split his head open. Everyone thought he would die but he didn't. He wasn't right though. For ten years he never said a word. He would simply sit in his chair in the living room or in a wooden rocker on the front porch and roll cigarettes and smoke without a word to anyone.

This irritated Jacob's grandmother. She was a tiny, feisty Irish woman with a short temper. She understood that there was something wrong with her husband, Leonard, now that he had his head split open and all, but she couldn't understand his silence. The doctors all said he could talk anytime he wanted to and this just made her all the angrier. It didn't bother her a bit that she had to live rather poorly now that he was no longer an electrician. The house was paid for and she had her garden and her fruit trees. But ten years of goddamn silence just about drove her nuts.

So towards the latter part of those ten silent years Jacob's grandmother made a habit of yelling at her husband. She yelled at him for everything from how he rolled his cigarettes to the way he dressed himself in the morning. Now Leonard had always rolled a sloppy cigarette but before he had fallen out of that pickup truck he had always dressed sharp. He always wanted his shirts and pants and even his boxer shorts pressed. But after he fell out of that truck he not only didn't care how he dressed, but he would sometimes button his shirt wrong, leave his pants unzipped, or only put on one sock.

This always sent Jacob's grandmother into a rage. She would scream and curse at him and tell him what a crazy old fool he was. One time she even threatened to take a butcher knife after him the next time he left his pants unzipped. But Leonard would just sit there, a little wide-eyed and silent.

Until ten years later (to the day, Jacob's grandmother will tell you). That was when Leonard was silently sitting on the front porch smoking a cigarette and watching his wife jump and leap and scream and shake her fists at him for forgetting to put his pants on that morning. Evidently something clicked inside his damaged head. He said, "Shut the goddamn hell up, Nettie."

Leonard's first spoken words in ten years startled Nettie. Those first words startled her so badly she leaped off the porch and did a belly flop right into her flowerbed. She wasn't hurt.

"Thank the Lord Jesus Christ!" Nettie proclaimed, as she climbed out of her flowerbed. She had chrysanthemum dust all over her. "Leonard can talk!"

And Leonard did talk. For five straight days and nights Jacob's grandfather talked and would not stop talking. He talked about everything he had not talked about for ten years. All five of his kids, who were more or less grown by then, came to listen to the voice of their father they had not heard for ten years.

Leonard told wonderful stories to each and every one of his children. He talked about when they were little and all the things they used to do. He talked about all the houses he used to wire back when he was an electrician. They excitedly asked him if he still remembered how to wire electricity. "No," Leonard said. One of his more ornery boys, Bill, asked him if he even remembered how to screw in a light bulb. Leonard thought about this. "Not right off the top of my head," he replied. But still Leonard kept on talking about everything else. In fact, he wouldn't stop talking. Occasionally Leonard would ask them how they had been and what they were up to but before they could open their mouth, he was already talking about something else.

So after five straight days and nights of hearing her husband talk non-stop, Nettie finally said, "Shut the goddamn hell up, Leonard."

THE ART OF CIGARETTE SMOKING

Earlier that morning, before the eclipse, Dorina and Jacob had gone to their grandmother's house. Nettie lived in an old house on a hill. There were several other houses on the hill also and right next to her house was a bootlegger's house.

Often Jacob and Dorina would go over to the bootlegger's house for a soda. A burly man with gray curly hair would be on the enclosed back porch and he would take their money and then they would open the red Coca-Cola cooler there on the back porch. Inside the cooler there would be more bottles of beer than soda. But Dorina and Jacob would just push aside the beer and pull out their sodas. Little chunks of ice would be dripping off of those soda bottles. Then they would say Thank You to the burly man and leave.

That morning before the eclipse when they got to Nettie's house, she was sitting in a rocking chair with her apron on rolling a cigarette. Her eyes were droopy. She said she was so tired she didn't know if she'd be able to get up again or not.

"I just overdid myself this morning, child," Nettie said, touching Dorina and smiling.

Dorina smiled back and her whole body seemed to warm up. "You'll be all right, Grandma," Dorina said, tapping Nettie's shoulder. Nettie looked at Dorina funny then cackled. "Why land's yes I'll be all right, child. If I was to die because of tiredness I'd been dead at your age." Then Nettie went back to rolling her cigarette and rocking slightly in the rocker. "I want you two to run a little errand for me as soon as I get a smoke."

Jacob stood at the other end of the porch turning the crank of a manual washing machine. The two beige cylinders of the washing machine squeaked as he turned the crank.

"You two ain't been down to see that crazy old river fart yet, have you?" For quite sometime now Nettie had taken to referring to her husband as a crazy old river fart.

"Nope," Dorina said, as she stood watching Nettie roll the cigarette. Her eyes were transfixed on Nettie's fingers and then on how she put the cigarette ever so carefully up to her lips and rolled the tip of her tongue along the cigarette to keep the paper in place.

"When you do," Nettie said, her lips pursed. "You tell that lazy son-of-a-bee I'm a fixin' chicken and dumplings for supper if he can get his lazy ass up here." She carefully removed a wooden match from a blue box, carefully closed the box, then put the cigarette up to her mouth. Dorina stood hypnotized beside her.

With the cigarette lit, Nettie took one deep, careful drag, then went completely limp, the process of making a cigarette finally completed. With her free hand she wiped sweat from her forehead with the edge of the apron she wore, as the hand that held the cigarette dangled over the arm of the rocker.

This whole process of cigarette smoking never ceased to mesmerize and entertain Dorina.

"My mama baked a pie this morning," Dorina said.

Nettie nodded. "That sounds good."

"Nope," Dorina said, rocking back on the heels of her tennis shoes. "They ain't never fit to eat."

Nettie cackled again, and said something about how she didn't raise her daughters right.

"They ain't never sweet enough," Dorina said, her hands folded behind her back.

Nettie kept smiling and rocking. "You're just gonna have to tell your mama to put more sugar in those pies."

Dorina turned one eyelid inside out and stuck her chin out.

"Okay," she said.

PRIDE

The errand Jacob's grandmother had them run for her was down to the grocery store. Nettie handed Jacob a dollar bill and a pack of food stamps. She said to Jacob the same thing she always said before she sent them down to the grocery store with food stamps.

"Now if these bother you any you don't have to go. I can get by till I can get to the store." Nettie tapped on the pack of food stamps Jacob held in his palm.

Dorina and Jacob would always look at each other curiously when their grandmother said this about food stamps. It didn't bother them at all to take food stamps down to the grocery store.

They didn't understand the concepts of pride and embarrassment they were supposed to associate with food stamps. They just thought it was fun. On the way to the grocery store they usually opened the pack of food stamps and marveled at how colorful they were. Time and time again both Dorina and Jacob thought it amazing that money that looked so much like play money could actually buy things.

They had no idea where food stamps came from or that food stamps meant that Nettie was poor and that they were supposed to feel awful about using them.

They would just hand them to the woman at the cash register and she would tear out however many were needed, give them change and they would leave. It seemed very simple.

They didn't even question the fact that they never ever saw Nettie use food stamps. They didn't even think about how Nettie, out of embarrassment and pride perhaps, always asked one of her kids or grandkids to use the food stamps for her.

"My Daddy is as black as coal!" Dorina yelled out as she skipped through the yard to catch up with Jacob. It was about a half-mile walk to the grocery store. They heard the squeak of the front door.

"Girl!" Nettie spat in her sharp, fiery tone. They stopped and looked back. "How many times I tell you there's people around here don't think that's anything to be proud of!"

They started walking again. Jacob didn't look at Dorina. He knew there would be a smile on her face.

"I am," Dorina said, just loud enough for Jacob to hear, as she kicked rocks in the road.

They headed on down the hill towards the grocery store. Jacob told Dorina they had to walk fast.

"There's an eclipse today," he said.

HACKLE-BACKS

Leonard took the motor-boat upstream from the dock then cut the engine. Dorina and Jacob were ready. When the boat drifted back to the dock Jacob grabbed a rope at the front of the boat and Dorina jumped right in. Jacob tied the rope to a post.

A limp cigarette dangled from the old man's lip as he sat at the back of the boat, his hand on the throttle of the engine. He had on a pair of overalls and no shirt. He was a skinny old man with a head full of thick snow-white hair. His prominent chin and long nose gave him the look of an animated scarecrow. He was smiling. Leonard was always smiling.

"By God it was a good day," he said, as he climbed out of the boat. Dorina gave him a big hug and kissed him hard on the cheek.

Then she bent over the large corrugated tin tub in the middle of the boat. Dorina couldn't believe all the fish in the tub. She told her grandfather he was the best fisherman in the entire world. Leonard let out a laugh. Jacob walked over and stood on the dock and also looked into the tub. It was filled with catfish mostly; dark, whiskered fish that always looked mean. But there were also a few white perch in there, along with one big Buffalo carp and even a sturgeon Leonard called a hackle-back.

The hackle-back interested Dorina. It was a pinkish color and, to Jacob, looked like Captain Nemo's submarine in *20,000 Leagues Under the Sea*. Dorina started to touch it.

"Don't you touch that damn hackle-back!" Leonard said as he rose up. "Those ridges on its back'll cut you like a razor!"

Dorina's eyes went wide as she withdrew her hand. "No, it won't."

"Hell it won't," Leonard said as he tossed the cigarette into the water. He started tying a rope to a post near the back of the boat. "You run up and get me a beer and I'll let you see what its mouth looks like."

Dorina stared more intently at the strange-looking fish. "It ain't got no mouth."

"Yeah it does," Jacob said. "Underneath it."

Dorina looked at Jacob, her face twisted up. "No, it don't," she said, as Jacob helped her get out of the boat. Excited, she ran up the dock and then up the riverbank, all the while yelling, "No it don't!"

Leonard shook his head as he watched his granddaughter run up the riverbank. "Damn." He unhooked the red gas tank from the motor. "If I had a fifth of that girl's energy I'd be a new man."

Jacob stared into the tub. He asked Leonard how big the biggest fish he caught today was.

Leonard ran his hands through his long white hair, cleared his throat and spit into the river. "Oh," he said. "I think that flat-head in there's about five pound." He stood up in the boat, pulled his smoke sack out of his overalls. He pointed upriver. "I saw a bobcat up around the bend. Crawlin' on a tree branch." Jacob's eyes lit up. Leonard continued. "Ain't seen one in years. You hear them every night but I ain't seen one in a long time. It must have been sick."

When Dorina returned with a can of beer Leonard and Jacob had everything secure. They set the tub full of fish on the dock. Jacob used an old rag to pick up the hackleback. It only weighed maybe two pounds. It was about as long as his fore-arm. Jacob held it upside down so Dorina could get a look at its mouth, which was round and looked like a suction cup. Dorina stuck her tongue out and made an awful face.

Leonard took a big drink from the beer, set the can on the dock. "They's the best eatin' fish there is," he said. "Take those three spines out and there ain't a bone one in them. Tastes better than catfish." He took out a blue bandanna from his back pocket, blew his nose hard. Then he carefully wiped his nose clean. He pointed at the hackleback.

"That's where you get--" Leonard couldn't think of the word.

"Caviar," Jacob said.

"That's right," Leonard said. "The eggs of those things are worth a lot of money to people somewhere."

Dorina continued to look a bit horrified at the fish Jacob held. "People eat fish eggs?" She asked.

"Uh-huh." Leonard emptied his beer. "Rich people think they're delicacies. They don't even cook them or anything. Just slap them on a plate and eat'em with a cracker."

Dorina was downright sickened at the thought. She shuddered.

"Not me," she said.

THE AGE OF AQUARIUS

With a sharp knife Leonard would slice open the belly of a catfish, reach in and pull out the insides, then toss the whole sticky, colorful mess into a trash barrel. Then with a pair of pincer pliers, he would pull the skin off the fish. The head was the last thing to go on a catfish. He would use a small axe to chop off the head. Then what remained of the fish went into a tub full of salt-water to take the fishy taste out of it.

As Leonard cleaned each and every catfish Dorina and Jacob watched him intently. They stopped watching him only long enough to run and get him another beer. The more fish Leonard cleaned and the more beer he drank, the more he talked. And he always seemed to talk about the same things over and over again.

When Jacob returned with another beer, his grandfather

was telling Dorina about the ninety-eight pound catfish he caught a long time ago. They had heard the story at least a million times.

He said the catfish's head was as big around as a car tire. He talked about how it took him all day to wear that fish down enough so he could get it into the boat.

"That trotline rope cut through my hands so bad I saw bone through my fingers," Leonard said.

"I thought you said you caught it in a net," Dorina said.

"Nope," Leonard said, as he tossed a cleaned catfish into the tub of salt-water. Jacob jabbed at the floating carcasses of catfish in the tub with his finger. "On a trotline," Leonard continued. He pointed the axe at Dorina. "That fish had swallowed fifteen of the hooks on that trotline."

Jacob asked him if he was using worms for bait.

"Nope. Crawdads," Leonard said. "Crawdads dipped in stink bait." Dorina reminded him that he had told them before that he was using worms for bait.

As Leonard continued on with his story, Dorina had wrapped herself around the tree beside the makeshift wooden table where he stood cleaning fish. Out of the blue, she said, "My Daddy is as black as coal."

Leonard stopped gutting a fish, took a sip of beer and looked directly at Dorina. Her cheek rested against the bark of the tree. She stared right back at him, her big eyes wide and no real expression on her face.

Finally the old man smiled and said, "So he is." He took a drink of beer and repeated, "So he is," then went back to gutting the catfish.

As Leonard got drunker he always got around to telling them about the Game Warden. It always scared Dorina and Jacob some when he began to talk about the Game Warden. Leonard hated the man and they didn't like him either. He was a large, ugly man with a glass eye that had a chip in it. Nobody liked the Game Warden and Leonard had particular reasons for not liking him.

He tossed an empty beer can behind him. "He killed my

best friend." Leonard scratched his thick, hairy white chest, his face serious. "Shot him dead with a sawed-off twelve-gauge shotgun."

Leonard finished cleaning the fish and they all went to sit around the fire. It was getting close to dark. Dorina and Jacob had to go home before dark.

Leonard stared mad and drunk at the fire as he continued to talk about the Game Warden.

"Bastard killed Henry Chalmers on the very same day in '56 he stole the motor off my boat," Leonard said, his eyes burning. He poked Jacob's shoulder. "Henry Chalmers was the best man I ever knew. He'd do anything in the world for you—I mean, anything!" Leonard's words were starting to slur. He blinked as he stared at the fire. His voice went low. "We grew up together."

Dorina drew stick people in the dirt between her legs with her finger.

"My daddy kills people in Viet Cong," she said.

The sun was a dull red and had fallen into the treetops behind them. Leonard looked at Dorina.

"I 'spect he does, child."

"Why'd he kill your best friend?" Jacob asked. He poked at the fire with a stick. Sparks flew.

His grandfather put his cigarette out and reached into the cooler beside him for another beer. He opened it with a yellow plastic opener. Yellow foam and then gold-colored beer spilled out and over his tar-stained fingers. He sipped at it.

"Bastard's mean is all. He was born mean. There's people like him all over." Leonard took out his smoke sack. "And he's stupid. Hell, he ain't got sense enough to shake after he pisses." He couldn't find what he was looking for in his smoke sack. "By god I'm out of rolling papers. Goddamn it." Leonard got to his feet and felt through every pocket in his overalls. "Goddamn it. I want you two to do me a favor." He pointed. "You know that old gray shack up the road?"

Dorina and Jacob looked at each other. They knew more than they wanted to about that old gray shack. It had strange people in it.

"It's the Age of Aquarius," Leonard said with a chuckle. "I want you to run up there and borrow me some rolling papers."

Dorina asked him what the Age of Aquarius was.

Leonard just laughed. "A bad age," he said. "Now you too get on up there and find me some rolling papers."

THE SHACK

There was always music coming from that old gray shack. The people inside the shack all had long straight hair that hung down the sides of their faces like curtains. Jacob noticed how they all wore the same clothes, too–old, faded blue jeans with huge bell-bottoms and flannel shirts over some kind of a t-shirt. There was always this one guy sitting on the front porch of the old shack with a guitar trying to play along with the music coming from the record-player inside. His name was Ralph.

Ralph never seemed to be able to keep up with the rhythm of the song. He always seemed about four or five beats slower. For instance, as Jacob and Dorina stood at the front of the shack the record player had stopped and four or five seconds later Ralph had plucked discordantly at the guitar and sang, "Hey, Joe." Ralph had a heavy black beard and tiny little black eyes that always seemed to be bloodshot. He looked at the two kids in the yard.

"Have you seen the Lord?" Ralph said.

"Nope," Dorina said.

"My grandpa is out of rolling papers," Jacob said, and just as he spoke a girl came out of the shack. She was followed by two other girls and a calico cat. The calico cat was very fat and seemed to have trouble walking.

"Children!" One of the girls said, as if delighted to see them. Then another girl spoke. "Are you looking for something?" She had red hair. Jacob found her voice very pleasing. He relaxed a little.

"My grandpa needs some rolling papers," Jacob said, and

he felt his cheeks redden as he spoke. "We'd just like to borrow a few. We'll pay you back."

"Narcs," Ralph said. One of the girls gave him a dirty look.

"Well, just come in!" The red-haired girl said. They all went inside. Jacob and Dorina froze. It scared them to go inside the shack. The last time they were inside it there was a blue light on that made their teeth glow. Jacob pulled Dorina along.

It was a two-room shack. They all evidently slept in the back room. In the front room a guy with his back to them slept on the sofa. It was an old red sofa with the stuffing coming out of the arms. The television was on but nobody seemed to be watching it. All that was on the screen was snow.

One of the girls bent towards Jacob and stared at him, a wisp of a smile on her face. Her skin was very pale and her lips were the thinnest lips Jacob had ever seen. The girls looked older than Jacob but he couldn't tell how much older. Maybe they were in their twenties. He didn't know.

"Your eyes are so blue," she said. Jacob scratched his chin and looked down at his feet.

The girl turned to look at Dorina. "What's your name?" Dorina told her.

"That's a pretty name."

"No, it ain't," Dorina said. "Charley Skinner calls me Door-knob." She walked over to where one of the women was putting a dark green cone into a shiny gold pot. Dorina asked her what she was doing.

"Incense," the woman said. She lit the cone with a match.

Posters hung all over the walls of the shack. Some of the posters were weird and brightly colored with strange designs on them, while other posters were just pictures. There was a poster of an American flag over the doorway into the other room, but instead of stars there was a black skull and cross-bones.

The red-headed girl called Jacob into the other room. There was a wood-burning stove in the middle of the back room. Wooden cots and sleeping bags surrounded it. Clothes were scattered everywhere. In one corner a girl was sleeping in a sleeping bag. Jacob was led to one of the cots that had been made. It had a dark green blanket on it.

"What color would you think he'd like?" She said, as she sat on the edge of the cot. For the first time Jacob noticed that there was a bandage on her arm. A touch of blood as big around as a quarter was in the middle of the bandage.

On the cot were scattered several packages of rolling papers. They were all different colors. Jacob had never seen different colored rolling papers before. He didn't see any like his grandpa used. He picked some blue ones. Dorina ran into the room.

"Look, Jake!" She stuck out her hand. On one finger was a small turquoise ring. "That girl gave it to me."

"Neat," Jacob said. "We gotta get home before dark. Thank you." He shoved the rolling papers into his front pocket. It bugged him in this place. He didn't know why.

They left the shack.

"This is the prettiest ring I ever seen," Dorina said.

"Yep," Jacob said. Everybody said good-bye. Dorina shouted out Thank You once again to the girl who gave her the ring.

ASLEEP

They walked fast back to Leonard's camp. It was near dark now and they didn't want to get in trouble.

"It fits big but she said I'd grow into it," Dorina said, still talking about her new ring.

"You will," Jacob said.

Dorina looked at Jacob. "I wish she gave you a ring, too," she said.

Jacob shrugged. "I don't like rings," he said. He stopped, reached down, picked up a rock and heaved it into the Wabash. It landed silently in the water just off the bank.

"Boys wear rings, too," Dorina insisted.

"Not me," Jacob said. He started to throw another rock

but changed his mind. They headed on back to camp.

When they got back to camp Leonard wasn't interested in rolling a cigarette. He was slumped back in his red-painted metal chair beside the fire sound asleep and snoring loudly. Jacob set the rolling papers next to him and they headed on home. Somewhere a motorboat ran. They headed down a gravel road towards town.

"You like them people?" Jacob asked Dorina.

Dorina shrugged. "Yeah. She gave me my first ring. I ain't never had a real ring before."

There was just a hint of red behind the trees now. It would be dark before they got home. Jacob thought about that girl who thought his eyes were blue. He still couldn't believe how thin her lips were. It was like she didn't have any lips at all. He grabbed Dorina by the hand, told her they had to run awhile. It was getting too close to dark.

So they ran.

EVERYTHING

There was perhaps another reason Delancey had come home to die. The reason came to him as suddenly as did the pain in his chest. He stood up, took a deep breath, or tried to anyway, and put the tiny nitro-glycerin tablet under his tongue. He sat back down on the porch swing. It was humid tonight. He unbuttoned the top button of his shirt.

"My daughter," he said out loud. He didn't know why he spoke out loud. Perhaps he just wanted to hear the words. He looked around and as he tried to rub the sudden stiffness out of his neck, he found tears burning in his eyes. "Daughter," he said again.

The pain spread for a moment and increased in intensity. Delancey held his breath and swallowed hard until finally the pain subsided. He stared into the gray-lit insides of a house across the street. Everything evens out, he was thinking. Delancey thought now about his daughter and how he hadn't seen her for over twenty-five years.

Everything, he thought again.

ALONE

The television in Jacob's house was broken. It had been broken for quite sometime. It was a black and white console television that stood on four short spindly copper-colored legs. There was aluminum foil around two antennas attached to the back. When it was working they could get three channels. Jacob sat on the couch in front of the television and wondered when it would be fixed again.

It was dark outside now. Crickets droned outside the open windows. His mother was sleeping. Later she had to work the midnight shift at a nursing home. She was a nurse. His father was working late at a fertilizer plant.

He was alone in the living room and as he sat there all he could hear was the hum and occasional click of the refrigerator. Dull, yellow light from the dining room was all that lit the living room. On the dining room table atop spread-out newspapers was a model car in various pieces. Jacob had gotten bored with putting it together and was sitting in front of a broken television wondering what show he was missing.

He thought about turning on the record player but he didn't. He didn't want to wake his mother up. So Jacob just sat there and pretended that the television was working. He pretended he was watching an adventure show in which he was the star and that girl who thought his eyes were blue was the co-star.

He did this for quite sometime.

LUCY

In the morning it was raining. It was a warm steady rain that was more pleasant than not in the summertime. Dorina led a pack of children through the street. The children did whatever Dorina did. They stopped when Dorina stopped. They skipped when Dorina skipped.

Jacob sat on his front porch. Across the street Dorina's mother sat on her porch snapping beans. Her name was Lucy. She was a slight woman with high cheekbones, light wavy hair, and hollow dark eyes. She was a very pretty woman except for her teeth. Her teeth were more black than white and whenever she would laugh she would put her hand up to cover her mouth. She didn't like anybody seeing her teeth.

Dorina was her only child except for her dead baby boy in the basement. Lucy stopped snapping beans and yelled at Dorina to not walk in the middle of the street.

Soon it began to rain harder and thunder clapped loudly overhead and the ground shook. Shrieking, the children all ran with Dorina to her front porch. The smallest child, a head shorter than Dorina, wrapped her arms around Dorina's waist. Since the kids were there Lucy put them to work. She had them all gather around her and the big metal pot she had between her legs. Shortly, they were all snapping beans.

BETSY

In the house next to Dorina's there lived an old blind man named Carl and his fifteen-year-old granddaughter, Betsy. Jacob took a keen interest in Betsy. She wasn't particularly beautiful or anything but she was still easy to look at. Betsy always wore short, cut-off blue jeans that fit real tight and blouses that showed off her breasts and usually showed her belly. Jacob liked to look at Betsy and lately looking at her caused him to feel pleasantly strange all over.

She and her grandfather didn't get along. Her parents had died in a car wreck when Betsy was eleven and her blind grandfather was her only surviving relative. But they had never gotten along so well and whenever Betsy didn't get her way she would rearrange the furniture in the house. This was the worst possible thing someone could do to a blind person.

This was why, as Jacob sat on the front porch, he could see Betsy's grandfather lying in the front picture window, curled up, and sleeping soundly atop a large console stereo. The couch had been there the day before, but today Betsy had moved it. They had evidently gotten into a fight and Betsy had moved the couch on him again. So her grandfather, unable to find the couch, had probably just said fuck it and curled up on the stereo.

Betsy, at the moment, sat on the wooden railing of her front porch with one leg pulled up in an upside-down V and the other leg stretched out straight as she read a *True Story* magazine.

Betsy was always borrowing *True Story* magazines from Dorina's mother, who had big stacks of these magazines in the living room. Jacob liked to look at the covers of the magazines but he didn't care to look at the black and white pictures inside. The pictures inside were always of women crying or running away from ugly men and Jacob didn't care for the pictures at all. Dorina, on the other hand, got a big kick out of showing Jacob the brassiere advertisements in the back of the magazines.

As Jacob sat there his eyes kept wandering back to Betsy. She had a sucker in her mouth and she kept twirling the sucker around in her mouth as she read. Her long brown hair hung across one side of her face.

Jacob was staring at Betsy when he heard a thump. Her grandfather had rolled off the console stereo and hit the hardwood floor of their living room.

Betsy didn't so much as glance up from her magazine.

TIRED

There was a trailer park on the outskirts of town. A gravel road wound through it. The trailers were all different sizes and colors. There were pink ones and blue ones and green ones. The trailers all had nameplates on the front of them. LIBERTY. ELCONA. SHULTE. HOLLY PARK.

The bigger trailers were set up on cement blocks to keep

them from buckling in two. The smaller trailers just set on small wheels. All the trailers had large, metal hitches attached to the front of them. In many of these V-shaped hitches flowers were planted.

Some of the trailers had old black tires on the roof. This was to keep their tin roofs from rattling in the wind. The wind was an enemy of the people who lived in these trailers. The wind made these traveling homes on wheels shake and rattle and the people inside, often worried that the wind would sometime turn their home over or if the wind was strong enough, just cause their home to explode.

Windy, gusty, midwestern days made the people who lived in these trailers very nervous. Few people ever quite got used to it, either. It was just something they had to live with.

In a green LIBERTY trailer in the park there lived a woman named Valarie. Valarie was a nurse who worked in the nursing home in town. She would go in at three in the afternoon and get off at eleven that night.

At the moment, Valarie sat in the back bedroom staring at herself in the mirror and she didn't particularly like what she saw. Her dishwater blonde hair was flat and plastered to her face and this seemed to make her prominent nose seem even more prominent. She tried to fluff her hair some. Her eyes were red and swollen and her mascara, which she had forgotten to take off the night before, ran and hid. She looked away.

Valarie felt incredibly tired. Tired of everything, in fact. Tired of her entire life, mostly.

The semen of a man she didn't even like oozed down her thigh. She shuddered and crossed her legs. The man was still asleep in her bed. His name was Bob and he was a doctor at the nursing home Valarie worked at.

Valarie hadn't wanted to sleep with him exactly but they had a few drinks after work, and then he eased his hand up her white uniform, and the attention he was giving her was something Valarie hadn't had for awhile. It had been a mistake, of course. Valarie felt that she was very good at making mistakes lately. Bob was maybe twenty-seven and married. Valarie would be thirty-five in a month and had been divorced for almost five years.

Valarie took her pillow and went into the living room. It was very cool in the living room. She had left her window air-conditioner running all night long. She didn't like to do this because it ran her electric bill up. The compressor on the air-conditioner kicked off and the whole trailer shook and this startled Valarie.

She fell onto the couch and tucked her pillow into her belly, pulled a blue blanket over her, and curled up. She brushed her hair out of her eyes and couldn't decide whether to cry for a while or just close her eyes and try to go to sleep.

Finally she closed her eyes and went to sleep.

THE ANGRIEST POET IN THE WORLD

Lived in the same trailer park as Valarie, two trailers down in a run-down ELCONA with leaky faucets and a broken hot water heater. Cold showers, the poet concluded, were his salvation, his penance for a bad life, his many bad lines, and there on the bathroom wall were the rejection slips he would wipe his ass on when the toilet paper was gone, like now. Ironic, isn't it, how the smallest publishing house had the softest paper and how the fucking *New Yorker* made him bleed?

He was thinking all of this and more as he sat at the moment on the pot reading Wallace Stevens. He yelled fuck at the top of his lungs and shocked his colon. He had left his pocket Oxford Dictionary somewhere other than the bathroom.

"Fuck life!" he yelled and then he arrived at some epiphany concerning the reading of poetry: If one cannot interpret a poem while on the pot without a dictionary, then fuck it, it shouldn't have been written.

His name was George. He worked at the same nursing home as Valarie. He was an orderly. He emptied bedpans and packed the asses of dead people, he would tell you.

George was wasting his college education but he liked his job at the nursing home. He liked particularly the stench of their elderly wisdom, the fiery sparkle in their eyes, but what George liked most was listening to their stories; bone-cracking truths condensed into single utterances and honed by time into these brilliant aphorisms that made George either laugh or cry, depending on his mood.

He finished and left the bathroom. He couldn't believe how humid it was after that fucking eclipse. He needed a goddamn air-conditioner. In the kitchen he poured himself a cup of percolated coffee and stared out his front window.

His neighbor, a young grade school teacher, was bending over her chrysanthemums. She had a great ass. George sighed and took a drink of coffee and stared at her legs, which stretched out of her red shorts like two erotic exclamation points punctuating any man's sexual fantasy.

George looked around for his pen and notebook.

THE BASEMENT

The basement was cool and dark and there was a hot water heater in the middle of it. Two small dirty rectangular windows let dull rusty light in.

Lucy sat on the old wooden steps that went down into the basement. The wood on these steps was so old the splinters from it were soft. Sweat dried cool between her breasts and on her arms. She rested her cheek in her hand. A cigarette dangled between her fingers as she stared empty right through that hot water heater.

There were fruit jars on a counter on one side of the basement. On the other side was a work counter. Tools lay scattered on it. There was a metal vice clamped to the counter. It was covered by a soiled and wrinkled baseball cap.

Lucy had things to do like clean the house but right now she sat cooling herself and on the verge of tears again. They came and went now all the time.

Her baby was dead. She had killed her baby and now it was wrapped in a blue blanket and tucked beneath the counter behind jars of peaches and apples and rhubarb.

Lucy hadn't meant to kill her baby. In fact, she couldn't even convince herself that she had killed her baby.

"Yes, I did," she said, her face wrinkling in pain as she blew smoke swirling into the basement. She finished her cigarette and got up and walked up the steps.

THE LAST TIME

The young doctor talked about how hard it was to move from California to here. He drank the coffee Valarie had intentionally made too strong and stared right through her when he talked. She sat indifferent to anything he said.

As he talked about what he used to do at the beach Valarie thought about what it would be like to wake up with a man that made her coffee. She noticed how clean his fingernails were.

He talked about how horrible it must be to be stuck in this small ugly town working in a rundown nursing home. Valarie's eyes went coldly back to him.

"You should go to St. Louis or Chicago," he said. "They pay nurses well in the cities."

Valarie's mouth tightened. "I should," she said.

"Well," he said. He set the cup hard upon the table. "I guess I better get going. I play golf at eleven." He laughed and Valarie decided she didn't like his laugh at all. It sounded like he was happily trying to spit up. "It's Thursday." His eyebrows rose. "Have you ever been to the club?"

Valarie stared at him a moment. "Hmm–" she said, as she thought about it. Then she looked him right in the eye. "I gave my ex-husband a blow-job in the parking lot one time in high school."

The Doctor winced.

"Well, you take care now," he said, awkwardly, as he started towards the door. He hesitated as he passed her, as if he didn't know whether to shake her hand or kiss her or what. Valarie just sat there, cold yet relaxed.

"Bye now," he said, opening the door. "See you at work."

Valarie started to say bye but she didn't. She didn't feel like it. She took a sip of coffee and heard his car door shut.

The last time, she was thinking, as he drove away. The last time.

MR. AND MRS. SIBBITT

When the rain stopped the sun came out and it got so hot and humid it was hard to breathe. Jacob had to mow a lawn before he could go down to the river. He pulled the mower out of the garage but couldn't find the gas can. The garage beside their house stood by itself and was old. It even leaned a little to the right after it had gotten moved off its foundation in a tornado a few years ago. The white paint was peeling off the sides and the door no longer shut very well.

Next to the garage beside their house in a smaller house with gray siding lived Mr. and Mrs. Sibbitt. As Jacob looked everywhere in the cluttered garage for the gas can he could hear Mrs. Sibbitt singing. She was always singing. Her voice was high and strange. An Amway salesman had called Mrs. Sibbitt's singing maniacal one time when Jacob was around and the word stuck with him. She was an old woman who wore an orange wig. Jacob, as did most everyone who met Mrs. Sibbitt, didn't think she was all there. For one thing she had a bad memory. Jacob and his family had lived in their house beside the Sibbitts for four years now and still Mrs. Sibbitt called him Randy.

"Come on in, Randy," Mrs. Sibbitt would say to Jacob after he mowed her lawn.

"Jacob," he always politely corrected. "Yes," Mrs. Sibbitt always replied, that ever-present faraway smile on her face. Then she would have Jacob sit down and she'd open a bottle of Pepsi, pour some into a glass, fill the rest of the glass with tap water, put one solitary ice cube in the glass, and set it in front of Jacob at the kitchen table. Jacob hated watered-down Pepsi. He had never known anybody to do such a thing before. But his mother had said Mrs. Sibbitt was from "the old school," which meant Mrs. Sibbitt was trying to make the Pepsi go further by mixing it with water. "She's cheap," his father had added. So every time Jacob mowed their yard he had to sit down, drink diluted Pepsi, and politely correct Mrs. Sibbitt every time she called him Randy. And occasionally she would offer him ginger snap cookies. Jacob hated ginger snap cookies. They were homemade and were always black on the bottom and hard as rocks. But, despite it all, for some odd reason he still liked Mrs. Sibbitt.

He liked Mr. Sibbitt even more. Mr. Sibbitt was a bent old man who was said to be eighty-eight years old. He still drove a car and this never ceased to amaze Jacob. The man couldn't see anything or anyone unless they stood directly in front of him. He also wore these humongous flesh-colored hearing aids behind each ear. The hearing aids were so large Jacob, when he was younger, used to think they were mainly responsible for Mr. Sibbitt walking so bent over.

But he still drove a green '51 Studebaker that had rust curling all around its edges, and Mr. Sibbitt seemed to become a young man again when he drove it. Jacob marveled at how Mr. Sibbitt could punch that car and throw gravel every time he backed it out of the garage. "Lay rubber!" Jacob or Dorina would call out to Mr. Sibbitt, then he would nod and smile and screech the tires in the street. Every time. Even when they wouldn't yell out for him to do so.

Jacob found the gas can and filled up the lawn mover. Dorina skipped up and leaped several times to try and touch the top of the garage door. She asked Jacob if she could go with him to mow the lawn.

Jacob checked the oil and the spark plug on the mower, said, "I guess."

"THEN WE CAN GO DOWN TO THE RIVER!" Dorina yelled, at the top of her lungs, head swaying back and forth like a crazy person. Jacob often got embarrassed by Dorina's crazy exuberance. He told her to settle down.

"I'm just playing," she insisted, as she tried to jump on the edge of the mower as Jacob pulled it along.

"Quit it!" he yelled at her finally.

"Oooh...tough boy, tough boy–" Dorina said, mimicking what Betsy had said to Jacob one time when they were playing.

Dorina ran on ahead, shouting and carrying on. Jacob just shook his head as he pulled the lawn mower on up the street.

SNOW

Atmosphere, Janet Kittel thought, as she moved the antenna around on the television set in her trailer. All she could get was snow this morning. Along with the sun blaring through the paper-thin curtains in the living room, the snow made the screen nearly impossible to see. She hated funerals anyway. There had been too many on television this year. She shut it off.

She was down to her last glass of rum. As she stood by the ice-box and poured it she pushed her robe off one shoulder. She felt how smooth that shoulder was. She ran her hand on down to her breast. She closed her eyes and half-sighed, half-shuddered. All naked and nowhere to go, she thought wistfully. Then, as she walked back into the living room she thought of her husband. She thought of a letter he might have written her today. She thought how she would tear up that letter without even opening it this time. He should be dead, she bluntly thought as she let the robe fall completely off as she curled upon the couch, her knees sliding up to her breasts as her heels dug into the back of her bare thighs. She wrapped an arm around her legs and eased a finger with a freshly-painted red fingernail up to part the curtain and look outside. She heard the drone and rattle of someone pulling a lawn mower.

That someone was a boy. A boy who had just recently become a man, if the thick, blonde hair sprouting on his legs was any indication. Saliva gathered at one corner of her mouth and her breathing left her just a touch as Janet stared at him. She watched him move in his tight blue gym shorts.

Janet watched as a black girl skipped up and tried to grab his hand. The boy scowled and pushed her hand away as he continued to pull the mower. The black girl, Janet saw, had to be a mix of white and black. She was so light-skinned and beautiful. She had curly black hair that was tied back with a white ribbon and fell almost to the small of her back. Janet saw her laugh and jabber at the boy, who just kept walking, expressionless and perhaps a bit troubled.

Janet eased a hand between her thighs. She could ease his troubles.

DOC GARRELTS

The lawn Jacob had to mow was for an old man named Doc Garrelts. He was no doubt the strangest old man in town. He was always doing weird things. One time last summer Jacob had come to mow his lawn and Doc Garrelts was standing out in front of his trailer dressed up like an Indian. He had feathers on his head, moccasins, war-paint, and everything.

Jacob had asked him why he was dressed up and all Doc Garrelts said was, "Protest." Then Jacob asked him what he was protesting and then Doc Garrelts took off running around his trailer, all the while yelling and whooping and shaking a rubber ax in the air. As Jacob watched the old man run around the trailer, he worried that he would have a heart attack. But he didn't. So after he quit Jacob mowed his lawn.

Today Doc Garrelts was on the roof of his trailer with binoculars.

"They're coming!" Doc Garrelts yelled down at Jacob and Dorina, who were standing on the ground trying not to laugh.

"Who's coming!" Dorina yelled up at him. Doc Garrelts stopped looking through the binoculars, nodded.

"God's messengers," he said. Dorina and Jacob were both

struggling not to laugh at Doc Garrelts. Everybody in town knew he was crazy. He had been for as long as anybody could remember. But they all liked him. And he paid Jacob three dollars every time he mowed his lawn, which was two dollars more than anybody else in the trailer park.

"You'll be ready for them I bet!" Jacob said, then covered his mouth. Dorina was doubled over in her attempt not to laugh.

Doc Garrelts put the binoculars back up to his eyes, said, "Oh, yes. The great God Jehovah has prepared me well for them."

Jacob shook his head and reached down to pull the cord to start the lawn mower. He told Dorina to watch out for the mower. He wanted to make quick work of Doc Garrelts' lawn. He wanted to get down to the river.

A POLITICAL STATEMENT

The door eased open and Janet, drink in hand, gave the two ladies standing on her patio, a politely bitter smile. They were smiling so eagerly it almost nauseated Janet. She absently rattled the ice in her glass as she felt her eyes begin to water. She looked out at the blue sky over the ladies' heads. The hat that one of them wore was extremely stupid-looking. The hat reminded her of her childhood somehow, when she would look at such a stupid hat with a certain kind of curiosity. It was just a stupid hat now.

"Would you like to talk about the Lord today?" one of the ladies said. The lady's voice was so perky it seemed to pierce Janet through her eyelids and splinter and crack somewhere in the back of her skull. It was partially the alcohol and partially the pills, Janet decided. She looked the lady right in the eye. And partially this woman's incredibly irritating middle-class voice. Janet wiped her bottom lip of spilled rum. She looked at the other lady and immediately sensed some hidden communion with her. As if they both secretly, and perhaps not so secretly, wanted to cut out the other lady's vocal chords. Janet sniffed and a tear eased down her eye.

She finally spoke. "My father–" Janet cleared her throat and took a sip of her drink. A cigarette was between two fingers but had long since gone out. "My father once said that the religious person is always looking for answers." The lady who had spoke, spoke again and said that this was true and that the answers always came from the Lord.

Janet's irritation grew. She took another drink and steadied herself against the door. "While," Janet continued. "The existentialist is always looking for questions." Janet let herself smile now briefly, then it turned into a slight show of pain. "He didn't say it to me actually. He hasn't said anything to me in a long time." She looked up at the sky again, then back at the ladies. They didn't know quite what to say.

"Do you know what humanism is? It's quite fashionable now." Janet flashed an acid smile. "Of course it is. My father is a pop historian, a glorious craftsman of abstraction." There was obvious pain now in Janet's eyes. Both ladies, leaning slightly forward and still at a loss for words, detected this pain. They still had no idea what to say. The weaker lady spoke and her voice was less offensive.

"Maybe you should talk to him." She said, as she looked at the other lady for approval. She didn't get it. The other lady told Janet emphatically that she should talk to the Lord.

Janet's eyes slowly met the stronger lady's eyes. It was 1969. Impoliteness was a political statement.

"Die horribly," Janet told the woman. Then eased the door shut in their faces.

A BRICK SHITHOUSE

Down on the Wabash the General sat on the ferryboat with his rod and reel. He had already caught a small channel catfish. It had stopped raining and it was getting hot now.

Dorina and Jacob walked to the front of the ferryboat where the General was and sat down. They took off their shoes and eased their feet into the warm, murky water.

"My oh my, it's hot, kids," the General said. He wiped his face with a red bandanna.

"Let's go for a ride in the boat," Dorina said, kicking up water with her feet. Jacob looked at the General.

"I don't know if there's enough gas to get you two very far," the General said, as he tightened the tension on his fishing line. The current was making his line slack. "I ain't put gas in it this week." He got a nibble on his line. They both watched his old, knotty hand ease toward the rod.

Jacob shrugged. "It's okay. I'll check the tank."

The General stared at the end of his rod and reel. "He's stealing my bait is what he's doing." He looked up at Jacob, his cigar butt moving to the other side of his mouth. His eyes were red and his cheeks splotchy and sun-burnt. In one pocket of his overalls was a half-pint bottle of whiskey. "Reminds me of a woman I used to know back during the Great Depression." He took his cigar out of his mouth for a second to spit pieces of it into the water. "She'd do just about anything for a loaf of bread." The General looked back down at his line.

"What's her name?" Dorina said.

The General hummed as he tried to think of her name.

"Gertrude," he said. "Gertrude McKinney." He left his line alone and took out the whiskey. "Built like a brick shithouse that woman was. Not a bad looker at all 'cept for she had a mole the size of a dime right on her chin."

Dorina looked at the General. "I ain't never seen a brick shithouse before."

"Hey now!" The General said scowling. "You ain't supposed to talk that way."

"You said it first."

Jacob motioned for her to come on. They got up and headed back to the bank.

"There ain't no such thing as a brick shithouse," Dorina said. "There's a wood shithouse behind our house."

Jacob kicked at a dirt clod on the ferry. It rolled off and splattered into the water. "It just means a fancy one," he said.

"Oh," Dorina said.

They jumped off the ferryboat to the bank and headed towards the General's motorboat. The bank was slick and muddy. Dorina slipped but Jacob caught her by the arm.

"I hope nobody ever says I look like a brick shithouse," Dorina said. "I'll bust'em."

The General yelled at them to put their life jackets on.

"Okay!" They both yelled back.

THE WATCHTOWER

Doc Garrelts lived in a pink-sided trailer at the end of the trailer park. In the small front yard of his trailer were two ceramic pink flamingoes. On the roof of the trailer Doc Garrelts lay flat on his back. He was stark naked.

Doc Garrelts was waiting for something. He heard a knock on his door. He smiled. That something had arrived.

At his doorstep stood two ladies in blue dresses. One of the ladies held a blue vinyl bag and the other lady held copies of *The Watchtower*.

Doc Garrelts crawled across the roof and peaked over the edge. In a quiet voice he said, "Can I help you, ladies?"

His voice startled the ladies until they looked up and saw his head peering over the roof of the trailer.

"Oh, hi!" One of them said, gathering herself. The other wore a hat that fell off her head when Doc Garrelts spoke. She picked it up.

"Nice hat," Doc Garrelts said.

The lady blushed. "It came with the dress."

Doc Garrelts nodded. "Nice dress," he said.

"Why thank you," the lady replied politely, straightening her hat.

"Can I try it on?" Doc Garrelts said. The two ladies looked

at each other.

"We," one of them continued, as she strained to smile. "Wondered if you'd like to talk about the Lord today."

Doc Garrelts smiled. "Sure," he said. "Come on up."

"Well," one of the ladies began. "We could come back–"

"Oh, no!" Doc Garrelts said. "I'd like to hear about the Lord right now!" He pointed. At the other end of the trailer was a ladder.

"I have lawn chairs," he added.

The two ladies looked apprehensively at each other again.

"I watched the eclipse from here," he said, as he gave the two women his warmest smile.

One of the ladies sighed. "Come on, Joyce."

"You think–" began Joyce.

"Just come on!" The other said.

They went to the ladder.

"I don't know, Marsha."

"Don't question the Lord, Joyce!" Marsha snapped.

Joyce tapped her hat down securely and followed Marsha up the ladder. The ladder was a little wobbly so Marsha quickly got to the roof and held the ladder as Joyce climbed to the roof of the trailer. When they were both on the roof they straightened out their dresses and looked around. The man was no longer on the roof.

"There's no lawn chairs," Joyce said.

"Christ!" Marsha said.

Joyce grabbed Marsha's arm and told her to look.

The man they had seen on the roof was shirtless and waving out the window as he drove a car through the trailer park.

Marsha's car.

A SANDBAR

The wind felt good in their faces as Jacob and Dorina cruised in the General's motor boat up the Wabash River. Dorina sat at the front of the boat, her hair flying in the wind and a big smile on her face. She dangled an arm over the side of the boat to feel the water. She was surprised at how warm the water was. There weren't many trees along the banks of this part of the Wabash. The farmers had plowed their fields as close to the water as they could and cut down all the trees that used to line the river.

Jacob sat at the back of the boat, his hand on the throttle. It was a beautiful day; hot, but in a boat in the wind it was perfect. The rain had moved north now and the sun was shining and the air was crisp and fresh.

They went up around a bend in the river. Dorina spotted where they were going first. It was a sandbar. Jacob cut the throttle back a little and told Dorina to sit back down. She always liked to move around in a boat too much and it always made Jacob nervous.

Jacob eased the boat right up into the sand. Dorina jumped out and ran with the rope up to a dead tree that had fallen over. She knew how to loop it around and tie it securely. Jacob had taught her. The sand was brown and cluttered with leaves and sticks and occasionally a dead shad. Dorina and Jacob thought it was the greatest beach in the entire universe. They stripped down to their underwear and ran splashing and laughing into the river. Dorina dove under first and Jacob yelled at her not to get out into the current.

"I know!" she yelled as she surfaced. Then she dove under again only to pop up shortly a few feet away, her arms waving as she gasped for air. Her curls were plastered to her cheeks and shoulders. "You're it!" she said, as she dove under again.

Jacob groaned. He would always be it. Dorina was as graceful and swift as a dolphin in the water. Jacob, on the other hand, considered himself as graceful and swift as driftwood. But he managed to keep afloat. He started towards where she had been and, of course, she popped up behind him.

"Jacob Belmo will not catch me!" Dorina said, over and over again, before diving under the water once again.

And she was probably right. Jacob would never catch her.

ACCIDENT

When they got tired of swimming Dorina and Jacob lay on their backs on the hard, hot sandbar. Dorina asked Jacob what an eclipse was. Jacob dug a finger into the sand, felt it under his fingernail.

"It's when the moon crosses in front of the sun," Jacob told her. They both watched an oddly-shaped cloud in the sky. Dorina scraped sand into her hand and tossed it on a dead shad that lay beside her. It looked like it had been dead for a long time. It was mainly bones and didn't seem to smell bad anymore.

"Why don't it happen more?" Dorina asked about the eclipse.

Jacob flicked sand off his finger. He didn't know the answer to that one. "It just don't," he said. He pointed at the cloud with his hand made into a pistol. He pushed his thumb down and fired. He looked at Dorina.

"Did your mother really kill your baby brother?"

Dorina did not move. She blinked once. "Yep," she said, shrugging. "He cried too much." She shrugged again. "She didn't mean to."

The thought sent a chill through Jacob. He went back to looking at the sky.

"I wish she didn't," Dorina said.

Jacob looked at Dorina. "How'd she do it?"

Dorina grimaced, reached up to her face and turned both eyelids inside out, and twisted up her lips before she spoke. "I got something you don't." Jacob looked at her again. He didn't like it when she turned her eyelids inside out. He told her to quit doing that, then said, "What?"

Dorina stuck out her bare chest.

"Boobs."

"God!" Jacob said, disgusted. He sat up and pulled his knees up to his chest. He looked away. "You ain't either. You're too young."

"No, I ain't. Look!"

Jacob refused to look.

"If you don't mean to do somethin' it's an accident, huh?" Dorina asked.

Jacob looked up the river. A thin trail of smoke rose above his grandfather's campsite. He had a fire going.

"I guess so, yeah."

Dorina slowly leaned towards Jacob, and then bit him hard on the arm, but only with her lips.

"Goddamn it!"

Dorina was up and running now, laughing and jumping. Jacob sat rubbing his arm. "Goddamn it! You gotta stop biting, goddamn it! I told you about that!"

"ACCIDENT!" Dorina yelled, before slipping ever so gracefully into the water.

PURPLE HAZE

There was going to be a funeral. When Betsy's grandfather fell off the console stereo in the living room of the house he and Betsy lived in, he landed just right and broke his neck. Even though he died instantly Betsy didn't notice it right away. She let him lay there all afternoon. Hell, she thought afterwards, he was always falling asleep in odd places.

When Betsy came inside and saw her grandfather there on the floor she just walked around him and put a Jimi Hendrix album on the stereo and cranked it. She didn't think anything about him being dead. She could have sworn he flinched.

So all afternoon as her grandfather lay dead on the hardwood floor of the living room, Betsy went about her business.

She even did an improvised strip-tease routine to Purple Haze. She had fantasies about being a stripper sometimes. Betsy wouldn't tell anybody but she especially got a kick out of stripping in front of her blind grandfather who always asked her what she was doing. "Dancing," she always told him.

So as Jimi Hendrix sang, "Excuse me, while I kiss the sky!" Betsy was on her tiptoes; her arms pressing her breasts together, as she gave her imaginary all-male audience her very best Marilyn Monroe kiss. She did this right beside her dead grandfather. And just as Betsy was about to give this audience her fondest thank you, her grandfather must have given the world his final kick, as he caused the needle to leap screeching across the record. This scared the hell out of Betsy. She gave her grandfather a dirty look and left the room.

Later that day, Betsy was painting her toenails a scarlet red when Dorina's mother, Lucy, came over. Lucy had planned to give Betsy a permanent. She had the Clairol box in her hand and everything.

But she took one look at Betsy's grandfather and knew something was wrong with him. She reached down and felt his neck. Quickly jerking her hand away, she let out a gasp. She touched him on the wrist.

Then Lucy looked up at Betsy. "Girl," she said. "Carl's dead!"

Betsy, who was biting gently down on her tongue, carefully finished painting her longest middle toe, looked up with an empty expression on her face and replied, "No."

BLUE CHEER

The day of the funeral Jacob took a peach upside-down cake his mother had made over to Betsy's house. He set it on the table with all the other dishes neighbors had made for her. Two old ladies sat in the kitchen eating chocolate cake and drinking coffee. Jacob grabbed a brownie from a plate.

"Poor thing," one of the old ladies said. "What's she going to do now?"

The other old lady shook her head. Jacob sneezed from all the stiff old-lady perfume that swirled almost visible in the kitchen. His mother had a bottle of it also. It came in a tall yellow-gold bottle.

"Bless you," one of them said.

"She certainly can't live in this big old house by herself," the other said. "She has to have relatives somewhere."

Jacob poured himself some Kool-Aid from a blue plastic pitcher. He stared a moment at the flap of pale white skin under the arm of one of the old women. It reminded him of the fin of a fish.

"Aren't you a Belmo?"

"Yes, Ma'am." Jacob bit into the brownie. It wasn't as sweet as he thought it would be. It was a little bitter.

Loud music suddenly coming from the living room startled the two old ladies. Jacob smiled and went into the living room where Betsy was bending over the console stereo. She turned the volume down. Jacob picked up the album cover on the console. It had BLUE CHEER written across the front. He caught a whiff of *Ivory* soap emanating from Betsy. He liked this smell much better than the perfume in the kitchen.

"Mabel and Eloise still in there?"

Jacob told her they were. He looked at the top of Betsy's head. Even slouching she was still taller than he was. He felt his heart speed up as he stood beside her.

"Old sluts," Betsy said, as she stared out the picture window. Her eyes were puffy and Jacob noticed how pale she was. She was as pale as he could ever remember seeing her. "Come on!" She said, tugging at his shirt-sleeve.

Jacob followed her upstairs.

THE LETTER

When the mail came there was no letter from her husband. There was no mail at all, in fact. Janet checked the box twice and the second time ran her hand all along the inside hoping something, anything would materialize. It didn't.

The mailboxes were all at the front of the trailer park in a row with a number on them. They had just recently been painted white. Janet thought briefly about checking each box on either side of her own for a misplaced letter but she didn't.

Janet Kittel taught English at the high school in town. This summer she was teaching a poetry workshop for adults on Monday nights. They had just read T.S. Eliot and for next Monday they were reading Sylvia Plath. Janet was married to a gym teacher at the high school. He was away for the summer in the National Guard.

Janet had a problem with her husband. She absolutely hated him. Sometimes she fantasized about his death. She fantasized elaborately at times how he got called to Vietnam and died a slow, painful, awful death. Sometimes in these fantasies she could feel the blood dripping from his body, feel his muscles twitch in pain. Sometimes these fantasies disturbed her so badly that she would drive to the Catholic Church in town and sit in the front pew and pray for forgiveness. But Janet really didn't want forgiveness. She wanted her husband to die so that she could be rid of him and she could breathe once again as freely as she had before they were married.

Janet stood on her broken concrete patio. Tiny red ants had built a mound in a crack in the concrete and were scurrying around very orderly and indifferent to anything or anyone. She squashed them out with her sandal. Then she went back into her trailer.

It was hot inside her trailer but she didn't like to run the air-conditioner. It was noisy and it either ran too hot or too cold. So to save money Janet usually just left it off.

She went to her desk in the second bedroom and began, for the hundredth time, her letter to her husband telling him that she was unhappy and wanted a divorce. She had to get the letter right and she had to get it written before he returned. She felt she had to tell him while he was away or she might never tell him. She stared down at the blank piece of paper. To think that she might never tell him how she really felt about him almost made her sick. Janet took in a breath and began writing the letter.

As she always did, Janet wrote the letter coldly and bitterly. She berated him for his ego, his ignorance, his callousness. Janet made sure to emphasize in the letter how she didn't like anything about him. How every aspect of his being left her with a residual feeling of nausea.

Janet wrote the letter in a fury, pressing down so hard upon the ballpoint pen that finally her fingers and wrist hurt. She wrote until she could write no more and then she jammed the pen so hard into the notebook it broke.

Shivering, Janet put her elbows on the desk and pulled at her hair and let out a low, ominous wail that reverberated ugly off the fake-paneled walls of the trailer.

DOLLS

Jacob and Betsy went up into the attic where lemon-colored sunlight through the window lit up slow, floating dust. When Betsy plopped upon the couch thicker dust flew everywhere. Out the attic window you could see the town's only grain elevator. Betsy put a cigarette in her mouth and Jacob reached over and lit it with a silver lighter that had belonged to Betsy's Dad. Jacob lit a cigarette too as he sat in an old rocking chair at the other end of the couch by Betsy's bare feet. The rocking chair squeaked. Jacob noticed how dirty the bottoms of her feet were.

Betsy took a deep drag off the cigarette and stared up at the ceiling. Jacob puffed at the cigarette but never inhaled. It always made him dizzy. He stared at a picture hanging on the attic wall across from him of Betsy and her parents. Betsy was younger in the picture and there was a yellow barrette in her hair. They were all three smiling. Her father's hand rested on Betsy's shoulder. Jacob looked around the rest of the attic.

Old dolls were everywhere. Betsy used to like dolls but she said she didn't anymore so now they were thrown everywhere in the attic. Betsy had tied one doll by the leg with a thin, white rope and hanged it from a rafter. It was a ratty blonde doll with tragic blue eyes. Betsy had made the eyes even more tragic by tracing them with a black crayon. The doll, Betsy had told Jacob one time, reminded her of a girlfriend she didn't like.

There was a strange feeling inside of Jacob as he sat there in the attic. He got this feeling lately when Betsy and he were together. It was a good feeling, he decided. He glanced at her lying there on the couch. She had one knee up higher than the other. She wore a green dress that was very short. Jacob tried not to look but he couldn't help it. He could see her panties.

Betsy's eyes were watery as she stared at the ceiling. The open window made the blonde doll hanging by a leg twirl slowly around.

She took a deep drag off the cigarette, and her voice sharp and low, Betsy said, "I hated that blind old man."

TWO JEHOVAH'S WITNESS HITCHHIKERS

Calvin looked in his rear-view mirror at the two ladies in the backseat. One looked a little scared and the other pissed. He tried to break the ice.

"It sure is a nice day today, ain't it?"

The one lady who looked pissed leaned towards the front seat of the police car. "I told you, Officer," she said very deliberately and cold. "That man stole my car."

"Well, yeah," Calvin agreed, nodding. He hit the button that made his siren wail. The scared lady nearly jumped out of her dress. It was a homely dress too, Calvin was thinking. He tried not to smile as he pulled the police car into the Sunoco gas station.

"I'll be right back," he said.

Marsha and Joyce watched him go into the station. They watched him get change and then make a call at the pay phone inside.

"What's he doing?" Joyce said. She was upset. It had taken her a long time to climb off the roof of that trailer. She had gotten up there and realized she was afraid of heights. They had walked all over town for two days now and still couldn't find Marsha's car. Finally they had run into the town cop.

"I don't know," Marsha said, disgusted, her arms crossed. "I don't like this town." She looked at the police officer in the station. She didn't know what he was saying but he looked like he was enjoying saying it. "He wears blue jeans. Where's he been the last two days? Did he say he was the only cop in town?"

Joyce had her compact out. Her hat was on crooked and sweat had almost ruined her make-up. "It's a small town, Marsha."

Marsha glared at Joyce. "I know that," she said. She looked out the window. Two children, neither much older than six or seven, dirty and barefoot, jumped up and down on the black cord that made the station bell ring.

Calvin returned.

"The man's probably in St. Louis by now," Marsha hissed.

"What's that?" Calvin said as he started the car. He pushed the siren button again, this time to the delight of the two kids. Calvin laughed.

"Damn, I wish I was a kid again," he said. "What about you two back there?" Neither of them gave a reply. Marsha started to then bite her tongue.

The 1964 Rambler police car pulled slowly out onto Main Street.

THE SHOEBOX

Dorina had a shoebox she kept under her bed. In that shoebox were some seashells, a ball of string, a broken compact, several broken crayons, a pink plastic bracelet, and now a turquoise ring.

Dorina took everything carefully out of the shoebox as she sat on her bed and lined it up on her pillow. She put it all in order of importance. The broken compact used to be the most important but now it was second to her new turquoise ring. Her eyes lit up as she carefully picked the ring up and studied it. There was a thin tiny crack that went all across the little round chunk of turquoise set in the ring. Dorina could not believe that this ring was actually hers. Her whole body shivered at the thought.

"It's mine!" she exclaimed. "Just mine!" Excited, she bounced off the bed and ran as fast as she could out her bedroom and down the hall to her mother's bedroom. The door was shut so Dorina turned the knob and swung the door open. She hadn't shown her mom her new ring yet.

Dorina didn't like what she saw. The bedroom was small and the bed was very close to the door. Close enough to the door that a large hairy bare foot shoved against the door then the door slammed into her.

Dorina got knocked backwards and out of the room. Her ring was knocked out of her hand and went rolling across the vinyl floor of the hallway. It noisily rolled all around and finally came to a stop against the wall. Dorina ran and got it, all the while fighting back tears. She picked her ring up and went back into her bedroom.

Sunlight shone bright through her bedroom window and this made her tears sting even more. She sat on her bed and closed her eyes and fought back her tears with anger. Dorina didn't want to cry and she wasn't going to.

Then she felt her lip. Her fingers were bloody and her lip was puffing up. Opening the broken compact, Dorina saw her puffed-up bloody lip on both sides of the crack that went down the middle of the compact.

"It don't hurt," she said. She put everything back into the shoebox and put the shoebox back under the bed. She ran her tongue over her swollen split lip and tasted blood.

With clenched fists and shoulders slumped Dorina stared out her bedroom window and yelled out loudly this time, "It don't hurt!"

DANCERS FROM ANOTHER PLANET

Was the name of the poem George pulled rejected from his mailbox. Pained, he read the rejection slip. *Thank you for submitting... It doesn't quite meet our needs at this time... you're a fucking lousy poet, asshole*, no, but it might as well have. Moaning, he headed back to his trailer, reading over the poem as he walked. He liked the poem.

Valarie stopped her car beside him and asked him when he worked.

"It's a good poem," George said, more hurt suddenly than angry. He handed it to her.

Valarie put her cigarette in the ashtray, then put the car in park and read the poem. It was a short poem about two people who shouldn't have fallen in love with each other. Valarie winced at the final line about taking a stab at romance and getting disemboweled. She sighed.

"There's so much ugliness in the world nowadays, George," she said. "Do you have to write about it, too?" She handed it back to him.

George thought about this. "It *is* ugly, isn't it?" He folded it up, stuck it back in the envelope. "I'm ugly," he said sadly.

"Oh, Christ! Get out of it!" Valarie said. "It's just a rejection slip. All writers get them, don't they? How about a drink after work?"

George looked in the car at Valarie. "Will we finally sleep together afterwards?"

"George!" Valarie put the car back in gear. "Five o'clock, Hank's. Go home and write a nice poem."

Valarie drove off.

"A nice poem," George said as he watched her car leave the trailer park. He looked up at the sky and then scratched his chin. "Fuck nice poems." He started back to his trailer. "Fuck all poems." He stopped suddenly and looked all around the trailer park. A lawn mower ran somewhere. The old lady who lived next door to him sat on her patio in a blue dress that may actually have fit her several sizes ago. She fanned herself with a folded-up section of the newspaper and looked at George out of the corner of her eye. The young woman with the pretty legs had gone inside. George had gotten a rejection slip.

He wanted suddenly to expose himself to the old lady, see

what she would do. No. Instead he would go inside and write a nice poem. Yeah, he thought, a nice poem. George stared at the cornfield behind the trailer park. Corn was so fucking ugly. A really nice poem.

"About screwing an epileptic during a seizure," George said through clenched teeth as he went inside, envelope crinkling in his hand.

A NIGHTMARE

The funeral home was an old white house with a green roof. A long blue awning stretched from the front porch all the way out to the street. In front of the funeral home was a large black hearse with COX FUNERAL HOME painted in white on the door.

Jacob and Dorina sat on the front steps of the funeral home. Betsy's grandfather was inside. Betsy sat inside also in a folding chair catty-corner from the coffin.

"We gonna go in there?" Dorina asked Jacob. Jacob was staring down at a June bug turned over on its back on the sidewalk. It spun around in circles, legs jerking.

"I guess," Jacob said. "Betsy's in there. I don't want to."

Dorina sighed and her whole body shook. "I'll have a nightmare tonight."

Jacob smiled. "Don't think about it."

"I *won't* think about it," Dorina said. "But I *will* have a nightmare."

Jacob stared at the shiny black car with the curtains in the back windows. It scared him. Dead bodies rode in that car.

"Let's go someplace else then," he said.

A PINK FLAMINGO NAPKIN-HOLDER

Calvin pulled into Doc Garrelt's driveway. Martha's car sat in front. The two Jehovah's Witnesses were all excited. One said that they had found their criminal as the other exclaimed something about returning to the scene of the crime. Calvin turned off the ignition.

"I think you two ought to follow me in." Calvin said, trying to sound serious. "Make an official identification."

Martha put her hand to her chest, and then in a half-whisper, "What if he's dangerous?" Calvin let out a strange laugh then cleared his throat. He leaned over and opened the glove box and pulled out a pearl-handled revolver that hadn't had a firing pin in it since Prohibition.

"I think I can handle him," he said.

The revolver took both Martha and Joyce aback.

"He didn't look all that dangerous," Joyce said.

Martha didn't agree. "You just never know," she said.

They got out of the police car and walked up to the trailer, the Jehovah's Witnesses almost cowering behind Calvin. He started to open the screen door, then looked back at Martha and Joyce.

"You two wouldn't mind a short little silent prayer right here and now, would you?" Calvin tipped his baseball cap back with the barrel of the revolver. "Baptists and Jehovah's Witnesses get along, don't they?"

Martha and Joyce didn't quite know what to think. They just bowed their heads along with Calvin. Then, after mumbling a few intentionally incoherent words, Calvin opened the screen door and knocked. No one answered. He knocked again on the metal door.

"It's open," Doc Garrelts said. His voice made the two ladies jump.

"That's him!" Martha whispered loudly.

Calvin nodded and then motioned for them to follow him in.

They went inside. It was a small trailer and as you entered there was a smoke-brown plastic partition stretching from the floor to the ceiling that partially hid a padded black bar that had the kitchen sink on one side of it. The kitchen table was small with two matching chrome-legged chairs that had red padded seats. The kitchen table was bare except for a napkin-holder that had two small wooden pink flamingoes on each side. The drapes were pulled shut in the living room. It was dark.

Doc Garrelts flicked on a hanging pseudo-chain-link globe lamp that had white plastic lattice-work covering it like a tacky spider web. Doc Garrelts said hello. He sat in a green swivel rocker.

Both ladies gasped. Martha pointed reflexively. "That's—" She wanted to say that was the man.

But the man sitting there had on a huge bouffant bright red wig and wore what had to be a fake mustache. It was a large greasy black mustache that curled almost to his ears. Calvin, as he rubbed his neck, had to look the other way.

THE FIRE STATION

The fire station sat on the corner at the end of Jacob's and Dorina's block. It was a small rectangular fire station that had once been a gas station. A fire truck and a red pick-up truck were inside the two bays. It had once been a green building but somebody had put a coating of thin white paint over the green. The white paint had not been very good paint and if you pressed your fingers to the fire station, chalky white dust came off on your fingers.

During the day a man with a large pot belly and a face like a rat sat in a metal yellow chair on the concrete in front of the fire station. His name was Lewis. The only noticeable thing about Lewis besides his belly was his pants. They were much too small for him and when he sat down the bottoms came up almost to his knees. Betsy once pointed out to Jacob that Lewis's family jewels, in those pants, didn't have anywhere comfortable to go, so they just bulged out ugly down his left thigh. Lewis was always rubbing this bulge, too, especially when Betsy was around.

Not long ago Dorina and Betsy had a little scam worked out concerning Lewis and the fire station. Betsy would stop and talk to Lewis and Lewis would ask her all sorts of questions as he kept rubbing the bulge in his pants. Betsy would smile and watch him rub as she coyly answered all his questions. And while Betsy was doing this Dorina would sneak into the fire station.

Inside the fire station was a refrigerator and inside the refrigerator there were always six-packs of beer, Powerhouse candy bars, and liverwurst sandwiches.

It didn't take Lewis long to figure out this little scam of theirs but for the longest time he liked Betsy's attention. In fact, he liked her attention so much he had his pants unzipped one time when she came up to him and as Betsy started talking to him and Dorina sneaked into the fire station, Lewis did something awful.

Lewis exposed himself and Betsy let out a scream and started running home. Dorina heard the scream and dropped the candy bars and liverwurst sandwiches and ran out of the fire station screaming also. Lewis just sort of crawled into the fire station and from then on he never talked to the kids in town.

But they still figured out ways to get into the fire station. Like now. Climbing Jacob's shoulders Dorina pulled herself up into a window in the back of the fire station. The frosted glass cranked out and Dorina was just small enough to climb inside.

Once inside Dorina walked on her tiptoes across the smooth gray concrete floor. She tiptoed around the fire truck to get to the refrigerator. It was an old refrigerator with rounded edges and a long chrome handle.

Dorina had to pull down hard on the handle to get it open. Inside there was a bottle of whiskey and three six-packs of Old Milwaukee beer in stubby brown bottles. She opened a small baby blue panel in the door labeled BUTTER. There, Dorina knew, was where the candy bars were kept.

Dorina, her heart pounding fast in her chest, took two candy bars and a six-pack of beer from the refrigerator.

A DROWNING

Jimmy ran away from home. Walked actually. His parents were at work and he wouldn't be missed for a few days anyway. He sat now and watched the river. It was up and moved fast like it was in a hurry to get somewhere. Jimmy was in a hurry to get somewhere but he just didn't know where. He had his sandals off and his backpack beside him on the steep riverbank.

He had hitchhiked straight down Route 1 to where he was. Jimmy was young and his curly blonde hair touched his shoulders and his gold wire-framed photo-gray glasses had white tape holding one side together. He had intense blue eyes, big lips, and bad skin. In his backpack were some clothes, a toothbrush, and two paperback novels: *Cat's Cradle* and *Dhalgren*. Jimmy had read *Cat's Cradle* twice and was a quarter of the way through *Dhalgren*. *Dhalgren* was the longest book he had ever tried to read.

Jimmy was deep in fourteen-year-old thought. He was about to knock on the door of that hippie house up on the bluff and ask for food. He chickened out. He came down to the river instead and now sat and for a moment regretted running away from home.

He took off his glasses and put them carefully beside him. The riverbank was steep here and it made him just a little uneasy. Jimmy couldn't swim. Everybody else could swim in his family but he was the youngest and they always said he was afraid of the water. He wasn't afraid of the water at all but no one had bothered to show him how to swim. He would someday learn how to swim, he had decided a long time ago.

His eyes hurt. His parents said he read too much. He spent all his money on books and his father in particular couldn't understand this. The only time his father wasn't of this opinion was after Jimmy was first shown how to drive a tractor and plow a field. It took him twice as long as it took his older brother and the rows were very crooked. His father looked at him and said this to him: "Maybe you should go read a book, Jimmy."

Jimmy heard something and was startled by a man suddenly beside him there along the riverbank. He relaxed. It was a man in a uniform. A rather fat man whose brown uniform didn't fit him very well. He seemed about to explode in it. The man was at least a head taller than him and at least twice as wide. He had the insignia of a Game Warden on his hat. He wore a holster but there wasn't any gun in it. Jimmy thought this was funny. Jimmy was the type of kid who didn't need much reason to find something funny.

The man didn't say anything. Jimmy was always saying something. He threw a rock out across the river.

"My dad and brother do a lot of river fishing. They say I'm not patient enough."

The Game Warden turned slightly to look at the river. He still didn't say anything. Jimmy stood up so he could see the man's face. The man wouldn't look at him. Jimmy got a little nervous. But not too much. The man wore a uniform.

The man spoke finally. He asked the boy if he lived in that house up there. Jimmy said he didn't. Jimmy told him his abbreviated story. He told the man he left home because he was looking for something. He said he took the road that led to Darwin's Ferry because he thought it was the most interesting name for a town he had come across along Route 1. So far anyway, Jimmy said.

Jimmy said he counted six box turtles on the road leading into town. He moved every one of them to the other side of the road. Two had already been run over by cars and smashed.

The Game Warden was still looking up at the hippie house. "I don't like the looks of those people," the Game Warden said. "In fact, I downright hate everything about that place."

Jimmy reached down to get his glasses and got them very carefully. The stem that wasn't taped was close to breaking also. He put them carefully on his face.

"I read in a book somewhere that you only hate what can hurt you." He laughed and most people liked his laugh. When Jimmy laughed it sounded like he meant it. The Game Warden didn't so much as smile. Jimmy was just making conversation, he thought.

Jimmy reached down to shut his backpack. He heard the man clear his throat deeply. As Jimmy rose up a forearm caught him in the jaw and with such force it sent him falling half-forward, half sideways. He stumbled bad. He went down to one knee but kept sliding. There wasn't anything to grab onto. Before he knew it Jimmy had slid into the water. He felt stupid and embarrassed. He told the man he couldn't swim. He just expected the man to help him.

The man didn't say anything. The man didn't move. He wasn't even looking at him. Jimmy went under. His hand popped out of the rapid, swirling brown water momentarily.

The Game Warden looked half around to see if anyone had seen what had happened. Then he thought about kicking the backpack into the water. He started to walk away. He came back and kicked the backpack in. He lit a cigarette and watched the backpack swirl and gradually sink also as it moved on down the river.

Then the Game Warden walked away.

REPOSSESSED CARS

The bank was the only new building in town; plenty of glass slanting down one side, and shiny black brick surrounding the glass. Very modern. Across the street from the bank old buildings stood swaying and tired. A little cafe was on the bottom floor of the corner building across from the bank. Daily specials were written in black magic marker on poster board and taped to the glass door. You knew the specials hadn't changed for a while because the tape had turned yellow. Next to the cafe was a used furniture store with a burnt-orange chair with thin cushions in the window. Beside the chair was a brass spittoon that was spotted and badly in need of polishing. $10.00 was written in pencil on masking tape stuck to the base of the spittoon.

The bank was next to the fire station. Not ten feet separated the two buildings. Behind the bank was a big gravel parking lot. The rocks were freshly laid and nearly glowed white and left powdery sediment on the bottoms of your shoes or in your hands if you picked the rocks up. It was the newest gravel in town.

In this parking lot were four repossessed cars and a repossessed pontoon boat. The pontoon boat had yellow tin sides and a blue square umbrella top. It sat up on cement blocks and had MABEL'S written in red across the front of the umbrella top. It was MABEL'S no longer. The bank owned it now. Inside the pontoon boat Jacob and Dorina sat on scratchy green indoor-outdoor carpeting. They were hidden inside the yellow tin sides. They sipped Old Milwaukee beer and ate Powerhouse candy bars.

Dorina put her mouth to the top of the beer bottle and tried to make it sound like a tiny foghorn. Then she asked Jacob why the beer they stole from the fire station always tasted so good and the beer his grandpa let them have anytime they wanted always tasted so bad.

Jacob smiled and leaned his head back against tin. He had no idea, but Dorina was right. He closed his eyes and felt a breeze cross his cheeks. Then Jacob started thinking about Betsy. He thought about Betsy as she sat on the couch in the attic in that short green dress. The image made him ache all over. The tips of his fingers seemed to go numb.

Next to Jacob, her eyes bright and serious, Dorina very carefully took her new turquoise ring off her thumb and, once again, rolled it around in her hands.

THE FLAG

All Betsy could see from where she sat in the funeral home was her grandfather's cold, powdery gray face and the blue knuckles of his thick, stubby fingers. She squirmed in the wooden folding chair and crossed her legs. Her hose made her legs tingle and itch. She hated to wear hose.

Looking at her grandfather made Betsy think of her parents' funeral. When her parents died the caskets were closed. All she could remember really of her parents' funeral was that there had been a flag on her mother's casket. Her grandfather had always told her she was wrong. The flag, he said, had been on her father's casket.

"Not on that goddamn floozy wife of his," her grandfather had said. "She weren't in no war. They only put flags on men who've been in the service."

But Betsy wouldn't believe it. She insisted that the flag had been on her mother's casket. She could see the flag and she knew which casket was which. Her grandfather was blind and she remembered telling him as much. Betsy also remembered her grandfather pulling her to him and talking harshly into her face.

"Your father was in World War II," her grandfather had said, as he practically spit into her face and squeezed her arm hard enough to make it hurt. "And while he was getting his ass shot at, your mother was showing her ass to every Tom, Dick, and Harry in town."

Betsy, at that time, didn't know anything about what her grandfather was saying about her mother. But the flag, Betsy defiantly insisted, had been on her mother's casket; where it was supposed to be. Her grandfather shoved her away so hard, Betsy recalled, as she stared at his cold, lifeless hand, that she stumbled and bloodied her knee on the hardwood floor of the living room.

"Then they fucked up," her grandfather had said finally, his empty eyes hollow and his face angry and bitter.

Betsy, as she stared now at the coffin of her grandfather, kept seeing her parents' coffins. She still didn't think anybody had fucked up. The flag was on her mother's coffin and that's where it was supposed to be.

WASTELAND

Like the hand of a mechanical card shark the record in the jukebox machine slid out of the stack and into place on the platter. The record popped and crackled a few times, then Hank Williams Jr. twanged lazily into his father's song- "Your Cheatin' Heart."

Valarie, after sipping from the frosted beer mug, crossed her legs and removed her shoes. She winced as a sharp pain sliced up her shin. She'd been on her feet all day. Her hose stuck damp to her toes. She took another sip from the mug.

Behind the bar Art Stanley wiped an imaginary damp spot on the bar as he poured himself another shot of bourbon with his free hand. There were two other people in the bar but he liked to stand by Valarie. Her nurse's uniform always clung to her full breasts nicely and she was one of the prettiest women Art knew. From where he stood he could see just where her short uniform ended and her white-nyloned thighs began.

"You look damn good today, Val."

"God!" Valarie said. "If I look half as bad as I feel you're full of it, Art." She put both elbows on the bar and tapped out a Winston Red. Art was right there with a lighter. She blew smoke high above her.

"You wouldn't believe the day I had." She brushed her hair back away from her face and pulled the top of her uniform together.

"I'm getting fat."

Art laughed. "You ain't never been fat since I knowed you."

"I'm either fat or bloated. I have to watch my salt this time of the month." She tapped ashes into the metal ashtray on the bar. She let out a sarcastic laugh as she stared at the ashtray. "Either that or buy a couple size-eight uniforms."

Art put the rag away and leaned heavily upon the bar.

"You know I read in *Reader's Digest* that women buy shoes two sizes too small just because they won't admit how big their feet are."

This struck Valarie as funny. "Those women aren't nurses."

Art took a sip of his drink. "I don't suppose so." He shrugged. Art was a burly man and the hair on his chest poked thick out of his T-shirt. "I don't think it said what they were. Hell, I don't believe half that shit in those magazines. Some General last month said we'd win that War over there by this time next year."

"Uh-huh," Valarie said, and just as she was about to say something George burst through the door of the tavern. He ran his hands through his shoulder-length hair as he walked down and sat beside Valarie.

"Hey, babe." He winked. "I'm free tonight." He went

mockly somber. "No, sorry. I'm not. I'm getting tied up around ten by these six blind nuns."

"Yeah," Valarie said.

"The unusual tonight, Art," George said. "I got my third rejection slip this week."

Art set a draft and a shot of whiskey in front of George. "Which poem?" Asked Art.

George winced and shrugged. "The greatest poem I ever wrote."

"Of course," Art and Valarie said in unison.

"Surprise, surprise," a bearded man at the other end of the bar said.

"Hey, shut up, Frank," George replied, as he looked down the bar. "Where's your old lady at? Oh, I forgot, the Redbirds are in Springfield tonight."

The man at the other end of the bar chuckled. "I should be so lucky. If she'd go I'd buy her a ticket and fill the truck up."

"And a press pass," George continued.

"Enough!" Valarie said.

George turned to Valarie. "Hey, are we a little uptight tonight. Bad day?"

"Bad day."

"Poor kid." He shook his head, eyed Valarie. "Puttin' on a little weight, Val?"

"Shut up!" Valarie said. "No." She tapped out another cigarette. "It's close to my period."

He gave her a strong hug. "Just kidding. You know me. I'm all wired up. Drank two pots of coffee trying to write a *nice* poem." Valarie asked him how it went. George shrugged. "I watched that schoolteacher next door sunbathe instead."

"George!"

"Well, hell. She lays there right in the goddamn street, all lathered up." George's eyes sparkled. "I kept putting this imaginary rotisserie through her, like they do in that cartoon." He gestured like he was turning the rotisserie. They all laughed.

"Sick." Valarie said, emptying her beer. "I wish I had time to lay out in the sun."

"Hell, make time. Call in sick."

"Ha."

Then they talked awhile about work at the nursing home, about how poorly run it was and how everybody was always quitting and leaving. Art put some dimes in the jukebox, punched in some more country and western music. The two other men at the bar got up and left.

"I have to work back to back shifts tomorrow," Valarie said.

"They can't make you do that."

Valarie's face twisted up. "Yeah, but if you don't somebody else will have to. It gets old."

"No kidding," George said. "Let's take off, Val. Let's go to Florida."

"Uh-huh," Valarie said. But George talked like he meant it. George, Valarie thought, always talked like he meant it. He talked about how there had to be a lot of hospitals in Florida. He talked about the beaches. He talked about the sun. George could always talk so passionately at times, Valarie thought.

"I gotta get out of this town, man," George said. He tapped nervously on the bar. Valarie, her head hurting, smiled and leaned her cheek in her palm. George nodded, bounced his knees rhythmically, as if he were about ready for lift-off.

"This goddamn Midwest is the biggest fucking wasteland." He emptied the shot Art put in front of him, then looked seriously at Valarie. "The goddamn flat fields and black earth. The grain elevators and tractors. Fuck that theory about room to breathe and think–Hell, if my mind becomes any more lucid I might have a seizure." Valarie laughed. "I'm serious. I want to try crowded streets and tall buildings–some concrete that isn't cracked–a beach even." He sighed deeply.

"Oh, George," Valarie said. She leaned over and quickly, yet tenderly kissed him just below the ear.

WHITE LIGHTNING

Leonard stood on a bluff overlooking a bend in the Wabash, pissing. He watched the dark yellow stream fall into the gray water entranced and back in the past somewhere, a young boy pissing under a bridge as a big old catfish bent his cane pole and nearly broke it. It had been a creek that day, not far from the farm he was raised on. Leonard was maybe ten. He shook vigorously and zipped up his overalls.

"Hey, old man!"

Leonard didn't know where the voice was coming from but he knew who it was. He turned and walking along the bank towards him was the General. He stopped walking just long enough to hold up a Mason jar full of clear liquid. Leonard took off his baseball cap and ran his hand back along his head, then put his cap back on.

"You're up to no good, Malcolm Talbert!" Leonard called out. He heard the General's familiar laugh in return.

"Why hell yes I am," the General replied, grunting, as he climbed up to where Leonard was. He was wheezing some. "When I ain't up to no good the Lord'll take me."

Leonard pointed at the Mason jar, his eyes wide and ornery. "That'll take you quicker."

The General stopped, looked curiously at the Mason jar full of White Lightning home-brewed corn whiskey, then looked at Leonard.

"I sure hope so," he said, seriously.

They both let out big laughs as the General unscrewed the lid of the Mason Jar.

BILL LANGLEY

The game warden's boat was an official-blue flat-bottomed sixteen-footer with the seal of the state of Illinois emblazoned on both sides. Bill Langley cut the black Mercury motor off and dropped anchor. He stood up and looked downriver and through binoculars he could see Leonard Downs and Malcolm Talbert nearly passed out on their backs. He looked all around and didn't see a soul in any direction. He reached down and pulled out a pump-action twelve-gauge shotgun from under the metal bench-seat.

Easy, he was thinking, as he looked through the sights of the shotgun at the two old drunks on the bluff. He could shoot those two old men dead and not a soul would know it. Bill Langley kept looking around for a while. There was probably nobody around for miles. Finally he put the shotgun back under the seat.

Then he pulled up one of Leonard Down's fishing nets and dumped all the fish into his boat. There were a lot of fish. Several large flat-head catfish and twenty or so channels and blue cats. He reached down and tossed two small perch back into the water. The old sod probably hadn't run his nets for days.

"Good for him," Bill Langley said as he sat down and pulled the rope on the motor. A small cloud of blue smoke came up behind the motor as it started. He turned the boat around and headed back upriver.

VIET CONG

Dorina finally stopped looking at her ring and lifted the bottle of beer up to her lips and sipped. Some dribbled on her chin. She wiped it off then stared in front of her intent and serious. Jacob seemed almost asleep beside her.

"When my daddy comes home," Dorina began. "I want us to take him to our beach." Jacob barely opened his eyes. He said okay. He asked her when her daddy was coming home.

"I don't know. Mommy says soon. When he don't have to be in Viet Cong anymore. She says we're gonna move to Alabama and start a church."

"Viet*nam*," Jacob corrected. "You always say Viet Cong. It's Viet*nam*." He glanced down at the ring on her thumb. She tapped it lightly on the beer bottle. He asked her if she had ever seen her daddy.

Dorina glared at Jacob a moment then shrugged. "Sure I have, silly."

"No you haven't."

Dorina jumped up and intentionally kicked Jacob's foot in the process. She leaned over the metal railing of the pontoon boat as she rose up on her heels.

"Let's pretend this boat is on the river."

Jacob poked his finger into the beer bottle. "The General said the Wabash ain't deep enough for pontoon boats anymore."

"Pretend!" Dorina said emphatically as she took a sip of beer. "You can't ever pretend." She let out a long, exasperated sigh. "I need a real friend."

Jacob turned his head and noticed a drop of blood on Dorina's tennis shoe. It came from when she got her lip smashed the other day. He needed a real friend, too, he thought. Dorina was too young and goofy. He took a drink of the beer. It burned all the way down. It didn't taste so good now.

Then all of a sudden Dorina jumped into his lap, her finger vertical over her mouth, her large eyes wide with fear.

"Too late, Missy!" Dorina and Jacob stared at each other. They both knew whose voice that was. It was Calvin, the town cop. Dorina's look turned from fear to disgust. She stood up.

"My name ain't Missy!"

"What are you doing up there?"

Dorina, as innocently as she could, replied, "Playing," as Jacob quietly gathered all the beer bottles together and tried to find a place to hide them. His heart pounded so hard in his chest he felt it in his ears. He opened a wooden panel beneath a seat and eased the bottles and the candy wrappers inside.

"Well now I've told you kids not to play around here before, haven't I?"

"Yes, sir, you have," Dorina replied, her face dropping into an expression she knew would have the right effect. Calvin stared at her a moment. Then he pointed a finger at her. "I'm going to give you one more chance, Missy. You know what I told you and that Belmo boy the last time. The Bank don't want you kids messing around here. I mean it! If I catch you around here again I'm going to take you down to the station and call your mom. You understand?"

Jacob, laying over on his side, looked up at Dorina. She was giving Calvin her very best helpless and hurt look. She looked on the verge of tears.

"All right," she said, pitifully. She wiped the corner of her eye with her fist.

Then Calvin told her not to get all bent out of shape about it. They just had to play somewhere else is all. "Come on down, now."

"Okay." Dorina walked over and climbed off the pontoon.

"Where's your buddy at anyway?" Calvin asked.

"I don't know," Dorina said, as Jacob, curled up in a corner under the seat, gritted his teeth and couldn't help but smile.

EVA BRAUN

Their legs dangled over the side of the bluff as both the General and Leonard Downs lay on their backs staring up at the darkening sky. The Mason jar was empty and on its side back behind them. The lid had long been inadvertently tossed into the river and was well on its way down the Wabash and on into the Ohio river. The General sat up and took out a box of stick matches and tried to re-light a cigar stub. His head spun but he got the stub lit finally. He puffed on it a time or two, then wiped his nose on his flannel shirt sleeve.

"Leonard, you ever heard of a woman smokin' a cigarette with her hole down there?"

Leonard had his wrist across his forehead and his eyes shut. One eye eased open. He thought about what the General had just asked him.

"No, Malcolm," Leonard replied in all seriousness. "I can't say that I have."

"Well by God they's some women who can." The General

puffed on his cigar as he put the matches back in his overalls. "They got movies you can watch, French or German, and some woman in those movies'll smoke a cigarette with her hole."

The General, unable to sit up any longer, went back on his back. Leonard had both eyes open now and they were very bloodshot.

"Malcolm," Leonard said. "I don't think I believe that."

"By God it's true," the General replied. "You know that Beechum boy who farms just upriver there?" Leonard nodded. "He said he saw one of them movies in Evansville and that very same night he paid one of them whores a twenty dollar bill to do the same damn thing."

Leonard thought about this. "Oh, hell," he said.

"Hell, he didn't. He ain't one to lie." The General pulled his whiskey flask from his pocket, dropped it, picked it up, then unscrewed the top and took a sip. He handed it to Leonard. Leonard took a shot. He looked at the General.

"Why'd a woman want to do that in the first place?"

The General shrugged, screwed the lid back on his flask. "Save her lungs, I guess."

They both laughed.

"Goddamn women," Leonard said.

"I hear you on that one." The General took off his baseball cap, laid it on his belly. "You remember Gertrude McKinney?"

Leonard put his hands behind his head, closed his eyes. "She had a mole on her cheek as big around as your thumb."

"Yep," the General said. "And tits like two balloons full of warm water." The General blew smoke. "I was thinking about her today."

"Hell," Leonard said. "I used to think about her every ten minutes when I was fifteen."

"You damn straight!" the General said, then added that he bet she could have smoked a cigarette that way. They both laughed and Leonard had to sit up as his laugh became a cough. He finally spit a mixture of blood and phlegm over the side of the bluff. The General sat up with him. He didn't like how Leonard's lips would turn blue sometimes when he coughed.

"You ever gonna get back with Nettie?"

Leonard, still coughing some, took out his smoke sack, started rolling a cigarette. He stopped rolling, said, "She thinks I'm a loony-bird."

The General looked at the old man beside him. "Why, you are a loony-bird, Leonard."

Leonard stopped rolling the cigarette again, his eyes showing some pain as he stared down the river. "I 'spect you're right, Malcolm."

"Oh, hell no you ain't," the General said, his hand on Leonard's back for a second. "No more than anybody. Now Roger Carrigan was as nutty as they come."

Leonard tried to remember Roger Carrigan. "Was he the one who used to run stark-naked after those Franklin twins?"

The General thought about this. "No," he said. "That was Daniel Eckert. He got killed in '44 right there in Berlin the same day they got Hitler."

"Yeah, I remember that," Leonard said, as he licked along the length of the rolled cigarette. He twisted the ends together. He looked at the General. "Probably runnin' naked after that Eva Braun."

They both started laughing and the General laughed so hard his cigar stub popped right out of his mouth and rolled down the embankment and on into the Wabash River.

RAY BRADBURY

As Jacob and Dorina cut through an alley and then a backyard on their way home they both talked excitedly about their close brush with the law. They talked about how one of them had to go back and get those beer bottles out of the pontoon boat. Jacob said he would.

"Just be careful," Dorina said. They walked in an alley where a thick row of grass grew in the middle.

They heard a gruff voice. They both stopped. They stood

in the alley behind a house they had thought long empty. Someone had broken a window on the back porch and it had remained there for a long time. The window was still broken.

In the middle of the backyard stood an old man with a cane. Outside of Jacob's grandfather, the old man had the longest gray hair of any old man Jacob had ever seen. It was thick and almost touched his shoulders.

They both thought about running but the man, strangely enough, didn't seem all that threatening. He was short and had a big belly and a soft, round face. He had a cane. He asked them what their names were. They told him. He nodded.

"Come here," the old man said, as he turned and headed back to the house. Dorina and Jacob looked at each other. Then Dorina started to follow the old guy.

"Dorina!" Jacob said, but she kept walking so he followed. Jacob's head was still a bit light from the beer.

They followed the man through the back porch and into the kitchen. The place smelled funny, just like Jacob's aunt and uncle's house. Mothballs. They followed the old man into the dining room where a huge glass chandelier hung over a dark, shiny wood table. The table sat on a strange, faded carpet that had yellow tassels all around it.

Dorina looked all around the place. "You just move in?" She asked. The man stopped walking, turned back towards the children.

"In a manner of speaking, yes," he replied. They both, right away, liked the old man. He had spoken to them like they were adults.

They followed the old man all the way through the house and out to the front porch. As they passed through the living room Jacob noticed that some of the furniture had white cloth draped over it.

Out on the porch the old man stood and looked out across the street. Jacob and Dorina didn't know quite what to think. The old man, as he leaned on his cane, rubbed his white mustache with his thumb and index finger.

"My wife and I lived in this house for thirty-one years." The old man pointed. "See those trees over there?"

They both looked at the lot catty-corner from the house at the end of the street. On the lot was a small patch of trees. They played in it all the time. They even saw a deer in it once.

"I took money out of the bank to buy that lot. I don't know why." He looked at them. "I don't ever want to see those trees cut down." The man put his cane in his other hand, shifted his weight. Jacob noticed he had one shoe with a thicker sole on it.

"We're gonna bury my baby brother–"

"I mow lawns in town!" Jacob loudly interrupted, his voice almost a yell. Then he glared at Dorina. He looked back at the old man. "I'll mow your lawn if you want me to. It needs it."

"It does," the old man said. "But another man mows it. Has for years. Ever since I left." He looked at Jacob.

"You read books, young man?"

Dorina jumped up on the concrete railing of the front porch. It was wider than she was. She sat with her hands under her legs.

"He's got the most comic books in town," Dorina said proudly. "You bend up the covers and he'll make you buy him a new one."

This made the old man smile and when he smiled his face lit up. His eyes sparkled. "Is that so, young lady?"

"Yep!"

"You read his comic books?"

"Carefully!" She said, sounding older suddenly. Dorina shrugged. "I like Richie Rich. He likes war comics. They're ugly."

Jacob stared at the boxes stacked in the corner of the front porch. He asked if those were all books.

"All books," the old man said. Then he walked over to one of the boxes. He bent down and pulled books out until he found the one he was looking for. Dorina got off the railing and stood beside him and watched.

"I only read one book before." Jacob said. "*20,000 Leagues*

Under the Sea." He shrugged. He didn't know what else to say. "I liked it," he said.

The old man nodded. He wiped the dust off the book. It was a gold-colored paperback with a man's face on the cover. The man wore thick glasses and looked as if he was staring up at something. Jacob's heart began to beat a little faster. There was always something magical about a book. A book of any kind really. He didn't know why he felt this way.

"You need to leave this place for awhile, young man." He handed the book to Jacob. Jacob took it. "Go to Mars for awhile."

This struck Dorina as funny as she leaned against Jacob to see the cover of the book. Jacob pushed her gently away, told her to quit leaning on him. She still thought it was funny what this old man said.

"He can't go to Mars!" She grabbed Jacob's arm. "Where is Mars?" Jacob shot her a disgusted look and kept staring at the book. He opened it carefully. For some reason he loved the smell of books. He looked at the back cover.

"That's yours, young man," Delancey J. McFadden said. He pointed at Dorina. "I'll find you something, young lady. You come back tomorrow."

"Okay!" Dorina said. "I don't read too good." She smiled at Jacob. "I want to go to Mars."

Jacob, embarrassed and disgusted with Dorina, told her they had to get home. He thanked the old man for the book. He stopped halfway down the concrete steps.

"I'll mow your lawn for this book."

"No, no," the old man said.

"Mars!" Dorina yelled out. Jacob whispered to her to shut up.

"My daddy is–" Jacob pushed her hard and told her to shut up again, this time louder. She almost fell. She glared back at Jacob, her fist doubled up and her eyes blazing. It was the first time he had ever tried to stop her from saying what she was about to say.

Jacob couldn't look at her. "We gotta get home."

Dorina kept glaring, her whole body trembling.

The old man sat watching it all, but his mind was elsewhere. Delancey sat on the porch swing, his cane across his lap and watched until the children faded out of sight.

MARY AND RON

Betsy sat and stared at the woman across from her at the table in the restaurant. Her name was Mary Biggs. She had grown up with Betsy's mother. When Betsy's parents died Betsy went up to Chicago and stayed with Mary a long time it had seemed like. They had kept in touch ever since and sometime each summer after that Betsy would go and stay with Mary and her husband, Ron.

Betsy thought Mary Biggs was as beautiful as a woman could be. Mary had long black hair, a pretty nose and mouth, and always wore her make-up perfect. Her hair always shined and always looked so healthy. Mary's body was so thin and petite she could have easily been a model. Sometimes Betsy would get sick with envy looking at Mary's body. She wished often to be that thin but this always made Mary laugh. Mary said she would swap bodies with Betsy any day and Betsy could never figure this out.

Mary was a social worker in a hospital in Tinley Park and sometimes this is what Betsy wanted to be someday, too. But other times the job as a social worker seemed a bit boring to Betsy. But most of the time Betsy wanted to be exactly like Mary.

Mary drank coffee and Betsy drank a coke. Mary wore a black mini-dress that flared at mid-thigh and her skinny little legs were covered with fish-net black hose. Betsy thought she looked so cute. They didn't know exactly what to say to each other. Whenever they got together before they always talked about what an asshole her grandfather was, but now on the day of his funeral, they both seemed at a loss for words. Finally Betsy broke the silence.

"My next-door neighbor, Lucy," Betsy began. "You know, Dorina's mother–she's married to a black man who's in Vietnam." Betsy's voice became almost a whisper when she said black man.

Mary said she remembered. "She had a baby awhile back. The cutest little thing you ever seen, big blue eyes. It wasn't her husband's. She ain't seen her husband since Dorina was born. Lucy wouldn't say whose it was but it didn't have any black in it." Betsy took the straw out of her glass, took a drink. "She gave that baby up for adoption, can you believe that?" Betsy blew her nose suddenly on a napkin. She had been on the verge of tears all day. It felt good to talk about something else. "I would have taken that baby. It just don't seem like Lucy doing that. I can't see anybody giving up their baby."

Mary was looking at the waitress, who was an older lady who seemed to be eavesdropping. She wore a stained green apron over a white uniform. Rosemary was written on her nametag. No one else was in the restaurant this time of day. Mary poured some cream into her coffee.

"Well, I don't know, Betsy. You do have choices in life."

Betsy laughed out loud. "Lucy just likes men too much is all. Always has, she says. She's nice and all. She yells at Dorina too much." Betsy caught her breath. "I worry about Dorina sometimes."

Mary looked at Betsy. When she jabbered so it reminded her so much of Betsy's mother. Emotion rose suddenly in Mary. She squeezed Betsy's arm. "Is she unhappy?"

"Who? Dorina or Lucy?"

Mary shrugged. "Either one. Both."

"Just to look at Dorina you'd think she was the happiest thing in the world." Betsy looked concerned. "I don't know, though. Lucy's the one I worry about. Her husband's supposed to come home soon and she's out practically every night with someone else. I don't try to be that nosy. You want a piece of pie? They make it fresh every day."

Mary smiled and said she didn't. She put her hand on Betsy's arm. "What about you, kid?"

Betsy looked at Mary. Her voice was so soft and pretty. She blew her nose on another napkin, took a deep breath.

"I'm fine. It's okay. Marge said I could live with them for right now. The Belmo's are great. Jacob's a little weird. I like him, though. He just don't say much. They got an extra bedroom, they live across the street, I can keep an eye on the house–" Betsy couldn't hold back anymore. She tried but she just couldn't. The tears rolled out and her whole body quietly shook as Mary moved over and embraced her.

Betsy stopped after a moment, blew her nose again, then rolled her eyes. "God, I'm ignorant."

"No, you're not." Mary kept hugging her. "You know, I've talked it over with Ron." Now Mary had to blow her nose on a napkin. They both, teary-eyed, looked at each other and laughed a bit. Mary continued. "But I've talked it over with Ron and after we get back from Mexico in August. We have that tour thing every year. In fact I wanted to ask you about that. I think we can swing an opening."

Betsy shrugged, then tentatively, "Mexico?"

"You have time to think about that. But in August our lease is up, too." Mary reached over, clutched Betsy's hand.

"We're looking for a bigger place. A house hopefully." She paused, then quickly Mary got the words out. "We want you to come live with us."

Betsy froze. She didn't even blink.

"Okay," Betsy said, weakly.

ONCE UPON A TIME IN THE MIDWEST

"Do not go gentle!" George yelled as he hovered, arms raised as he stood on his knees straddling Valarie in the doorway. "Into that good trailer!" Valarie was laughing. They were quite drunk as they had both stumbled going into her home. George eased himself down to Valarie, kissed her on the cheek.

"George," Valarie said as she pulled away from him slightly.

"Dylan Thomas was the best goddamn poet there ever was. There ever will be! Power!" He climbed off Valarie, found a light switch. Valarie pulled her legs inside, set up and felt a wave of dizziness.

"Oops," she said, holding her head. "I drank too much."

"It's good for you," George said. He parted the kitchen curtain. It was dark now. Across the street the lady strained to look out her front trailer window at the spectacle that had unfolded at Valarie's steps.

"Is that all she's got to do?" George said. "Look out windows." He let the curtain drop back into place. "Is that all I got to do?" His head spun, too. "Once upon a time in the Midwest." He sat down beside Valarie. "We're goddamn voyeurs. Bored white Protestant self-righteous shithead voyeurs." He slurred his words. He kissed Valarie's cheek. "Once upon a time in the Midwest. I will write this poem. The words will crackle and sparkle like Technicolor gems embedded in the face of the Princess of Truth!"

"Oh shut up, George," Valarie said, her voice hardly loud enough to hear. "Kiss me again and I'll slug you." She closed her eyes and started backwards. George caught her, eased her to the vinyl floor of the kitchen.

"You know something, George."

"What?"

"You're not a very good poet."

George shrugged. "I know that."

"I have a headache."

"It's an obnoxious time. The world is on fire."

"Yes," Valarie said. "Now go home, George."

George stared down at Valarie's long eyelashes, glanced briefly at the swell of her breasts.

"Okay, Val."

KIDS

Night settles thick on the Wabash. The trees that line the banks become pitch-black and the river itself becomes an increasingly denser shade of iridescent gray. Tiny shad fish flick upon the dull-shimmering surface of the water as the current slows and settles into a quiet rhythm.

Leonard had gotten his fire going for the evening and stood staring out across the water. He had a lingering headache from too much home-brew but that was nothing new. Staring down at the river at night made everything better and it was a beautiful night. The stars were out in force tonight without a cloud to be seen and there was a cool breeze coming off the water that was slowly killing off the heat of the day.

Leonard stood mesmerized, pausing only to take a puff off a cigarette. He had four bank poles made from tree branches stuck in the ground down by the water; a big crawfish impaled on each hook. There were two hooks on each line. Hopefully by morning there should be a catfish on each hook. But fishing hadn't been all that good lately. Someone was running his nets. The Game Warden came to mind and anger flared suddenly in Leonard. He turned to walk back to sit by the fire and was startled by two girls from the shack upriver. They were always startling him. They were always as quiet as ghosts. He greeted them and they, as usual, said very little and simply sat down on the big log beside the fire. They both, like all those kids up at the shack, were hard to tell apart. They all wore tight faded bell-bottom blue jeans and over-sized flannel shirts with hair that hung long and straight down their faces.

"It's a beautiful night, girls," Leonard said. He picked up a metal cup and began pumping water from the red-painted metal pump beside the fire. The heavy clang of the pump caused an echo on the other side of the river. "A beautiful night," they both said in unison, then giggled. Leonard sat in his chair. He opened a can of beer. Kids spooked him terrible nowadays. "So what's new?" He asked staring into the fire. He immediately regretted asking.

Both girls just looked at each other. They couldn't think of anything new. Leonard glanced at them and bet they were stoned. A couple of them always liked to get stoned and come sit with him when he got the fire going. These same two girls came the other night. He pulled his gaze away from the fire. One of them was lighting a fairly large cigarette rolled in green paper. He was right. "Damn kids," he muttered under his breath.

After the sweet smelling smoke had gotten more of a hold on them one of them began to talk. She said she was from Calumet City. She had gone to college for a year but nothing was happening there so she dropped out and ran off with a guy named Harpo who said he was half-Indian. "I don't think he was," she said. "He wrote haikus." Her eyes were wide and empty as she stared into the fire. "I caught my mother in bed with another man when I was seven." Leonard sighed and took a drink of beer and said, "Yikes." He handed them each a Sterling beer. "That's awful."

The girl looked blankly at Leonard. "I slept with him when I was fourteen."

Leonard scratched the back of his head. They were fucking with him again. They were always fucking with him it seemed like. He didn't like that at all.

"Were you ever unfaithful to your wife?" One of the girls asked him.

"What?" Leonard opened another beer for himself. "No, no. Uh-uh." He took a sip of beer, took out his smoke sack. "Nope." He glanced at the girls. They were staring blankly at him, like two young does. *I will not get the heebie-jeebies*, he was thinking as he looked at them. There were faint smiles on their faces, like newborns breaking wind.

"We sleep together," one of the girls said.

Leonard never even blinked. He returned his gaze to the fire. "That's–" He didn't know what to say exactly. He didn't say anything. He lit a cigarette.

The girls grew quiet. An owl began to hoot. Somewhere a dog was barking.

"I'm pregnant," one of them said finally, chin uplifted, awaiting his response. He gave none. He had no response to give. Kids, Leonard thought.

A MIRACLE

"I want to live with Mary and Ron," Betsy said. "But then I don't."

Jacob and her sat on the Belmo front porch. Jacob sat on the porch swing and Betsy on the front steps. There were no lights on in Betsy's house across the street. Jacob thought the house was scary since Betsy's grandfather had died in it. It didn't seem to bother Betsy. Jacob listened to her as she talked about moving to Chicago at the end of the summer.

"They might not like me."

"They will too," Jacob said, as he looked across the street. He could see Dorina bouncing on the couch in her house. Her mother must be taking a bath or something. She'd yell at Dorina to stop bouncing otherwise.

"One time last summer when I stayed with them, you know?" Betsy said. "Ron kinda looked at me funny, you know?"

Jacob looked at Betsy. He couldn't see her face in the dark but he could see the shadow of her legs. Cicadas joined crickets in filling the air with a loud familiar summer noise. He did not know what Betsy was talking about. She let out an exasperated sigh.

"Sometimes I just want to die," she said.

Jacob grabbed hold of the porch swing, kicked the floor with his tennis shoes to get it to rock some. "Not me," he said.

Betsy pulled the jeans jacket she had on tighter around her. Jacob didn't know why. It was still awful warm.

"They said I could have died when Mommy and Daddy did but I didn't."

Jacob, still looking across the street, saw Dorina leap off the sofa again. She seemed to be having a good time.

"They said it was a miracle," Betsy continued. "They all said it was a miracle. All those strangers. Nurses and police." She got up and went and sat beside Jacob in the swing. She looked towards the fire station down at the end of the block. Jacob looked too. Bugs buzzed thick around the solitary light that hung outside the fire station. There was a round hood over that light, like a plate. "It kinda made me feel special. Even though my Mommy and Daddy were dead I still felt kinda special." She looked at Jacob. "Ain't that awful?" Jacob looked at Betsy. He could see her face now. She was upset. He told her he didn't know. He didn't know what to say really.

"Except Grandpa. He never once said it was a miracle." She grabbed the chain hanging loose beside her, wrapped it around the chain that held the swing. "I bet he wished they would have lived and I would have died." She asked Jacob if she knew what she was talking about. Of course he didn't. He was only twelve. He said he did, though. "My parents took care of him," Betsy said. "Then he had to take care of me." She pulled a leg up on the swing and wrapped her arm around it. She rested her chin on her knee. Her bare leg and its proximity to Jacob made his throat dry. He could see her face now and the dim light coming from inside the house was just enough to make her eyes sparkle. He looked away.

Dorina stood on the cushions of the couch in the house across the street with her arms outstretched and her fingers bent, pretending, it seemed like, to be some kind of monster. Jacob watched her leap off the couch once again. He worried about her mom catching her. He thought about getting up and going over and warning her. He didn't, though.

"I'm glad he's dead," Betsy said again. She picked at nail polish on her toes. "It's awful but I am."

1894

The intermittent clack of the typewriter was all that could be heard in the house, that and the incessant if not annoying noise of nocturnal nature coming through the open windows. Delancey J. McFadden had glared earlier out the window at those noises but it was too damn hot to shut it. He sat hunched over the gray metal machine with two fingers poised, mouth open, and chin protruding. Beads of sweat joined the brown age spots on his bare forehead.

Occasionally one of the two fingers he typed with struck the keys, sometimes swiftly and other times with trepidation. The typewriter sat on a large roll-top desk in the den. Empty dark mahogany bookshelves lined all the walls of the room from floor to ceiling. Over the doorway was a framed picture of a young man and a woman. It was Delancey and Edith McFadden on their wedding day.

Delancey was writing the story of his life. The story began in 1894. It would end sometime soon, Delancey wrote in the introduction. He paused to sip a drink of water. He was working on the introduction. He re-read the three paragraphs he had written this evening. He shook his head and frowned. They weren't any good. He let out a big sigh and sat back in his rocking chair. He was much better at writing about someone else's past. He leaned forward and ripped the paper from the black cylinder, crunched it together and tossed it over his shoulder.

He went out on the front porch. It was a nice evening and he wasn't dead yet. He sat down in the swing and laid the cane across his legs. No, he wasn't dead yet and there was still time to enjoy the evening.

Then he saw someone sitting on the concrete porch steps. A woman. A cigarette flared red in front of her face.

"Hi, Dad," she said. "What's up?"

Delancey was silent for a moment. He didn't believe it was her at first. He hadn't expected to see his daughter. Perhaps, he thought, she is why I have come home. He pushed this thought away. He glanced up at the full moon. It hung in the sky over the town like a big light bulb.

"Hello, Janet," he said finally.

THE BUNDLE

Dorina moved aside two jars of peaches, a jar of apple butter, and three jars of green beans to get to her dead baby brother. He was wrapped completely in a soiled blue blanket. The bundle didn't seem much bigger than a loaf of bread. She unwrapped the head slightly to make sure that he was still there. An ugly smell hit her strong in the face and Dorina had to jerk her head away as the odor took her breath away. She wrapped it quickly back up.

It was almost daylight outside now. Blue light came through the basement windows. The sun would come up soon.

Just a few minutes ago Dorina had lain in bed shivering, immobilized. She had a nightmare just like she said she would and the fear she felt in that nightmare she could not explain. There had been no monsters in the nightmare like she sometimes had and nobody yelled at her or chased her. But it was an awful dream just the same. She had been floating. It was all black and she spun helpless all around and her head seemed to go one way and her body the other and she screamed in the dream and nobody was around. She woke up freezing cold and unable to move or breathe.

After rising straight up in her bed it came suddenly to Dorina that today was the day she should bury her dead baby brother in the woods. "Poor baby," she said, giving the bundle a quick, firm kiss.

JACOB'S DREAM

Jacob had been dreaming, too. It was a pleasant dream and a horrible dream all at the same time. His whole body tingled pleasantly all through the dream but in the dream he was running. At first he was running just for the sake of running. Then he felt a presence of some sort. It was chasing him and engulfing him and in addition to the pleasant feeling that ran through the body of a young boy rapidly becoming a man, Jacob felt an overwhelming sense of fear that if he stopped, the presence would scoop him up. He ran as fast as he could in the dream and he never tired. He leaped a fence and ran up and over a hill and his belly pleasantly left him as he ran fast down the hill but still the presence got closer to him and his dream grew increasingly darker.

In this dream Jacob ran until he ran into what seemed horribly to be something resembling intestines. Something between balloons rubbing together and the entrails of some animal. They were sticky, these entrails, like those of a squirrel and rabbit. Jacob had often seen his father and grandfather pull from the animal's bellies these entrails while cleaning them to eat. He got all tangled up in these entrails and couldn't catch his breath and suddenly the dream was no longer pleasant.

Jacob awoke with one side of his face against something soft and warm. That something was Betsy's belly. She had on a t-shirt. Jacob froze, his mouth going wide. Betsy was curled around him in his own bed. He moved his eyes but not his head.

His hand rested on her ankle, electric suddenly, as he felt the knob of that ankle. His face a curious blend of something between abject fear and revulsion, Jacob eased his hand away from her ankle. He ever so carefully rose up in bed. Betsy was sound asleep and had his pillow. Her face was contorted, her cheeks damp and red. She had been crying. The pillow, Jacob could see, was soaked. "God!" He whispered, near panic. He carefully climbed over Betsy to get out of bed. His erection brushed against her and he almost died. He grabbed his jeans and snuck as quietly as possible out of the room.

THE MEANING OF LIFE

Who was it that said that if he could not travel the world over to find the meaning of life, he would step out his back door and look for it in a blade of grass? Delancey took in the rejuvenating aroma of fresh-cut grass and pondered this, but only for a moment. Such thoughts he was trying, here at the end of his life, to avoid. He rubbed his forehead. Besides, it had probably been some graduate student of his, one of those countless blisters and chancre sores that passed through his office door at the University, on their way to some pompous and unproductive academic position of their own. He took in a deep breath. It was time, he kept telling himself, at seventy-five, to relax.

Delancey put his feet on a box of books and watched a man

named Martin Baines mow his lawn. Martin was perhaps four years younger than Delancey. He had a long, full face, and huge hands. He waddled back and forth as he pushed the red mower, a victim of an arthritic hip. Martin and Delancey had went to the same high school way back when and while Delancey went on to college Martin had stayed home to farm just outside of town. Now Martin and Delancey were retired and, Delancey couldn't help but notice, both were at the wrong end of their lives.

Martin stopped a moment to wipe sweat from his face and catch his breath, as the lawn mower droned and vibrated loudly in front of him.

A garbage truck stopped at the end of the street and a man hopped off the back, dumped a trash barrel into the truck and got back on. The truck rumbled on. The town was alive in its strange and mundane way and this inextricably bothered Delancey as he sat on his porch this morning. Even at his old age he had half-expected to return home again and find everything more dead than he was. He wiped sweat from his forehead. It just wasn't so, he thought, as he watched that cute little mulatto girl skip down the street, a blue bundle in her arms. He watched her go into the patch of woods on the corner lot.

NO RICE

It had been windy off and on all morning and this bothered Janet to no end. It made the tin sides and the roof of her trailer rattle. She had the necessary old tires she needed to put on the roof like a lot of other trailer dwellers, but hadn't yet asked anybody to put them up there for her. She crossed her legs as she sat at the front kitchen table and tapped cigarette ashes into an ashtray that had a blue dolphin embossed on the bottom of it. She sure as hell wouldn't put them damn old tires on her roof by herself. It looked tacky anyway. She stared absently at a bottle of Valium on the table beside her first cup of coffee. There were only six left.

Her father was home. Big deal. She hadn't written him or

even so much as talked to him for over a year, and now he had limped back home again. She had tried to talk to him, last night, and they couldn't say ten words to each other. Janet squinted her eyes and held the hot cup of coffee up close enough to her chin to feel its heat. The wonderful, the magnificent, the womanizing Delancey Joe McFadden.

Janet put her hands together around the hot cup of coffee to keep from trembling as she stared through her coffee cup. And she wasn't even his biologically. Her eyebrows rose. Or his emotionally, or anyway really, she thought.

She looked outside her window and snarled. Who was that man who sat out there on his broken old patio writing so furiously into those same blue notebooks? She snarled even more. And what did he write? Nausea rose in her once again. Exhibitionist. Sitting out there *composing* something no doubt.

Janet got up quickly and poured herself another cup of coffee from the metal percolator on the yellow counter and mused to herself once again about how the percolator had been a gift from the mighty McFadden, on the event of his daughter's wedding. "His health however," Janet began oratorically as she poured two, then three teaspoons of sugar into the cup, "prevented him from attending and giving her away." She sat the spoon down, leaned her hip hard against the counter, thinking once again what she had thought time and time again, "I was never his to give away."

Outside, on the patio across the street in a ragged, faded blue terry-cloth bathrobe George drank his morning coffee out of a ceramic beer stein that had a gargoyle on it. He looked up from his notebook and had to re-focus. It was a bright sun this morning. After reading the morning paper he was trying to write an anti-war poem. People were dying for no reason, George surmised by reading the headlines. Innocent people were getting in the way of American and Vietnamese bullets. He stared at the few lines he had written, then ripped the pages from the notebook. Every goddamn poet in America was trying to write an anti-war poem this morning.

He looked up at the heavy-set woman named Gladys who came to sit out on her porch across the street. He waved to her and she nodded back and began to fan herself with the same newspaper George had been inspired by this morning. She had boils on the inside of her thighs that never went away, she told George one time. He saw them now, close up, inflamed and sore. At eleven o'clock she would crack open her first bottle of Old Milwaukee beer. She would drink one every hour until two. Then she would waddle painfully back to her bedroom in the black-sided NEW MOON trailer, turn the fan on, sigh, and go to sleep. George turned to a fresh page in his notebook. *As helicopters sprayed defoliants and sneaky, indigenous Orientals carefully sat cute little oriental babes on top of hand-grenade booby traps.*

Old fat Gladys would dream and it would be an old-fashioned dream. Of manners and politeness. *There would be no rice in her dream*, George wrote in his notebook.

BETSY AND JACOB CONVERSE

"The problem is," Betsy began as she leaned towards Jacob. They sat at the wooden dining room table. They were the only ones at home. Jacob's father always left before dawn and his mother hadn't gotten off the night shift yet at the nursing home. Betsy took her pinkie and picked a piece of cornflake from between her two front teeth. Jacob was having trouble eating his cornflakes. Betsy still had just her panties and t-shirt on. She reeked of Dove soap. She sipped from a cup of coffee. Jacob didn't think she was really old enough to be drinking coffee. He glanced at one of her bare knees that poked scary and wonderful up next to him beside the table. Well, maybe she was old enough, he decided.

"People don't know what's really inside each other," Betsy continued as she looked blankly up at the ceiling and tried to explain to Jacob what she meant. Then she suddenly looked hard at Jacob and he felt himself almost jump. "If people knew exactly what was going on inside each other–" Betsy sighed through her nose. She still wasn't quite sure what she was trying to say.

"We'd be better off," Jacob said, trying to help her out.

Betsy frowned a little. "Maybe." She sipped her coffee. "Sometimes I think things I wouldn't want anybody in the world knowing what it was." She crossed her legs then Betsy looked Jacob intensely in the eye. "I'm in love, Jacob." Jacob's heart stopped. "I never been before. I know what it is, though. I feel it." Her eyes were moist. Jacob had almost stopped breathing. Betsy's voice had grown suddenly very serious. "He's a poet. Do you know any poets?"

Jacob didn't know any poets. "I ride my bike out to the park every Thursday and he is there and I love him." Betsy stared out the window. "He writes the most beautiful poetry I have ever heard. He reads it to me sometimes." Jacob looked at Betsy very carefully. She looked on the verge of tears. He asked her quietly what his poetry was about. Betsy paused. "I don't know," she said. She put her coffee cup down. "He don't even remember my name half the time. We just talk. He drinks a lot. I love him more than anything in the entire universe." Betsy swallowed hard. "One time, though, I let him–" Betsy stopped, then she stood up. "Some day I'm going to tell him how I feel." Betsy pulled her hair back. "I'm going to tell him I love him."

Betsy left the room. Jacob stared into his cornflakes and tried to think of what Betsy had let the poet do. As Jacob sat there and tried to think he found it impossible to swallow.

LOVE

The phone rang and Valarie could hear it but she couldn't exactly wake up. Yet it kept ringing. Finally, with tremendous effort, as if she were underwater, she lifted her arm, grabbed the black phone and said hello.

"What is it that's in those other poems that aren't in mine?"

Valarie, slowly waking up, sat up and wiped matter from her eyes. One piece of matter was so embedded in her eye it made her eyes water when she removed it. "George?"

"I want to know."

Then Valarie realized her clothes were off. Her head hurt, too.

"Did you take advantage of me last night, George?"

"Three or four times," George said. "No, just kidding. Only once. It was nice though. You were great. Thank you."

"Hog," Valarie said.

"My poems," George said.

Valarie sat up more in the bed, brushed her hair out of her face. "George, it's too early in the morning."

"You said there was something in those poems that you never see in mine."

"God, George. What time is it?" She looked at the clock on her bedside stand. It was a square travel clock with green illuminated hands. It said seven-thirty.

"You going to take me fishing today? I'll pack a lunch."

"My poems."

Valarie sighed. "I don't remember what we were talking about. I have to stop getting drunk, George. It'll make my face look older than it already is." She strained to look at herself in the mirror on the other side of the bedroom. She felt one cheek with her fingertips. It was ignorant to go to bed with her make-up on.

"You have a gorgeous face. And a gorgeous body and a great ass. JESUS CHRIST! What's in those poems that aren't in mine!"

Valarie rolled her eyes. She took a deep breath. Finally, "Love," she said.

CLICK! Went the phone. Smiling sadly, Valarie put the phone down, curled back up in bed, pulled the baby blue comforter up over her, and closed her eyes. She could see exactly what George was doing at the moment. And he was.

"JESUS FUCKING CHRIST!" George stormed across the floor of his kitchen and stared out his front window, his face angry and pained. "LOVE?" He yelled. "FUCKING LOVE!" He hit the splintery paneled wall with the flat of his fist. "I'M NOT GODDAMN ROD McKUEN. ROADKILL MY ASS! SHIT A FUCKING BRICK, MAN! THE GUY'S PROBABLY A FUCKING CHILD MOLESTER!" George looked for a moment as if he might die. "LOVE?" He made a noise deep in his throat.

He threw his bathrobe off, then angrily took off his boxer shorts and tossed them into the kitchen sink. It was time for a nice, cold shower.

"FUCKING WATER HEATER!" George screamed halfway through the living room.

"LOVE?" He screamed right before he slammed the bathroom door shut.

BREAKFAST ON THE WABASH

Mornings on the Wabash were Leonard's favorite time. There was an unbelievable crispness in the air and the mild chill of the night always mixed nicely with the approaching heat of the day. He sat in a rusty metal chair on the bluff. Curled in faded army green sleeping bags around the still smoldering campfire were the two hippie girls. They slept hard, oblivious to the morning dew that coated their empty young faces.

Leonard took a sip of strong coffee from a dented, tin cup and stared upriver. The heavy rains up north had caused the river to rise considerably. He might have to move his fishing nets. He watched a deer step slowly out of the trees across the river. He watched it bow its head, nip tentatively at a blade of grass, woman-like.

Leonard started coughing and the deer bolted immediately back into the trees. The cough was a deep rattle that made his face red and his whole body convulse. He kept coughing and finally spit out a blend of phlegm and blood on the ground in front of him. He finally stopped coughing and stared empty-eyed at the blood. He looked back out at the river. It might be a good idea to move his nets somewhere else anyway.

"Goddamn game warden."

The coffee was cold now and had nothing but grounds at the bottom of the cup. He emptied the cup on the ground and then took out his smoke sack. And as he leaned his elbows on his knees and rolled himself a cigarette, his thoughts went to his buddy, Henry Chalmers. The man the Game Warden shot and killed in cold-blood in 1956 not a hundred feet from where Leonard sat right now. Once again Leonard felt heat crawl up his neck. His head spun some as a wave of dizziness caught him suddenly.

Then Leonard looked down at his cigarette, completed rolling it, and decided once again that he would get that Game Warden someday. He lit the cigarette and leaned back in the chair. Henry Chalmers and Leonard had grown up together. As kids wherever one went the other wasn't far behind. Leonard's eyes glazed some as he went back in time and saw him and Henry in matching dark blue overalls and shiny black patent leather shoes on their way home from Sunday school. They had climbed over a fence to steal strawberries from an old man they knew was sitting in the second pew of the Calvary Baptist Church.

Leonard's thoughts were interrupted by one of the girls who came and stood beside him on the bluff. The sleeping bag was draped around her. She stared at the water, expressionless and still sleepy-eyed.

"You like strawberries?" Leonard asked her.

She turned to look at him, her face blank. Her shoulders went up and down. "Sometimes," she said. Then a wisp of a smile crossed her face. She said she was hungry.

Leonard laughed. They all knew about the breakfasts he could make. Upriver came two fishermen in a small green-painted, v-shaped, wooden boat. They both wore baseball caps. One sat at the front of the boat and the other sat in the back with his hand back on the throttle of the motor. It was a small motor that whined like a chainsaw and could barely move the boat through the water. The fishermen waved and Leonard and the girl waved back.

"I believe, I believe, I believe in God," Leonard proclaimed as he stretched away what remained of any morning stiffness. He asked the girl if she believed in God. Her shoulders went up and down again. "I don't know." Then she said she was hungry again.

"You are, you are, you are," Leonard said. He took the last drag off his cigarette, flicked the butt over the bluff. "Breakfast," he said. He got up. He would fix them the greatest breakfast ever made.

Shortly the smell of frying bacon filled the air around the camp. The two girls stood peeling potatoes over the wooden table where Leonard usually cleaned fish. Leonard came up behind them with three large brown duck eggs, the last of a dozen the General had given him last week. They stopped peeling potatoes and stared curiously at the duck eggs. They hadn't seen duck eggs before. One of them asked if he had any regular eggs and she evidently meant chicken eggs. Leonard thought this was funny. He reached under the table where his metal cooler was, took out a can of beer.

"These are better eggs," he said, shoving the opener into the can of beer. "I guarantee it."

The two girls looked like they weren't quite sure about that. One wrinkled up her nose.

After Leonard got everything together he sat two cast-iron skillets on a rusty hollowed-out top of an old stove that sat directly over the campfire. He put more wood under it. It wouldn't be long before it was blazing away again. He looked over at the girls. On the same table where they had peeled potatoes and onions and a green pepper, they were now rolling a cigarette in a pink wrapper. Leonard looked hard at the two girls.

"You kids got to stop that shit," he said. "It ain't good for you."

They both twisted the ends of their freshly made cigarettes to perfection. Then they both stopped and looked at Leonard, who held a beer in one hand, as a limp cigarette dangled from his lip.

Leonard shook his head and went mumbling back to the fire about how he was a goddamn old man and they were just goddamn kids.

ONWARD

Marsha and Joyce stood on the steps of the house and knocked. An old man, reading a newspaper, got up, looked out his picture window, saw the women, snarled, and sat back down. The two Jehovah's Witnesses looked at each other. Marsha said something about God's ways.

"My feet hurt," Joyce said.

They both had been taking their time. They knew where they were. One block away was the trailer park and neither of them was in a hurry to get there. Marsha, in a green polyester pantsuit, looked at her watch.

"I'm having fried chicken tonight," she said. "And fried potatoes with onions, and green beans."

"That's sounds good," Joyce said. "I made a casserole last night. I overcooked it."

They walked to the next house. Marsha knocked.

"Good morning. How are you today?" Joyce chirped. They both gave the old woman at the door their biggest smiles. She slammed the door in their faces. They weren't having much luck today. They headed up the street.

Joyce took out an emery board she got free from the hardware store and began doing a nail as she walked. Marsha told her not to do such things in public.

"I have a hangnail," Joyce said.

"Not in public," Marsha insisted, her face hard as she walked. She didn't like having a door slammed in her face. She stopped walking. "Sometimes I don't know about God."

Joyce stopped doing her nail, looked at Marsha.

"That's no way to talk. He sure won't be unless you believe."

"I believe!" Marsha said. "My husband said women shouldn't be calling on people." She continued as she switched the blue bag to her other hand. This made Joyce laugh. Marsha asked her what was so funny.

"If we left it up to our husbands to call on people the church would look like a soup kitchen during the Depression."

This made Marsha smile. Her husband was a slovenly, pot-bellied carpenter and Joyce's husband was an almost identical coalminer. They continued on to the end of the street and walked around the corner. They were on Main Street now at the end of town. They sat for a moment on a square concrete cistern on an empty corner lot. Joyce took off her blue high-heels and rubbed her feet. They could both see the entrance into the trailer park now.

"I don't think I like anything about that trailer park, Marsha." Joyce put her shoes back on. "What if we run into that man again?"

"He has a soul," Marsha said. Joyce looked as if she wasn't quite convinced of this.

"Why would he dress up like a woman like that?"

Marsha blinked. "I don't know, Joyce. The devil is as conniving as they come." Marsha got to her feet, picked her bag back up.

"It's time to tread into the devil's territory." A grain truck rumbled by with a large black dog poking its head out the passenger's window.

Joyce said she didn't know. "I think we'll end up in a nuthouse before we get to Heaven, we keep going back to that trailer park."

Marsha struck a fist forward. "Onward!" She exclaimed.

THE POEM

George had all of his fishing tackle in a dark green metal box he kept under the three wooden steps leading up to his trailer. With the sound of metal scraping concrete he pulled the tackle-box out onto the patio. He couldn't believe how caked with red clay dirt the tackle-box was. It had been raining the last time he had been fishing and he hadn't washed it off afterwards. He tried to now with a stick and knocked some of the dirt off but decided to give up. Hell, it'd just get dirty again.

Even though he kept everything he owned in the way of

fishing tackle in the tackle box, he opened it anyway to make sure everything was there and in the right place. The smell of dried dirty river water mingled with a few bits of crusty hard, long-dead night crawlers made George move his head back. There was even a dead minnow that George quickly removed. He had to stop getting so drunk when he fished and clean out his tackle-box better.

Those ugly smells were unexpectedly joined by an at once delicate-sweet and familiar smell. George jerked his head around and there Betsy sat on his front steps. His pulse rate, heart, and blood pressure all went off at the same time like so many alarm clocks. His pupils dilated as that same litany once again went rumbling through his libido smacking and beating at his id as his ego curled fetal in the back of his skull, yelling: "Jailbait, jailbait, jailbait."

"Going fishing, Mister Poet Man?" Betsy inquired, her voice, George noted, as before, a macabre blend of contemptible innocence and a centuries old sexual understanding.

George, frozen, his face somber, eyes fearful, replied, "Yes."

Yes, indeed. It had been an accident really, one of those momentary lapses when an individual teeters on the brink of disaster, yet sees that brief, blinding glimpse of infinity and leaps. George didn't leap, he concluded, just slipped.

It began after George had written (as he had often done) his greatest poem. But this *was* his greatest poem; he felt it. Precision-polished and honed into something as close to brilliant as George could get, he believed. It was a prosaic sort of poem about a murder, a double-entendre poem about a middle-aged couple who killed their spouses, dumped one body in a cistern and burned the other beyond recognition in a staged automobile accident. All for love, they said. A true story George had read in the newspaper and decided to write a poem about, comparing the couple to a menopausal Romeo and Juliet, two aging love-struck psycho-paths too aware of their own mortality to kill themselves, but deciding instead to eliminate their respective spouses. And it almost worked, George wrote, like love itself, almost.

When he finished that poem it felt so right. It had fucking brilliant etched in gold all around it; so goddamn perfectly symmetrical, black letters on erasable bond paper unsmeared by a mistyped letter. Yes! George danced, he leaped in the air, fists rising as he did a victory dance. He sang! The poem was his Grecian Urn, his Prufrock; then abruptly, he stood crouching in defiance, staring coldly at all those faceless poetry editors, their four-eyed cronies with their half-assed English degrees shivering as they handed those editors the poem. George sneered as he imagined them reading a poem so great it made their clits and balls visibly retract. The language, the form, the content, the obligatory classical allusion, the goddamn sheer exuberance that comes howling only out of the bowls of genius. At least once. At least once. And it had.

So then George placed the poem on his clipboard with great ceremony, walked out of his trailer, cut through a bean field, and around a junkyard, an irrepressible smile on his face. He stopped for a moment on the edge of the junkyard to stare at four rusty old cars stacked on top of each other. All four were precisely the same rusty-brown color of rotten and fermenting apples, one right on top of the other, technology fucking each other in the ass, dead, Keats and Yeats, Rimbaud and Baudelaire. Yes! There had been color there in each one once, a sweetly humming engine, firm, unscarred cushions and fresh tread, as they cruised through their time with loving grace and headlights on; assimilating, feeling, depositing not only their bodily fluids, but also the scratchings of immortality! George saluted these dead cars that were his influences, then he crossed the street to Hank's Tavern where he read Art his poem. Art, innocent of all figurative relationship to his namesake, still gave George a resounding ovation and a free drink.

"That'll make it," Art said nodding, as he handed George the drink. George nodded back. It would make it indeed. Then George asked for a jug of red wine. It was time to celebrate.

George left Hank's with the wine and walked to the other side of town to a small, secluded park and sat on a picnic table and drank. It was a warm spring day and only a few transparent clouds stretched jagged across the sky. From where he sat he could catch a glimpse of the river, just a glimpse, and that was all he needed at that moment. He drank the slightly chilled wine, wiped his mouth. Then he drank some more.

George drank until the jug was empty, his head spinning with a fruitful drunkenness, his mind afloat with imaginary interviews on style, influences, and purpose until finally, a good two hours later, he fell over backwards on the picnic table, laughing as he fell, laughing as he slipped into something between unconsciousness and sleep. My poem! he felt his mind scream. My Kingdom for a poem!

George awoke to that same aroma that now, as he stood on his patio, totally replaced the smells emanating from his tackle box. But back then, on his back beneath the picnic table, it was such a delicious and intriguing smell that he felt he could get more of if he sat up on his elbows. He heard Betsy ask him if he was okay.

What his eyes first focused on were two ripe young breasts bursting from a flowery sleeveless blouse that was held vicariously closed by a large white button. Underneath those breasts a perfectly round little hole encased her belly button. One brown knee touched his hip as the other gently rested against his side.

"You're drunk," she said.

George, on his elbows, felt her knee slide up close to his face. Betsy, smiling a wry yet somehow baffling smile, gently, slowly, her fingers heavy on his flesh, brushed his hair out of his face.

Suddenly George was struck with a feeling like something between rubber and lightning, an alcohol-induced epiphany, perhaps. Yes. Now suddenly, there were more important things in the universe than poems, than words written to synthetically, second-handedly, capture the unbridled energy of life and matter. There was, as George was immediately absorbing, the immediacy of the moment (Carps in Denim was that college phrase he coined himself). So George leaned towards that smooth brown bare knee and docked his lips gently there, kissed it.

He barely remembered how it ended up as it did. Soft electric flesh, toes in his mouth, inner thighs alive, warm burning wet tightness... Perhaps it was her who straddled him and not him who pulled her upon him. In any case, it wasn't long before her tongue was driven deliciously into his at once scared and burning mouth, not long before his hands tingled as they played across flesh as forbidden and compelling as anything Nabokov could conjure up.

"Fifteen," he remembers her saying, her breath as hot as the inside of an Easy-Bake oven, as her mouth once again fell hard against his. At least she's not twelve, he remembers thinking, as her legs retracted up to his armpits like erotic landing gear on a Barbie and Ken Lear Jet.

His last thought? His last thought before he plunged completely, horribly, regrettably, inside?

The poem is great. It is.

PEOPLE

"And how are you this morning, young lady?"

Delancey's voice startled Dorina. She sat on her heels, her knees spread upon the ground as she dug between her legs with a small metal toy shovel. The blue bundle was behind her. When she saw it was that old man from across the street she went back to digging.

Delancey leaned hard on his walking cane, stared through the trees at a tractor plodding though a field outside of town. Clouds of dust billowed up behind the contraption the tractor pulled. Delancey didn't know if it was a plow or a cultivator or something else. He knew nothing about farming and had been proud of this fact for virtually his whole life. He had been more than a farmer, he had always believed. He was educated. An academic. Now suddenly, it embarrassed him.

"Perhaps I've learned all the wrong things in life," he thought aloud.

Dorina stopped digging. "What?"

Delancey turned a heavy head towards the little mulatto

girl. He smiled. "What are you digging for, child?" He pointed with the end of his cane. "Gold?"

Dorina sat her shovel down and dug out a rock the size of an apple, tossed it aside and went back to digging. "Nope."

Delancey looked back at the tractor. He watched the farmer on the tractor look back behind him. "My father wanted me to be a farmer," he said. "He thought I had enough schooling after the eighth grade." Delancey laughed an unnatural laugh. "Imagine that."

Dorina, her face serious as she stared down and dug, said more coldly than she usually said it, "My Daddy is as black as coal."

Delancey jerked his head around. "He is?"

"Yep." Dorina stopped to catch her breath. It was going to take longer than she thought it would to bury her dead baby brother. It was hot today. Her knees were sore.

Delancey's eyes squinted serious. "There's nothing wrong with that, you know."

Dorina glanced up at the old man, and half-sighed, half-laughed. No matter who she said it to, they always had something to say about it. She dug hard into the dirt.

"My mommy says he gets out soon and he's gonna come get us. We're gonna move to Alabama and start a church. You got a bigger shovel somewheres?"

"Where is he?" Delancey asked, thinking impulsively that the little girl meant out of prison.

"Viet Cong," Dorina said. "Vietnam. He's got a purple heart now. They put one in him. Part of his belly got blowed away. He can't eat as much as he used to."

Delancey stared hard at the little girl.

Dorina looked at the old man. "You said you had a book for me."

Delancey nodded, said he did. "It's right on the porch."

Dorina got to her feet and Delancey could see the bundle behind her now. Dorina wiped her hands clean on her yellow shorts.

"What's it about?" She frowned. "It got pictures?"

Delancey shrugged. "No pictures." They started walking. "It's about what all good books should be about, I suppose."

Dorina asked what that was.

Delancey gave the tractor one last look. "People," he said. Then he told Dorina not to forget her little blue bundle.

She didn't even look back. "It ain't going nowhere," she said, as they headed back to Delancey's house.

IN VAIN

When Betsy left and the house was empty Jacob tried in vain to get the television to work. Nothing but hiss and snow, with an occasional blurred image now and then. He was too restless anyway. He went outside, sat on the porch, and tried again in vain to read the book the old man had given him. That didn't work either. There was a hot empty place in the pit of his stomach. Betsy had caused this somehow.

Jacob jumped up and hurried into his bedroom, slammed the door behind him. He plopped hard upon the bed and stared at the ceiling. The ceiling was cracked and peeling. There were yellow stains cutting jagged across the peeling ceiling. It reminded him of a piss-stained mattress he had seen at a junkyard one time. He closed his eyes and tensed up. Something was really wrong with him today. Really wrong. He jerked his eyes open, tried to think of something, anything other than Betsy. He couldn't. He pulled the pillow to his face, tried to catch a whiff of her smell still lingering on it.

Then he threw the pillow hard against the wall. He had to figure out something to do. And fast. He leaped out of bed and practically ran out of the room.

GUILT

Valarie stopped in the middle of the road between her trailer and George's to tie her hair back with a black ribbon. It looked like a beautiful day to fish. She hadn't been fishing all that much except with George but each time she went she enjoyed it. George was always fun to do things with. He made her laugh and sometimes this was the greatest thing a man could do for a woman. She continued walking and thought about all those years she never laughed once with her ex-husband.

Valarie passed two well-dressed ladies holding *Watchtower* magazines. They all smiled and exchanged hellos. Valarie felt a bit self-conscious as she passed them. Perhaps her cut-offs were too tight or maybe she was a little too top-heavy and maybe even too old to be going bra-less in a white t-shirt. Oh, hell with it, she thought, her nose wrinkling after the ladies passed.

Then guilt rose suddenly in her again for calling in sick at the nursing home. They would be short-handed today. But that was nothing new. They were short-handed every day on every shift really. Valarie stopped suddenly to check the paper sack with their lunch in it. Four bologna sandwiches with cheese, carrot sticks, and two plastic butter tubs filled with potato salad. That should do them. George loved her potato salad and it was all she had left of it from the weekend.

As she came up to George's trailer she saw Betsy on his front steps. George sat on the patio cleaning out his tackle-box. Valarie said hello to Betsy and suddenly remembered that her grandfather had died.

Betsy rose from the steps and as she did she carefully brushed off her bottom in that slow, sensual way Valarie brushed off her bottom in front of a man when she was that age; as if that slow, intentional stroking was somehow detectable to the eyes of a man. It was the way of youth and innocence. George picked dirt from his lures, not even looking at Betsy.

"I hope you catch some big ones," Betsy said. Valarie took Betsy's place on the steps. Then she told Betsy she should come with them. Valarie didn't notice George freeze but Betsy did and this made Betsy smile ever so wider.

"No," Betsy said. "I don't like to fish all that much."

"You could get some sun," Valarie insisted. "That's what I plan to do."

Betsy's eyes lit up. She could always use more of a tan.

George shoved a lure hard into the tackle box. "It's supposed to cloud up I heard," he said. "Rain probably later."

Betsy smiled. "I'll throw my bathing suit on, lay in the backyard. You two catch a mess." She got on her bike and rode off.

Valarie stretched out a leg, took a pack of cigarettes from her right jeans pocket. "I ran around with her mom in high school. Wild as a March hare." She lit a cigarette with a metal lighter. "You think she's like that?"

George shrugged as he unraveled a rusty metal fish stringer. "Listen," he said. "If we fill this up today I'll clean and fry every one of them."

Valarie eased smoke out of her mouth and sucked it up into her nose. "A deal." She rested her chin in her palm, cigarette in between two fingers. She smiled.

"I feel lucky today." He gave Valarie's legs an exaggerated eye.

"You better be able to swim then." She snarled as she took another drag off the cigarette. "When I knock you out of the boat."

"Damn," George said. "Relax."

Valarie laughed and got up, bent down to pick up the lure made out of hairs from a squirrel's tail. "You ever wonder why men *always* have to say that to women?"

George gave her a dirty look, went back to picking at his tackle-box.

A WAR DANCE

Doc Garrelts was dancing with a dummy on the roof of his trailer. It was a ragtag dummy in new overalls with slanted eyes that smiled kindly, like someone on very good medication. Its hair was a coal-black and straight wig. Yellow thongs were sewn into the bottom of the overalls. Rice was strewn on the roof of the trailer.

There was no music but Doc Garrelts, in a tattered tuxedo without any trousers on exposing bright red boxer shorts, danced anyway. He dipped and spun his dummy. He threw it up in the air, caught it just before it hit the roof, bent over and kissed it on its black magic marker lips.

It was a war dance that Doc Garrelts was doing. He had been watching war dances all summer and then his little television quit on him and now he had to make up his own war dance.

It was pretty successful actually, as war dances go. It was working even better than that current war dance in Indochina, as for horrifying the two middle-aged white women who stood in the street below watching him. Joyce and Marsha. They watched Doc Garrelts with the same sort of abject fascination that they had perhaps watched other war dances. But this time, instead of simply changing the channel or going in to check the pot roast, they were now, at that moment, doing what all civilized people should do when confronted with a war dance.

They were running like hell.

EROSION

The Wabash River was a murky brown today. George re-baited one rod and washed his hands of worm shit over the side of the boat. The water was almost hot. He sat at the back of the boat next to his old ten-horse Johnson motor. The motor had a white dome on top of it like an old toaster without the slots. The throttle jutting forward on the right side was wrapped in black electrical tape to keep it held together. But the motor ran though and it only cost him fifteen dollars at a rummage sale. He had to take it apart and clean it, but it ran like new after that.

Valarie was stretched out on her back at the front of the boat, her elbows on the front board and her head tilted back with her sunglasses on. Her T-shirt was rolled up under her breasts to give her belly some sun. There were two small ripples in her belly, one slightly bigger than the other. George couldn't help but stare at her. She had one of those classical full bodies like Jane Russell and Marilyn Monroe, a great body, George thought, unlike those new, emaciated women like Twiggy.

"Twiggy," he said, as he sipped from a beer and stared at his three lines stretching taunt out into the water. The water current was strong and slowly bent his rods, only to release them occasionally with a jerk. When the current was this strong it was hard to tell whether you were getting a bite or not. It was how river fishing always was.

Valarie reached up, put her sunglasses up into her hair. "What?"

George looked at her. "I said Twiggy. You know her?"

Valarie relaxed, exhaled loudly. "The skinny little bitch." She put her sunglasses back on, stretched out comfortable. "This is great, George. We should become professional fishermen."

George laughed. Valarie hadn't so much as looked at her lines. They dropped anchor next to the Indiana side of the river beside a tree that erosion had toppled horizontal almost entirely into the water. Its leaves were still green even though half its roots were pulled up out of the ground and pointing grotesque at the sky. The tree would be entirely dead soon. George felt some sort of sad irony for that tree, for having been born too close to a volatile body of water instead of, say, in a quiet little place among countless other trees in a woods somewhere. Yes. Perhaps a short run beside the active motion of a river beat the hell out of two hundred years frozen among your peers.

"Are you circumcised, George?" Valarie asked.

George, not listening, fumbled around in his pockets for the little three-by-five blue spiral notepad he always carried with him. He would call the poem "Erosion." "What?" he said.

Valarie chuckled. "I'm a Nurse Perverse," she mused. She looked at George out of the corner of her eye. He was writing something down. Then abruptly he stopped writing, looked at the notepad with, what looked like to Valarie, incredible disgust. He slammed the notepad shut.

"I will never be a poet."

Valarie sat up. "Oh, George." She pulled her T-shirt down and lit a cigarette. Then she leaned her elbows on her pulled-together knees, stared at George. "Neither will I."

George looked hard at Valarie. He thought about this. He wiped sweat from his face. He thought about it a little too long. Valarie smiled seductively, satisfied and happy all of a sudden. George was just so weird.

"You want to make love, George?"

PARIS

The book was old and one end curled up. It had a lion and a witch and a big coat on the cover. Dorina didn't like to read. She couldn't read really. She tried like all the other kids her age but she just couldn't. She stared at the cover anyway.

"Any people die in the book?"

Delancey was far away and tired. He sat in the porch swing. He thought he shouldn't have gotten so tired just walking the short distance that he did. He didn't like how he was feeling at all. He stared at the little girl, smiled. "I don't know. I haven't read it. I bought it–" He looked through the little girl suddenly. His daughter lived in this town. "I bought it for my daughter when she was about your age." He scratched at his chest. "Someone told me it was a good book." He put his cane across his lap. "For kids."

Dorina sat on the concrete steps of the porch and picked at a dead bug with her thumb. "My mommy says when babies die they go to a special place in Heaven."

Delancey nodded. Thick clouds were moving in from the west. There was a storm coming and very quickly. A sharp feeling of despondency shot through him. His daughter was in town.

"I don't believe that." Dorina said, as she kicked the dead bug off the steps with the heel of her tennis shoe. "I don't believe hardly nothing."

Delancey looked at the little girl. What she just said and the way she said it reminded him intensely of how his own daughter had been. He let out a quiet laugh.

"You must believe in something." He lifted his chin, saw his daughter as a child, saw her innocent and clean. Saw her happy and uncluttered. Saw her running towards him. Saw himself lifting her up. He let his mouth shut.

Dorina shook her head. "Nope." She brushed her hair out of her face, squinted at the old man. "Jacob, maybe," she said. She lifted one shoulder. "Maybe." In the west a flash of lightning caught Dorina's eye. She jerked her head around.

"I gotta go," she said. Dorina went off and left her book on the step.

Delancey could see it was raining in the west now. It would be raining soon here, too. Windows would be shutting and children would be running inside and pavements would steam. The thought took Delancey back to Paris ten years ago when his loins were still alive and her name? Becky. Becky Something. Delancey wiped sweat from under his nose. She came with him to Paris for three days. He shook his head. Even ten years ago he felt he would never grow old, and now? He took in a large painful breath. Where was his daughter then? The air was heavier now.

Thunder rumbled. He could hear the rain coming. Still, for a moment, he let his eyes glaze and tried to feel again what he had felt for Becky what's-her-name. He tried hard. Or was it Betty?

"Oh, God," he said, tapping on his cane. The hissing of the rain grew louder and a cool breeze appeared. The sky grew increasingly darker. Delancey watched the first few raindrops splatter on the broken sidewalk in front of his house. The raindrops were the size of silver dollars and left dark spots on the concrete.

His daughter was somewhere in this town and he hadn't said ten words to her yet. "My time is running out," he said.

NAKED

When she felt the first few raindrops upon her bare legs Betsy began peddling her bicycle as fast as she could. She cut through an alley and was headed towards the Belmo house when she decided to take a detour to her old house. She rode though the thick unmowed yard to the back of the house. Everything was locked up except a back window. It was raining hard now and the wind was strong and cold. Lightning flashed and thunder followed the lightning immediately. Betsy was soaking wet before she was able to climb inside.

After she did climb inside and got completely to her feet the familiar scent of the house caught her by surprise. It shouldn't have but it did. She looked impulsively around for her grandfather. Of course he wasn't there. The house was dark except for an occasional flash of lightning.

Betsy stood in the utility room. She unzipped her wet cut-off blue jeans and let them drop to the floor. She kicked off her tennis shoes. Everything was much like it had been. Laundry detergent in place. Someone had bought the dryer but the washing machine was still in its place. Betsy watched herself, since she was very young, put that old man's smelly clothes in that washing machine. Sometimes his clothes would smell so bad she would gag. It was an ugly, thick smell that threatened to suffocate Betsy if she didn't get the detergent in and the lid shut in time.

As Betsy walked through the kitchen she took off her damp t-shirt. Everything in the kitchen had been boxed up now except for a blue plastic cup on the sink. The tile floor of the kitchen was dirty and gritty feeling. It had never been that way when she lived there. She cleaned it every Saturday.

The living room was as it always had been. Lightning flashed and her grandfather's rocking chair ignited in blue flames for a moment. Betsy's eyes hardened with a strange fascination as the chair rose in the air as lightning flashed and thunder rumbled. This had been her home.

Betsy stepped out of her panties and let them fall upon the carpeting. She was naked now. The thin, worn carpeting felt particularly coarse beneath her feet. Betsy didn't remember it being that way before. She vacuumed the carpet every Saturday with an Electrolux. As she looked around Betsy noticed for the first time just how old everything in the house was. The dark green couch that had been there as long as she could remember had sunken, ill-fitting cushions and the seams were split, exposing yellow beneath the green. She hadn't noticed this about the couch before. Just like she hadn't noticed just how old her grandfather had become until she saw him at the funeral; hadn't seen those deep wrinkles in his face, or the wrinkles in his fingers that seemed exaggerated by death. A wave of panic went through Betsy as she stood there in the living room. Her body was dying and changing too, no doubt. It was just the way it was.

Up the stairs Betsy went and the dirt and dust collecting on her feet was almost more than she could take. It was as if with every step she was filling up with it all. She stopped upon the stairs and shut her eyes as she leaned against the wall, her arms wrapped tightly beneath her breasts. She found herself crying. At first she didn't even know it was her that was crying. It was as if someone else was crying and she was only listening. She could hear this person crying but it wasn't her. And then it came suddenly to her that she was crying and Betsy felt it now and began to cry even more.

For the first time Betsy found herself crying for the loss of her mother and father. It came strong and powerful to her now as she leaned against the wall on the stairs that her parents were gone and they would never come back. Why it had not come to her before she did not know.

As the storm outside shook the house, Betsy let it all out and cried so hard her legs finally gave out and she crumpled slowly upon the stairs, naked, and crying like there was no tomorrow.

THE STORM

The storm came up suddenly as storms often do and brought with it the sudden devastation that never really surprises anybody who lives in the Midwest. The brunt of the storm was a thick black mass of clouds that materialized seemingly out of nowhere and abruptly enveloped the town like some satanic apparition now solidified and convulsive. It wreaked a horrible punishment of thick cold rain and continual staccato lightning followed by a massive percussion of thunder that rattled windows and shook foundations.

Delancey stared out his living room window and marveled at this fantastic display of cosmological anger. Oddly enough he forgot for a moment his own mortality and dwelled instead on this storm perhaps affirming the possibility of a higher order of things. Such fury and passion had to originate from something outside mere mortality. His eyes widened as, at that very moment, one of the larger trees in his lot on the corner bent like the string on a harp, and then snapped in two. This made Delancey smile a curiously pallid smile. The window he peered out of gave and went like an accordion on opium. His eyes continued to widen. He was viewing the most delectably incredible natural orchestra ever conceived, and it was touring the Midwest, stopping briefly here at this very spot at this very moment, and he was sitting front row and center. It was grand and wonderful. It was a strong affirmation to Delancey at that moment that there was an energy, a force that transmuted, ripped to shit if you will, any of those fashionable thoughts he once held so dearly about existential finality. Yes! There was indeed a God and he might make it up there to see him yet.

Then he began to hear what sounded remarkably like a freight train. The house began to shake. He turned and headed immediately for the basement. His time with God could wait.

Just three blocks away Dorina stopped running. There was a storm raging just behind her but not where she stood. Dorina didn't know quite what to think. The world had stopped moving, it seemed like. Not a leave rustled or a bird chirped. It was the calm before the storm but Dorina didn't know this. It was as if everything had frozen into something like a painting. Dorina didn't know exactly what was wrong but it made her tingle all over at first and then suddenly she became so scared her legs began to shake.

Dorina spun all around in a sudden panic as something like lead pressed heavy in her chest and she thought she wasn't going to breathe anymore. She tried to scream but all that came out was a little squeak. It was like there wasn't any air to breathe anymore. Stars filled her eyes as she stumbled sideways dizzy and frightened and made her way to the yard of Mabel Blanchard.

Now Mabel Blanchard's yard needs some explaining. It was one of the tackiest yards on the face of the earth. It had the largest collection of plastic and ceramic figurines that could ever be assembled and placed on any quarter acre of front yard. There was a little ceramic black boy holding a lantern, three birdbaths, five plastic pink flamingoes, seven various other birds, a gray ceramic elephant, two stone cats, and a ceramic black poodle with a nose cracked off. Not to mention four different birdhouses of varying heights. And that was only about half of the shit that was in that yard.

But the one thing that Dorina instinctively went for in the yard was, by and large, the ultimate symbol ever created by the garish American middle-class psyche. It was also the most unfathomable of all front yard creations. As the storm dropped viciously upon that front yard, bringing with it wind and rain, violence and noise, Dorina flew head first into an upright, half-buried bathtub and wrapped her arms tightly around a small ceramic Mother Mary, her arms outstretched and robe painted a baby blue. A blue almost identical, Dorina noticed as she shivered and clung to Mary, to the blanket that was wrapped around her dead baby brother.

So as the storm beat into the bathtub and threatened to scare poor Dorina to death, all she could think about was this similarity in color. As that storm continued to rage and spit upon the earth outside that bathtub, Dorina's lips began to tremble and she began reciting a litany that she believed was a combination of her dead baby brother and the baby Jesus Christ.

"BabyJesusBabyJesusBabyJesus," Dorina just kept repeating over and over again, as she clamped her eyes shut and shivered.

Finally she felt a warmth between her legs. It was a slow, spreading spot of urine in her panties that turned cold very quickly. Dorina just kept shivering and reciting her litany until it became almost a scream.

The storm brought with it two or three tornadoes that tore several grotesque paths through the town that day. Trees had been broken and ripped from the ground at random and glass was blown out of a hardware store window. Down at the high school the metal fence behind the baseball diamond had been uprooted and placed twisted and warped upon the adjacent football field.

In the trailer park on the edge of town was where the devastation took its heaviest toll. The storm had cut a path through the trailer park like a mad surgeon might ravage a surgical ward with a chainsaw.

One trailer heaved once as if catching its breath before it was lifted into the air and stood on end for a moment before crumpling over and splitting in two. Another trailer had been bent in two to such an extent that it suddenly burst apart into many pieces as if a bomb had gone off inside it. Still another trailer was lifted a few feet into the air and then deposited on its side on top of a pick-up truck that was parked in the driveway.

It had been no picnic for the people inside these trailers. Some had been smart enough to run to the ditch between the cornfield and the trailer park and lie flat there. Some had simply stayed in their trailers without caring one bit whether the storm hit them or not. Still others had panicked at the last moment and ducked under their beds.

Janet Kittel, however, was beneath her kitchen table with a bottle of wine and two unlit candles. As a child, storms had made her so incredibly excited with a pleasant fear that she had on two occasions done exactly what Dorina did; pee her pants. She hadn't done so this time yet. Even as Janet's trailer shook and clattered and once even left the ground it seemed like, her pants remained dry. But still that same feeling of excitement had now replaced a more appropriate feeling of fear that she should have felt. She was an adult now. Her mind should be all cluttered up with the concept of finality. There should be thoughts of what she had done with her life and how it had all been wasted and so on. If nothing else, Janet should at least be thinking about the one article she remembered her father having written years ago for some historical/philosophical periodical. Janet had looked it up while sitting in the library when she was a junior in college. She took a sip of wine and tried to remember the title. It came to her.

"*Bringing in the Leaves... Bringing in the Leaves...*" Janet smiled. The article was subtitled *The Religion of Existentialism.* Janet, as the storm shook and rattled her trailer, could only smile and drink more wine.

Her father, Janet postulated as she sat there beneath her kitchen table, the Great Delancey J. McFadden, was such an asshole.

SEX ALONG THE WABASH

George and Valarie lay upon a bed of moss amidst a clump of trees along the Wabash. They had tied their boat to a log. Trees surrounded and overhung them and a coolness rose up from the damp moss and collided with the heat of their naked bodies. They were heated up and writhing together slowly. George's tongue ran thickly along the inside of Valarie's thigh. A bitter-sweet taste of perfume clung to his tongue like a horny leech. The image of her spraying the perfume there flashed neon in his head. Valarie's eyes were closed and her face reminded George of the face of the stone statue on the Virgin Mary he had seen at the Catholic Seminary in town. Her lips, both vertical and horizontal, were absolutely perfect, George concluded, as he lapped heavily at a bead of sweat dangling on the lip of that holiest of places between her legs. One of her thumbs danced a rhythmic caress over an erect nipple of her full left breast, as her other hand dug into George's scalp, as his tongue plunged and pushed upon her most delicate button. In short, George was going down on Valarie with such a delicate, firm precision, that her whole body began to convulse.

DEATH

Jacob had followed Betsy into her grandfather's house and now he stood staring at her panties on the carpet. They seemed to almost glow, as if they were the only object in the house in color. He kept staring at those panties and, for the longest time, could not take his eyes away from them. He tried to but just couldn't. Finally he did. He looked around the house.

Death hung in the house so thick he could almost feel it. Jacob looked back down at Betsy's panties. They were blue and were alive practically. Death hung everywhere else, but Betsy's panties, Jacob believed, were alive. He fought an impulse to pick them up. He looked back around the house.

Suddenly it struck Jacob that Betsy had taken off all of her clothes. He swallowed hard and could not stop an intense excitement from rising up. He continued on through the house, slowly, his breath nearly gone.

Upstairs, in the attic, Betsy turned sideways. Her suspicions were true. The attic wasn't very well lit and the full-length mirror had copper-colored splotches all around its edges but still she could see her naked body. What she saw upset her.

Outside the storm had passed. Thunder grumbled but only in the distance.

Betsy had missed two periods. She stared a moment at her belly and then at her face. She didn't look like herself. There was someone else in the mirror maybe but it certainly wasn't Betsy.

She closed her eyes.

MARTIN LUTHER KING

The General's house was built into the side of a hill overlooking Darwin's Ferry and the Wabash River. The house was more or less protected from the storm. It shook some but Leonard and the General, who sat on the screened-in porch that faced the Wabash, didn't let that bother them. They drank beer after beer and talked.

"Goddamn," the General said as he stared down at the ferry-boat. "The sumbitchin' storm's rippin' my poles out." The General was talking about the two cane poles he put at the end of the ferry-boat. The storm lashed water against the boat with such ferocity as to jerk the poles straight up into the air. They both watched as the poles detached from the ferryboat and slammed into the water.

Leonard laughed. "Probably a catfish on one of them the size of your leg."

"By god that'd be my luck, wouldn't it?" The General emptied his beer can, reached for another. "Hell, I don't care, shit." He shook his head. "You know, Leonard, I been thinkin'."

Leonard stared at the General. "Well by God that's good for you, Malcolm." Then Leonard took his dentures out of his mouth, cleared away a chunk of breakfast with his thumb, then put the fake teeth back in his mouth.

Thunder clapped loudly and unexpectedly, as if right on top of the two old men and it startled them. Leaping into the air, they both yelled in unison, "HOLY SHIT!" Then they settled down and cursed the storm some more. They each took deep breaths. Leonard fumbled with his smoke sack and Malcolm continued.

"I don't mean just thinkin' thinkin', you know what I mean?"

Leonard looked at Malcolm. He took a tiny white sugar cube from his shirt pocket. "You ever heard of LSD, Malcolm?"

The General repeated the word. "Nope. Can't say that I have."

"Well these two girls gave me this here cube and said if I ate this I'd understand more things than I've ever understood in my life."

The General blinked. "Leonard, I'm trying to tell you about these six niggers I saw on a street corner in St. Louis when I was a kid." The General coughed. "You know that little nigger girl who's always sayin' her daddy is as black as coal?"

Leonard stared at the General through slit, bloody eyes. "She ain't a nigger, Malcolm." Leonard moved the sugar cube around in his hand. "She's my granddaughter."

"Well I know that goddamn it to hell." The General shook his head. "I don't mean nothin' by it. That's just what I'm gettin' at, goddamn it." Malcolm wiped his nose on his sleeve. "What I mean is, that was the first goddamn niggers I ever seen in my life on that street corner. Leonard, I was only six year old and I nearly shit my pants. They *were* as black as coal, by God. I mean they were so shiny black and all you could have goddamn seen yourself in'em."

Leonard laughed. "By God you're right there. You get right up close to'em you'll see yourself in'em." Leonard held the sugar cube up to his eye. "Every time."

The General shook his head. "You ain't listening to me, old man. What I mean is it ain't like it used to be."

Leonard plopped the sugar cube into his mouth. "What do you mean it ain't like it used to be?"

"Just what I said. It ain't like it used to be. That little girl runnin' around here. That nigger up there in that shack with all those whites. Hell, on that TV in there before it was broke. You seen that Martin Luther King?" Malcolm pointed the stub of his cigar at Leonard. "Shit, if he weren't a nigger that sumbitch might have been President they hadn't killed him."

Leonard thought about this, then shrugged. "Hell, it wouldn't bother me none," he said. "Nigger, Jew, White. I goddamn still wake up some morning and not know where the hell I am." Leonard didn't think the sugar cube tasted very good. He washed the taste out of his mouth with a new can of Sterling beer.

"You ain't listening to me, Leonard. What I'm saying is--"

Malcolm paused. "The goddamn world's changing or somethin'."

"Oh changin' hell," Leonard said. "White people'll always hate black people and black people'll always hate white people. As long as people shit in different outhouses, people'll find somebody to hate."

Malcolm stared at Leonard for a moment, puzzled. He asked him what he meant.

"All shit looks the same, Malcolm. No matter what asshole it comes out of," Leonard said. "People just don't think so."

"I suppose you're right there," Malcolm said. "Maybe if we were all the same color as your granddaughter, it would be all right."

Leonard eased his eyes shut, felt his head spin in an odd direction. "You got something there."

Malcolm nodded. "Maybe the goddamn old dogs gotta learn some new tricks."

Leonard laughed sarcastically. "You can teach an old dog new tricks," he said. "But the goddamn cats will still shit in the middle of the goddamn floor when company comes over and you neglect them."

Leonard and the General looked at each other. Malcolm was a little irritated at Leonard, who was staring at him funny. Leonard had a strange look on his face. Shortly, Leonard believed that the General was turning silver and starting to levitate.

"What the hell's that supposed to mean, Leonard?"

Leonard looked up at the pink sky and then out across the yellow and orange and purple Wabash, said he didn't know.

PREGNANT

Her voice, Jacob could hear, was as soft as the inside of her thigh where his hand had been earlier that morning. Her eyes were wet and sparkled almost unnatural as they sat on the bed up in the attic. All Betsy had on was a flannel shirt held precariously shut by one button. It had been her father's shirt. It was open almost to her belly button and each breast swelled out of the shirt with such force as to render Jacob near peristaltic. He could see for the first time in his life, a nipple. It was a brown little thing that made his heart pound in his chest like a Benzedrine jackhammer. It also made his head feel so light he was afraid it would float away.

Betsy sat looking at Jacob on the bed with one ankle tucked under her, as her other leg dangled over the side. She held the shirt she wore closed between her legs with her hands. One tear eased out of her saturated left eye and found a resting spot on the edge of her top lip.

Even though her face was contorted in pain, Jacob could never remember her ever being so beautiful. For the first time, Betsy was no longer ordinary in any sense of the word. She sniffed and gently brushed away the tear from her lip. She looked Jacob straight in the eyes but somehow was looking through him. "I'm pregnant," she said.

INSURANCE COMPANIES

The one trailer that was affected most by the storm was the pink-sided Holly Park that Doc Garrelts lived in. The people in the ditch watched with eyes wide as Doc Garrelts' HOLLY PARK twisted off the cement blocks it sat on and was spun high into the air like a huge metal balloon that had suddenly been pricked by a needle. The trailer stood on end for a moment high in the air, its sides twisting obscenely as if some invisible creature was trying to rip it apart.

One of the people in the ditch looked frantically around in that interminable moment during a disaster, and tried to find Doc Garrelts. No, Doc Garrelts had chosen to stay in his trailer. Their hearts sank. Regardless of his obvious insanity, Doc Garrelts was, far and above, the most beloved individual in the trailer park. As they watched his trailer rise horribly into the air, tin sides twisting and aluminum window frames bending, they all recalled the various antics of the old doctor.

One recalled how Doc Garrelts had once fired up the

Sherman tank on the edge of the cemetery in town and drove it through the streets in protest. It had not been driven in over twenty years and they still couldn't figure out how he got it running. And in protest of what? They all asked him. "Of War!" He proclaimed, green helmet on and nothing else. A state trooper arrested him and then let him go as the bank in town, the owner of the cemetery and the tank, refused to press charges.

Another recalled how Doc Garrelts, when the circus once came to town, had arranged to hang-glide over the entire area with pink flamingoes attached to the wings of the hang-glider. Why? They all asked him. Why was he doing it? Protest! He proclaimed, sunglasses on, as his boxer shorts flapped in the wind and his pink flamingo hang-glider swooped down upon the gathered townsfolk.

Yes, every one of them had a different memory to recall concerning Doc Garrelts. In some odd way he was the town hero. And now he was surely dead.

As Doc Garrelts' trailer hung in the air as if by strings, and all the people stared horrified, one window blew out the back of the trailer, taking with it a huge stuffed pink flamingo. The flamingo shot straight into the sky and vanished. Several of the people on the ground who stared up at the twisted and distorted trailer hanging in the air had to look away. It was just too painful to watch.

Finally, horribly, with a boom that rivaled that of ten jets shattering the sound barrier all at once, Doc Garrelts' HOLLY PARK trailer came right back down upon its concrete blocks upside down. The boom that it created as it hit was later said to have been heard ten miles away. And after it hit the trailer collapsed and wheezed like some huge, dead monster.

They all, as the storm died and vanished as quickly as it had struck, ran out of the ditch and up to Doc Garrelts' upside-down trailer. Someone watching sniffed back tears. Another voiced a brief prayer. Still someone else cursed the Divine Injustice of it all. It was a horrible and tragic sight. A front window, unable any longer to handle the severe trauma it had just been subjected to, popped and shattered.

Everyone had twisted, pained expressions on their faces. No one wanted to go inside that trailer. One, though, had sense enough to run for a phone and try and call an ambulance. The others just stood dazed and in shock.

Finally, they heard a noise in the trailer. Their mouths collectively went wide. Then they heard another noise. And another.

Then finally the screen door swung slowly open, as if by its own volition. Everyone outside the upside-down trailer crept closer and strained to look inside.

To everyone's shock, Doc Garrelts popped out and down the steps, with a glass in his hand. He wore a Bob Dylan T-shirt and green sweatpants.

He smiled at everybody, took a sip from the glass.

"Damn," he said. "I almost spilled my drink." Then he winked and smiled. "Thank God for insurance companies, huh?"

CHESS

After the storm passed Janet lit both candles and finished off her bottle of cold duck. She got up once to call her father. She vaguely hoped the phones wouldn't be working after the storm but it rang. She let it ring twice and then hung up. She sat back down.

Janet let her eyes become mesmerized by the two flickering candles, as her thoughts went back to when she was nine years old. Her mother was throwing things. Her father sat in the front porch swing reading a book and quietly putting notes in the margins with a fountain pen. A gold-tipped fountain pen that had a thick, black body and always felt heavy when Janet snuck around and picked it up.

Her mother was throwing things in her father's den. Her mother said nothing as she threw things. She simply threw something, picked up something else and threw that. Her mother threw marble chess pieces at the moment. Blue marble they had bought in Mexico some time ago. Her father liked to play chess, and usually with young men Janet fell immediately in love with as soon as they said hello to her at the door.

Janet remembered watching her mother throw the chess pieces as she hid beneath the dining room table, much like she had just done to protect herself from the storm.

The chess pieces thudded against books on the shelves and clanged against the metal typewriter. Her mother took careful aim at a picture on the wall of their little family.

Her mother threw the queen, the most powerful chess piece, her father had once told her. Her mother missed.

Now there was only one chess piece on the board, the largest piece, but also, Janet would learn, the one piece that could only move one place in any direction. *Bringing in the leaves... Bringing in the leaves...*

Janet's mother, without missing this time, threw the King through the window in the den. Janet, as she emptied her wine glass and took three Valiums, remembered quite vividly glass breaking and shattering everywhere.

NETS

Meanwhile Leonard called out to the General not to spill the bottle as they both staggered down the riverbank to get to the General's sixteen-foot Johnboat. It was time, they decided, to run Leonard's fishing nets.

"I'll have the biggest goddamn fish fry you ever seen, Malcolm!" Leonard proclaimed, as the General tried to jerk on that old Mercury ten-horse. It just sputtered and died. The General said it needed a new spark plug. Leonard stood up in the boat, bottle held in the air. "Don't we all, goddamn it! Don't we all!"

Finally the old engine fired off.

Old logs and other debris that had been stirred up by the storm bobbed thick in the Wabash now. It made the river look like some kind of stew. Drunk as he was, Malcolm still knew he had to be careful when he drove the boat. He told Leonard that it had been a bad storm. Leonard, who sat at the front of the boat facing the back, agreed with that one. The Wabash was already rising. It would rise some more before morning. A fast-moving log the size of a man's torso scraped the side of the boat. Leonard jumped but Malcolm had swerved to keep the log out of the engine prop.

Leonard took out his smoke sack. The heat was coming back. He felt it on his shoulders.

"There ain't gonna be much in my nets, is there?" Leonard said. They both knew a storm scared the hell out of fish. They lost their sense of smell and wouldn't be able to find their way into Leonard's nets where that rotten cheese was. Another log brushed against the boat. They both shook their heads and laughed as Malcolm, engine throttle held steady under his arm, unscrewed the lid of the bottle and took a big drink.

THE LAST BARGE

Something jabbed George behind the eyelids as he lay near-sleep, exhausted from sex, upon the bed of moss. He woke completely up, his heart pounding. He sat up on his elbows. Valarie was asleep entirely, her belly hard against George, her thigh heavy between his legs. George stared at the curve of her back, the fullness of her hips, felt the prickly coarseness of her pubic hair against his leg. He stared at her face where her hair fell across her cheek. Her lips were parted slightly, her eyes shut. Restless suddenly, George eased away from Valarie, who stirred slightly but stayed asleep. George pulled on his jeans.

Sunlight trickled through the thick tree branches over them. There was no longer even a hint that there had been a storm. He stared back at Valarie there upon the moss, lit a cigarette, then stared out across the Wabash. The poor man's Mississippi, he thought. The Wabash was about dead now as a river. The last barge made it through in 1965. It was too dried up and shallow now, like all the people who lived along it. Racists, George thought as he blew smoke into the air. His thoughts went to that little mulatto girl in town and a cross burning they had just downriver somewhere awhile back. He stared at the riverbank and the receding water line. There wasn't even enough water for a Nigger Jim or a Huck Finn to float down in the Wabash. George smiled.

Something brewed ugly inside George. It always had and probably would never cease until he reached that blissful blackness at the end of his life. Poetry wasn't the answer and neither was emptying shit out of bedpans. He drew hard on the cigarette, watched a blue-painted boat in the middle of the river pull up a fishing net.

"I wish I was black or female," George thought abruptly. He flicked the cigarette butt away. "Just to have license to be so angry." He laughed under his breath.

The man pulling up the net out in the middle of the river had on a uniform of some kind. George didn't know who the Game Warden was. He didn't know that the Game Warden was stealing from Leonard's nets. George turned and walked back to Valarie.

A DEAD SQUIRREL

Dorina pushed aside tree branches and pieces of bark strewn everywhere to look for her dead baby brother. A panic rose in her as she searched all over the lot. He had to be somewhere. She climbed over a broke-in-two tree and slipped and scraped her leg. It burned terrible but it didn't slow her down any. She kept looking. She about started crying.

Then, beside one of the trees that got uprooted by the storm she found her blue bundle. The storm had unwrapped it's little black feet. Dorina stared. Those little feet were wrinkled and curled-up so tiny they hardly looked like feet any more. She couldn't believe how black the feet were. Her baby brother had been white. She shuddered and wrapped the little feet back up. Then what she saw made her drop the blue bundle.

There was a squirrel there on the ground. A dead one. Its

eyes were wide open and its legs stretched out rigid. It had a white belly of fur. Dorina studied it carefully, her face wrinkled in something between fear and curiosity. She picked up a stick.

Finally she poked the squirrel gently. It didn't move. Then she poked it again. It still didn't move. It was dead. She tucked the blue bundle under her arm.

"My daddy is coming home," she told the dead squirrel.

Dropping the stick and tucking the blue bundle under her arm Dorina walked down the street where the old man lived. He was sitting out on his porch. His eyes looked strange.

"Look how beautiful it's become after the storm," Delancey said. Dorina sat down upon the steps, shrugged.

Delancey nodded. "We have to always question everything." He looked at Dorina. "I've written five books and three times that many articles. My heart isn't working very well. I'd trade everything for a little more time."

Dorina wasn't listening to the old man. She tapped her tennis shoes upon concrete, told the old man about the dead squirrel. Delancey stared in front of him, his chin out and eyes glazed. The storm had raised his blood pressure to a dangerous level. He felt the pain in his chest. He had taken two little tablets. His breathing was heavy.

"I have a daughter," he said. "She doesn't think I'm much of a father." He laughed a quick deep laugh. He looked at Dorina again. "I wasn't," he said, tapping on the cane in his lap. One corner of his mouth rose into a strangely sad smile as he still breathed heavily.

"So what?" he said without much conviction.

THE EDGE OF A WATERFALL

Dorina heard that familiar sound and jumped off the porch steps and ran into the street. She left her blue bundle on the steps.

"Where you going? Where you going?" Dorina yelled as she jumped up and down in the street. "Can I come? Can I come?"

Betsy put the skids on her bike and so did Jacob. As Dorina climbed onto the crossbar of Betsy's bike, Jacob called out for them to look at the corner lot where the storm had tore through the trees. They all looked at it with awe but not for long. They wanted to get down to the river.

They continued on through town a little slower now, as they checked out all the damage.

Delancey, back on the porch, dozed for a moment, awoke, and there in his nostrils he believed, was the stench of his own death. It wasn't. It was the dead baby wrapped in a blue blanket on his steps. It didn't matter much anymore, he decided. Like reaching the edge of a waterfall and teetering there, Delancey's life began to flash before him. He tried to think of his accomplishments as neon credits flashing by after a grand and wonderful movie. It didn't work. His failed relationship with his daughter loomed heavily over everything else. There was perhaps, he concluded, nothing he could do about it. He tried to think of something and nothing came to mind. He dozed off again.

MORE SEX ALONG THE WABASH

It was a more quiet, more intense love-making the second time. When George slid into Valarie that second time they could feel each other far up into their lungs, it seemed like. Valarie's eyes were watery and sad as her lips parted in what looked like a frown. George's expression fell somewhere between winning at blackjack and witnessing the saddest event in the universe. He moved inside of Valarie almost imperceptibly slow. She clutched at the small of his back as he slid his thumbs over her eyebrows, her lips; it was the greatest, most extraordinary love-making George had ever experienced. The animal side had left them and now their bodies were a part of some unspoken, inarticulate revelation that could only be passed between them now, at this very moment, in this very manner. Finally, they both let out moans that made every animal in the woods around them pause.

Afterwards, on his back and his pupils dilated, George, out of breath, turned and looked at the beautiful woman lying next to him. Valarie, her body relaxed suddenly, stared up at the beautiful trees as she blinked away salty tears. George wanted desperately to say something, the right thing, precisely. It came to him.

George, in perfect rhythm with the times, told Valarie that she was the greatest fuck that he had ever had in his lifetime.

Valarie stared through the tree branches at the beautiful sky, took in a deep breath and the wonderful smell of the earth that surrounded them, and concluded quite emphatically, that George would never, *ever* be a true poet.

BLOOD

Jacob stared at the trees, the road, the thin slice of the river off to his left. But his grandfather's yelling wouldn't go away. They stood in front of their grandfather's shack. Jacob looked at Dorina who clung to Betsy's waist. Dorina had never seen her grandfather so angry. He staggered into his metal chair, still yelling. Leonard got to his feet and pointed his finger at the river. He would kill that Game Warden, Leonard kept yelling. He stopped yelling just long enough to cough deeply and spit up blood. It was all blood this time, no phlegm. When Leonard wiped it away from his lips he smeared it all across his face. He kept pointing and yelling. Dorina began to whimper. Betsy grabbed her around the shoulder, told her it would be okay.

"He robbed my goddamn nets!" Leonard yelled. "Goddamn it!" He pulled himself out of his chair and staggered towards his metal cooler. His voice was hoarse now as he yelled. Then he stopped and glared at the children. He was having trouble staying on his feet. His eyes were so wide and his expression so angry Leonard seemed to be looking right through them. When Dorina saw the blood across his face and the veins popping out on his forehead she buried her face in Betsy's shoulder and began to cry.

"I'll kill that sonofabitch!" Leonard yelled, body swaying, as he continued on towards the cooler. "I'll blow him right into that goddamn river or my name ain't Leonard Lee Downs!" He stumbled and fell to a knee. This unfroze Jacob. He ran towards his grandfather. Even Jacob was on the verge of tears now. He couldn't stand to see his grandfather in such a state. He said "Grandpa," very weakly as he helped the drunken old man to his feet. Leonard jerked his arm away from Jacob.

"Goddamn it!" His voice rose. "I ain't too old to kill that sonofabitch! Threatened to shoot–" He hesitated, stared at his grandson, one eyelid drooping. "That sumbitch threatened to shoot and kill me and Malcolm both and I caught that peckerwood red-handed stealin' fish out of my own goddamn nets!"

Betsy rolled her eyes. "Come on, Dory," she said. "It's time to go home." Dorina was crying heavy now. She didn't want to leave Jacob or her grandfather. Betsy continued. "He's drunk again. He's always drunk." Betsy kicked up the kickstand on her bike and climbed on. "Come on, I said!"

Dorina whimpered, then called out to Jacob. Her grandfather was shaking his fist towards the river and still yelling. Jacob motioned Dorina to go on as he followed his grandfather, who stumbled again, this time to all fours. This brought on another coughing fit.

Jacob went on ahead of him and took a beer out of the cooler. As Betsy and Dorina rode off, Jacob could see Dorina looking back. He hated it when she saw her grandfather like this.

Leonard, on his feet now, stumbled into the cooler and fell right on his ass, still cursing the Game Warden. Jacob helped him sit up, handed him a beer. Leonard wiped off his face with his shirtsleeve, took a big drink.

He was breathing hard. His eyes had blood in them. He had stopped yelling. He looked at Jacob.

"I ain't crazy, boy." He swallowed hard, spit on the ground. "That sumbitch ain't gonna get away with it this time. He killed my best friend, he ain't nothing but shit, he steals my fish, and by God I'm gonna get him back this time." Leonard fumbled around in his overalls for his smoke sack. He took another drink of beer. When he found his smoke sack he seemed to relax some. Jacob sat down beside him. Leonard looked tired suddenly.

"Did I ever tell you what happened to me?" Jacob opened himself a can of beer. Leonard went on, for about the hundredth time. "I was making over two hundred dollar a week as an electrician. They said I could wire a house faster than any three men around." He nodded. "I could." Leonard swallowed hard and began rolling a cigarette. He moved so he could see the Wabash. Jacob stared at the label on the beer can, swiveled it in his hands. His grandfather's voice was hoarse. "Hell, they had politicians and everybody calling me up to put electric lights in their houses. I'd do it, too. Hell, it didn't matter to me who they were. Shit." Leonard licked along the length of the cigarette he just rolled, twisted the ends together. His hands were shaking some and his voice trailed off. "Then I fell out of that truck." He took a deep drag off the cigarette. "Split my head open like a goddamn cantaloupe." He looked at Jacob out of the corner of his eye. Jacob refused to look at him. "You ever sit down to do somethin' you know you can do but you just can't do it?" Leonard looked back at the river. "By God that's how I was." He laughed sharp and quick. "Hell, it was just like my son said; I couldn't make up my mind which way to screw in a goddamn lightbulb." He laughed again. "But I knew how to fish. I couldn't talk but by God I remembered every damn thing there was to remember about fishing." He bared his yellowed, ill-fitting dentures. Jacob smiled, too. His grandfather stopped smiling.

"That's why I'm gonna kill that sonofabitch this time." Leonard got himself to his feet. "Go get my gun, Jake."

HOME

Lucy couldn't believe it at first. After the phone call she couldn't think straight. Her husband was finally coming home. It had been over eleven years and he hadn't ever seen his baby daughter. Now he was coming home and if his letters meant anything, he was going to take care of them now.

Lucy put her blouse on backwards and couldn't find her barrette at all. She was definitely flustered but she liked what she saw in the mirror. Even though it had been such a long time since Lucy had met up with her husband she didn't think she'd lost a thing in that time. Then she froze. Her eyes. Her eyes didn't look as good as they had. There was pain in her eyes and she had no idea how to get rid of it. She went back to looking for her barrette. She got on her knees on the hardwood floor and looked under her bed. Dorina might have taken it.

But life had to go on, Lucy told herself as she looked under the bed. Then suddenly it again came back to her what she had done to her child. It had been an accident. Suffocated the poor little thing in her arms to keep it from crying. It was an accident. She loved her baby.

Lucy got to her feet. But her baby boy was dead. She took lipstick off the dresser and it fell out of her hands before she could get it to her lips. Suddenly her hands were shaking. She couldn't look at herself in the mirror. She froze now like a statue.

The father of her dead baby boy had been a farmer named Jerry. Lucy unfroze and rolled her eyes. Jerry was white. She didn't know how she was going to explain her baby to her husband, who was black, anyway. And he was on his way home right at this very minute. Maybe, just maybe, she had killed her baby on purpose. Lucy closed her eyes and rubbed her temples. It was all too much. Nothing made sense and nothing ever happened like it was supposed to happen. But life had to go on. It was her philosophy and she would stick with it.

Lucy called out her daughter's name. There had been a storm and Dorina hadn't come home yet. She went out on the front porch and yelled out her daughter's name several times. Lucy looked up and down the street. Finally she stopped yelling for Dorina. She knew somehow her daughter was all right. Her daughter would always be all right. Dorina had that much in her—to stay fine in the face of disaster. Lucy ran her fingers very deliberately through her hair. First her right hand, then her left.

Then she walked into the kitchen. Her husband would be home soon and this time it would be different. Lucy sat down at the table, put her elbows hard upon the table, and started crying.

OVER EIGHTEEN

Leonard stumbled on the way down the riverbank and went head over heels down the embankment. Jacob, his grandfather's gun in his hands, stood at the top of the embankment and prayed quickly that his grandfather would not tumble on into the Wabash. He didn't. Jacob called out to him.

Leonard rolled over on his back, still cursing. He sat up slowly. "My gun goddamn it! What time is it?" He fumbled around in the front pocket of his overalls for his pocket watch. He got it out and in his hands and stared at it intently. He was too drunk to read the hands. He put the watch back in his front pocket. "That goddamn Game Warden will be by at four and I'll kill that sonofabitch this time! Jacob!"

Jacob looked at the gun, then at his grandfather. He made his way down the hard clay and rock embankment. He stepped on a red and white plastic fishing bobber and it shattered under his tennis shoe. He made it down to where his grandfather sat breathing hard and the first thing Jacob noticed was the bits of clay and rock in his grandfather's long snow-white hair. Leonard put the gun across his lap. His eyes were shot and he didn't look like he felt any good at all, Jacob noticed.

"Go away now, boy," Leonard said. "Murder ain't nothing to watch."

Jacob sat down beside his grandfather. They both stared into the Wabash. The river had went down some since yesterday.

"I said go away," Leonard said, his voice not so loud or convincing anymore. "You got to do what you got to do in this life, boy." Leonard knocked more dirt out of his hair. "So you don't feel like shit at the end." He pulled his smoke sack out, began rolling a cigarette. After he got it rolled and lit he told Jacob he wanted to show him something. He took his pocket watch back out, opened it up. Inside there was a picture of Jacob's grandmother. She was very young and her coal-black hair was parted in the middle and pulled tightly back. There was barely a smile on her face. She looked beautiful.

"Did I ever tell you about our wedding?"

Jacob tried to remember. He was certain he had heard the story before but unfortunately it eluded him at the moment.

"We ran off together to Lynchfield, Kentucky. To a preacher named–" Leonard couldn't remember the preacher's name. "Anyway, before we went into that church, Nettie started digging around in her purse. I told her to hurry up, we were gonna be late. Besides, I said, her daddy might catch up with us and shoot me dead." Leonard shook his head. "Her daddy liked me about as much as he liked those damn dollar-sized bunions he had on his feet. He got them standing all day in a meat-packing plant up near Terre Haute where he worked." Leonard took a big drag off the cigarette and was catching his second wind, it seemed like. Jacob looked upriver where the Game Warden's boat would be appearing shortly.

"I ain't kidding you, Ol'Man Kingary had feet goddamn this long." Leonard held out his hands. Ashes fell from the cigarette that stuck to his bottom lip and onto the front of his overalls. "He could walk across that river there and not sink with those feet a'his." He chuckled. "He kicked my ass good with one of them one time too when he caught me and Nettie together." He took a big drag off the cigarette, coughed, and continued his wedding story.

"Anyway, I said, 'Nettie. What are you doing? We got to get in there and get married before your Daddy finds us.' 'I need something to write with,' Nettie said. I asked her why and she told me it was none of my business. So I looked around the car for something to write with. It was a brand-new Model-T Ford. The same one your mommy broke off a pair of scissors in the ignition one time. Anyway, I found Nettie a piece of paper and she tore it into two little pieces and wrote something on each of them. Then she took off each shoe she had on and put a piece of paper inside. I kept telling her to hurry up, we had to get in there and get married. Besides, my feet were getting colder by the minute. Hell, I was only sixteen and your grandmother fifteen." Leonard shook his head. "You ain't got no business getting married at that age anyway. Or any age. Hell, you're fucked in the head to get married at all anymore really.

"But I went on ahead and waited for Nettie on the church steps." Leonard took out a red bandanna from his back pocket, blew his nose on it. "The first thing I remember in that church was the Preacher's wife." Leonard's eyes lit up. "Fred! goddamn it! That was his name. Fred Gatlin. His wife wore the godawfullest yellow dress you ever seen and I bet you she weighed every bit of two hundred pounds." Leonard laughed and his dentures slipped in his mouth. "Damn, we were scared. I don't think it would have bothered neither one of us one bit if ol' Fred would have told us to turn right around and go home because we were too young to be getting married. But that's what people did back then. Hell, they probably still do it."

Leonard eased back upon the embankment, let out a big sigh. "Damn, I'm tired."

Jacob looked at his grandfather. He asked him about those pieces of paper his grandmother wrote something on and put in her shoes. Leonard put his hands behind his head and continued.

"Well, we walked on up there to the altar I guess it's called, and were both shaking like leaves. Nettie about broke my arm she grabbed it so hard. I felt like any minute one or both of us would turn and run right out of that church. And I'll tell you this; Fred was the meanest looking Baptist preacher I think I ever saw in my life. His eyes were like two piss holes in a snow bank and he had this mustache that hung over his lips like he was a goddamn walrus or something. And he had on this black suit that made him look more like a mortician than a damn preacher." Leonard let out a laugh. "Hell, he probably buried more people than he married, I don't know, but he scared the hell out of Nettie. She took one look at him and I had to hold her up to keep her legs from givin' out. And hell, my legs weren't exactly rock hard. The sumbitch was mean-looking. And you know what the first thing he asked Nettie before he started to marrying us?" Leonard paused now, his eyes going shut.

"What?" Jacob said. Leonard's eyes opened.

"Now Nettie ain't ever told a lie in her life. It's how she was raised and by God if that woman's ever told a lie I ain't never heard it. But that preacher looked her right in the eye and said, 'Are you over eighteen?'" Leonard shook his head. "Right then and there I thought it was over. I could see Nettie just running crazy right out of that church, but you know what she said?" Jacob shook his head. "She held her chin right up and said, 'Yes, sir, I am.'" Leonard sniffed loudly and let his eyes shut entirely. He had just about talked himself to sleep. Then, in a last gasp, "We were married and spent our wedding night in Martha's Cottage Hotel on old route 40 one mile out of Parrington, Kentucky. Nettie cried all night and it took us a good two weeks to figure how to do what we were supposed to do." Leonard fell fast asleep. He began to snore even.

Jacob stared at his grandfather and was glad he was asleep. He would hopefully sleep through the Game Warden going by in his boat. But he still wanted to know what was written on those pieces of paper inside his grandmother's shoes. "Grandpa?" Jacob said, his voice low. He said it again. His grandfather opened one eye partially. Jacob asked him about those two pieces of paper his grandmother wrote on and stuck in the bottoms of her shoes before they got married.

"Why Nettie wrote EIGHTEEN on each one of those pieces of paper. I told you your grandmother ain't never told a lie in her life, didn't I? She knew what that preacher was going to ask her. And when he asked if she was over eighteen, she wasn't lying, now was she?" Leonard cleared his throat, let his eyes ease shut. "You better study more in school, boy." Leonard said, then he went back to sleep.

Jacob thought about what his Grandfather had just told

him. It wasn't long before his grandfather was snoring.

Sighing, Jacob looked out over the Wabash where the Game Warden's boat would be appearing soon.

THE TOURIST

"You probably don't remember me, do you?"

Delancey opened his eyes. He had dozed off and was beginning to dream. He suddenly couldn't remember any of it though. Leaning against the porch with his arms crossed was a thin young man with a thick beard. He wore a flannel shirt and faded bell-bottom jeans. The man wrinkled up his nose and sniffed. He paid no attention to the blue bundle on the porch steps.

"I believe you got something dead under your porch, Mr. McFadden."

Delancey sniffed also and was quite relieved. Perhaps it wasn't him that reeked of death after all.

Delancey looked at the man. "No, I can't say that I do remember you, young man."

"I used to date your daughter."

Delancey looked at his cane. His daughter. The man sat down in a chair beside the porch swing.

"I just got back from Vietnam." The man scratched his beard. "I'm all right, though. Yep." Then he yelled, "INCOMING!" and leaped out of the chair and dove flat on his belly on the floor of the porch. The man lay there a moment, then he got back up laughing. Delancey was trying to steady his heartbeat. The man sat back down.

"Everybody thinks us vets'll do that the rest of our lives." He laughed some more. "I got drafted but went in as a conscientious objector. I'm a Quaker." The man nodded. "They sent me right in there with the Fifth Infantry along the De-Militarized zone." The man unwrapped a piece of chewing gum, stuck it in his mouth. "The only thing I ever shot though was a camera. You want to see something?" The man pulled out an Indian-bead wallet from his back pocket, removed a snapshot.

Delancey took his bifocals out of his shirt pocket, looked at the picture. It was of a Vietnamese family. Three children and the mother and father. They were quite possibly the homeliest oriental family he had ever seen. Waving behind them in the picture was the man sitting beside him.

"Dr. Toe and his family. I wanted to marry his daughter. I never got a picture of her, though." The man pointed. "She's the one that took the picture." The man put the picture back in his wallet. "I didn't marry her though. She was kind of a bitch. She talked too damn fast anyway." The man relaxed in the chair. "I handed out supplies. Me and this other conscientious objector–a guy named Bill. One day we were under this tent watching that John Wayne movie *The Green Berets*, you know? And there's this scene in it where they have this big battle where all hell breaks loose. Well, we were all just sitting there watching this John Wayne movie and there were bombs going off on the screen and man, it seemed too goddamn real." The man looked at Delancey. "Well, we found out it was real. We were under enemy fire at the same time John Wayne was under fire in that movie and everybody started running and all and as all hell was breaking loose all I had around my neck was my camera. Click-Click. There were all these gooks popping out of the ground like slant-eyed gophers, and all I was shooting was pictures. Click-click." The man laughed, put his feet on a box of books. "Everybody started calling me the Tourist after that."

Delancey tried not to smile as he put his bifocals back in his shirt pocket. "War must be an awful thing."

The man seemed to think about this a moment, then he shrugged. "Yeah, it was pretty bad really..." the man's voice trailed off. "They had a hell of a black market over there though. Did your daughter make out all right in the storm?"

Delancey asked the man what he meant and the man told him about how the storm tore through the trailer park where his daughter lived. Delancey got immediately up from the porch swing.

MABEL BLANCHARD

Dorina scooped up her blue bundle from the porch steps and headed away. The Vietnam veteran still sat on Delancey's porch. He called out and asked Dorina what she had wrapped up in that blanket. Dorina stopped in her tracks and stared at the man.

"My dead baby brother," she said.

The man scratched at his beard a second, then yelled out "INCOMING!" as he leaped out of the chair, and hit the deck of the porch. Dorina ignored him.

She went behind Delancey's house and down the alley walking fast and thinking about Jacob and her Grandfather. They were the two most important people in her life. Maybe, Dorina believed, her Daddy would become the most important person in her life when he came and got her and her mommy. Dorina thought about this as she cut through another backyard. Two small, skinny hounds in a metal cage began to bark at her as they moved frantically back and forth in the cage. She had to get to the river.

But if her Daddy came and got her and her mommy, then that meant leaving Jacob and her Grandfather. She tried not to think about this. Maybe her Daddy wasn't coming at all. This seemed to be the most real thought to her. And maybe she would be afraid of him. She hadn't ever really seen a real black person in her life. Everybody called her black but she didn't think she was black. Her skin was exactly the same color as the inside of a Milky Way candy bar and that wasn't black at all. It just didn't make any sense. But Dorina knew one thing. She loved Jacob and her Grandfather more than any two people in the world.

Dorina fought back tears as she was almost running now. She absolutely hated it when people got angry. It was stupid and it scared her. She stumbled on loose rocks in the gravel road that led to the river, fell to her knee, and scraped her elbow trying to protect her blue bundle. She wanted badly to let loose and cry but she didn't. She got to her feet and went on.

Dorina stopped in Mabel Blanchard's yard and placed her

baby brother inside the half-buried bathtub. She leaned the bundle against the ceramic Mother Mary. Then she got to her knees, clasped her hands together and prayed.

She prayed first that her dead baby brother had somewhere to go when it got to Heaven. She was certain God had a place for all dead babies but she prayed for him just in case. Her Grandmother had once told her extra prayers never hurt at all, so that's what Dorina always did. Then she prayed that her Grandfather would be okay. Everybody said that he would die soon if he didn't stop drinking and smoking but Dorina couldn't even imagine him ever dying. Then she prayed (and she knew it was a selfish prayer, but she prayed anyway) that her and Jacob would always be together even when they grew up.

Dorina almost stopped praying but then she decided to pray that her Daddy would love her and take good care of both her and her mommy. Amen, she said.

Dorina got to her feet and just as she did so she was hit in the back of the head and up-ended. She landed flat on her face on the hard grass. Dorina rolled over, stunned more than hurt.

Towering over her, broom in hand was Mabel Blanchard. And she looked very old. She was so old Dorina couldn't tell if she was mad or angry or anything. She wore a faded blue paisley dress that had long sleeves with yellowed lace around the ends. Her hair was so gray it was almost blue. Her skin was a ghostly white and there were so many wrinkles in her face it was hard to figure out which one was her mouth. She wore black cat-eye glasses that were very thick and made her eyes look bigger and scarier than they actually were. She looked ten feet tall hovering over Dorina.

When Mabel Blanchard spoke her voice was a croak and hardly loud enough to hear, let alone loud enough to frighten Dorina. Dorina could not believe a person could look so old.

"Get out of my yard, you little black heathen," Mabel spat.

For some reason Dorina did not fear this woman. She was so old her voice had lost all authority. She was funny almost. For some reason Dorina thought of the Statue of Liberty she had seen on television one time. The broom quivered in the old woman's arms, as if she could barely hold it. Dorina rolled away from her and stood up. The old woman drew back the broom. This made Dorina mad. She doubled up her fists and squinted her eyes. It was the first time in Dorina's life she ever felt like striking back at an adult.

For some reason Dorina could not explain, she suddenly wanted to hurt this old woman. The old woman again told her to get out of her yard. Dorina, spitting out every word this time, told Mabel Blanchard that her daddy was as black as coal, then she glared at the old woman as she had never glared at anyone before. The wrinkles on the old woman's face moved in odd directions. Then she made a feeble swipe at Dorina. Dorina, her fist still doubled-up, easily got out of the way.

Dorina gave Mabel Blanchard one last glare of defiance and then headed on down to the river, the blue bundle under her arm.

THE SIX O'CLOCK NEWS

The water lapping against the riverbank reminded Jacob of sheets ruffling, of Betsy making her bed earlier that morning. He tried to blink the thought away. Beside Jacob, snoring, was his grandfather. The gun that lay across his lap had no shells in it. Jacob had removed the shells before he brought the gun to his grandfather. Jacob looked upriver. The Game Warden's boat would appear soon. Jacob looked up at the sky but he just couldn't help it. Betsy once again resided over all of Jacob's thoughts at the moment. He tried to figure out why this was so. He took in a deep breath and followed the trees lining the Indiana side of the river. Nothing stirred there except a few birds. He had known Betsy since they were small and there was even a time when he had hated her two summers ago. She had made fun of him and this had left a deep scar. He couldn't remember exactly anymore what it had been that she had made fun of, but the scar still remained. But now he had felt her flesh against his this morning and seen her naked this afternoon during the storm. Jacob now could not look at Betsy as he had looked at her before.

Jacob picked up a smooth gray rock and flicked it high above the water. It fell soundlessly into the fast moving Wabash. Then he jerked his head upriver. The Game Warden's boat appeared.

Jacob's grandfather lay on his back upon the riverbank, his head to one side and mouth wide open. He was sleeping hard. Jacob hoped to God he would not wake up. He thought about taking the gun from his grandfather's lap but this would surely wake him. Jacob pounded his fists on his forehead and looked all around. Maybe he should have left the shells in the gun. Emotions of fear primarily welled up through his neck and burned at the top of his skull. There was trouble ahead.

The Game Warden had killed a man. Henry Chalmers, Leonard Downs' best friend, late one afternoon in 1956. Shot him twice with a double-barrel twelve-gauge shotgun and he hadn't minded pulling the trigger at all. It had been easy. He didn't like Henry Chalmers.

Henry Chalmers was a handsome man who everybody liked. The Game Warden had a glass eye and was extremely ugly and everybody hated him. So all the Game Warden had to do was point the shotgun at Henry Chalmers and pull the trigger. He had done the same thing to a cat once. And a dog.

After the Game Warden pulled the trigger and that first blast hit Henry Chalmers, a curious thing happened. The Game Warden had expected it to be like in the movies. He expected Chalmers to throw his hands high in the air and fall in slow-motion to the ground. But Henry Chalmers didn't react that way at all. It wasn't like the movies at all.

Instead Henry Chalmers stumbled to his knees after the Game Warden had shot him, then jerked his head around and glared at the Game Warden. He called him a son of a bitch. Then Henry Chalmers tried to get up and come after the Game Warden. This surprised and even scared the Game Warden some. So the Game

Warden shot him again and directly in the face with the twelve-gauge shotgun. This time Henry Chalmers fell back like some drunken soldier and then eventually fell forward. Sort of like in the movies, the Game Warden thought.

He stared awhile as Henry Chalmer's body jerked some and then finally went still. Fascinated, it reminded the Game Warden of the Six O'clock news and how they showed this gook in Vietnam put a gun up to this other gook's head and pull the trigger. He had later seen the same picture on the cover of *TIME* magazine. He would later watch this same clip over and over again on the news and anywhere else on the television. It was on all the time. Then his television stopped working and even more than the *Andy Griffith Show* The Game Warden missed seeing the expression that gook had on his face right before that other gook put a bullet through his temple.

Then the Game Warden walked away, satisfied more or less.

But Henry Chalmers didn't die immediately. He had been fishing that day and he was supposed to meet Leonard Downs and drink some beers and clean all the fish he had caught. Henry Chalmers wanted once again to hear Leonard's 98-pound catfish story. It changed every time Leonard told it but it was always interesting. But Henry would never hear the story again.

Leonard Downs found his best friend face down in his own blood. He eased his best friend over and one side of his face was a mass of blood and broken cheekbone. Leonard cursed and his eyes blurred with horror and sadness.

"Goddamn," Leonard said.

A smile creased the one side of Henry's mouth that hadn't been struck by the shotgun shell. And according to Leonard, Henry was able to utter one word to his childhood and lifelong buddy.

"Friend," he said. Then Henry Chalmers died.

For years no one knew for sure who killed Henry Chalmers. The rumor had it that two niggers from Evansville, Indiana did it. There were always stories of niggers coming up from Evansville and doing this and that. But many people believed that the Game Warden had done it. He was known to be a cruel man and suspected as a thief and he only kept his job because his uncle was a politician in Springfield. No one knew exactly.

But Leonard Downs knew. He knew for a fact that the Game Warden had done it. He didn't see it and no one told him but he knew for certain. And in between his drunken stupors he vowed that some day he would revenge the murder of his best friend, Henry Chalmers. He had been making this vow for over ten years now.

Leonard had planned to at this very moment but he was sleeping and there were no shells in his shotgun.

Jacob pulled his knees up to his face as he sat beside his slumbering grandfather and pounded his chin on his kneecaps. He half-held his breath and kept praying over and over that the Game Warden's boat would not wake his grandfather up.

But the drone of the motor kept getting louder as the Game Warden's boat kept getting closer. Jacob fidgeted horribly and wanted to cry suddenly. The Game Warden had turned his boat toward shore.

He could see as the boat approached, that the Game Warden had his shotgun across his lap also. Jacob looked desperately up at the sky, perhaps in hopes of some divine intervention.

None came.

TELEVISION

On television one time when it was working Dorina remembered watching a bunch of sailors wrap a dead body up in a blanket and toss it into the water. She remembered them all being very serious about this type of burial. It had meant a lot to them and so it must be a very important way to bury someone. Dorina decided, as she walked down the street, that she would bury her baby brother in the river like they did on television.

She ran into the old man as she walked down the street. Delancey had stopped to catch his breath. He was trying to get to the trailer park to see if his daughter was okay. He took out his handkerchief and wiped his forehead. He was breathing hard and was a little disoriented. Dorina asked him if he was okay. He smiled at the young girl. In his state he mistook her for his daughter.

"Where's your mother, Janie?" He had always called his daughter, Janet, Janie. It had been his sister's name.

Dorina told him her name wasn't Janie. "Where you going?" She asked him.

Delancey looked up at the sky. It blurred. The sun was a bright, blurry yellow. Clouds surrounded it conspiratorially, Delancey decided. He also decided once again that he was very close to death.

They stood at the end of a dead-end street. To their left a large stretch of freshly-mowed grass was between them and the First Baptist Church. It was a simple white church. To their right was another stretch of freshly-mowed grass. At the far end of the grass was a brand new house. It was a large rectangular one-story house, half-brick and half-stucco. The roof wasn't completely finished yet. Rectangular strips of tar were stacked upon the roof.

Delancey pointed at the house. "The Death of Western Civilization," he said.

"Huh?" Dorina said.

Delancey nodded. "It is." He kept pointing. He touched her shoulder, told her to come along.

They walked up to the house. Delancey stopped and Dorina stopped beside him. She switched her blue bundle to the other arm and looked up at the old man. She told him it was the banker's house. Dorina stared almost eye-level at a little ceramic black boy in a blue riding suit holding a brass ring. It was the only decoration in the yard. Delancey stared at the house.

"What's missing?" He said.

Dorina looked up at him again. She shrugged and told him she didn't know.

"The Machine Stops," Delancey said. He fumbled in his shirt pocket for a pill, put it under his tongue, his hands quivering. "You see, child," he said. "America is slowly–no rapidly, turning into a collective society. Thinking, drinking, talking the same way. This house–" He caught his breath. "It all makes sense now." Delancey looked out of the corner of his eye at Dorina. "I was a bad father." He paused. "I didn't know how to be a good father. Still don't." He looked down at the little girl holding the blue bundle.

"You see, we had front porches. Everybody had front porches. We sat out on these front porches and saw only as far as we could see. But we looked and we kept out minds open. If it rained we watched and listened. When the birds chirped we heard them. We sat out on our front porches and we held hands and talked. We talked to neighbors and strangers. We talked to anybody that walked by. We watched the Heavens move! for God's sake, on those front porches." Delancey looked back at the house. "Look." He pointed again and he had talked himself out of breath. "Castration of the American Dream." He was pointing at the little cement slab at the front door of the house. The slab was barely big enough for the green WELCOME mat to fit on. It was all the front porch this new house had.

"No front porch." Delancey said. "The death of America, child. Now that front porches are gone the Seal is complete. All houses will be built without front porches from now on! Hermetically-sealed, synthetic wombs lit only by one light." Delancey laughed. "One light!" he said.

Dorina looked at the house. She couldn't see any light. "What light?" she said. Delancey, sniffing his own death once again, pulled Dorina along with him to the picture window. He stopped and let out a satisfied exclamation as he looked inside. He was right, by God.

Dorina strained to look inside but she wasn't tall enough. "What light?" She kept saying.

Delancey had a scornful, satisfied smile on his face as he looked inside the house. He was no longer writing history now but he was most certainly witnessing it at this very moment. His hands rose in the air. "The death of front porches and the bastard birth of the New Order!"

"I want to see!" Dorina said. She wasn't sure what she wanted to see, but she wanted to see something.

The old man looked down at her. His expression was one she would never forget. He pulled Dorina to him, lifted her slowly up. She helped him by gripping her tennis shoes to the bricks. Delancey, winded, held her there as she looked inside.

There was indeed, only one light in the room in the new house. It sparkled brightly and lit the entire room.

The source of the light was a television. A brand new Zenith color console television. It had big round silver dials on the right side of the screen. It was the biggest television set Dorina had ever seen. And it was working.

CATS AND DOGS

The two Jehovah's Witnesses stood outside Doc Garrelts' upside-down trailer staring at each other.

"God is testing us, Joyce," Marsha said.

"I've failed," Joyce was thinking. She didn't say this to Marsha, but she didn't want to go into that upside-down trailer. She didn't want to confront that man again. "Maybe we should come back tomorrow."

Marsha let out a partially disgusted sigh. "The world is an awful place, Joyce. We have to take whoever we can to meet the Lord."

Joyce wrinkled up her nose. The Lord didn't want to meet this man who danced with dummies and stole their car. Marsha wiped perspiration from her face with a lace hankie. She asked Joyce if she'd read that article in the *Watchtower*. "About this guy they thought was crazy because he tried to grow tomatoes in the African desert. He prayed to God every morning and night for seventeen days for rain. On the eighteenth day it rained cats and dogs," Marsha said. She tucked the hankie neatly back into her black vinyl purse. "*Real* cats and dogs." She looked at Joyce. "The cats ran all over the place and the dogs dug up all the tomato plants. The man gave up and went back to Tucson, Arizona and got a job selling insurance."

Joyce looked at Marsha and thought about this. She thought about asking Joyce what the moral of the story was but she didn't. She looked up at Doc Garrelts' trailer.

"The problem was that man didn't believe, Joyce." Marsha said, as she sucked in a deep breath. "But I believe." She looked at Joyce. "Do you?"

Joyce looked tentatively up at the sky. She hoped Chihuahuas and not St. Bernards would fall from the sky if worse came to worse.

They headed towards Doc Garrelts' upside-down trailer.

THE STROKE OF MIDNIGHT DECEMBER 31ST, 1969

Dorina ran out into the freshly plowed field where that same girl who gave her the turquoise ring sat. Dorina pulled the ring out of her pocket and put it on her finger. She sat down beside the girl, putting the blue bundle behind her.

"It falls off if I wear it all the time," Dorina said, out of breath, as she brushed her hair out of her face. She was a little glad to get away from that old man. She shrugged then looked at the girl. Her eyes were wide as she sat Indian-style in the red clay dirt. The girl had no shoes on and her feet were dirty. There was a green butterfly sewn on to one thigh of her bell-bottom blue jeans. The girl, seeing Dorina, smiled finally. Still, she said nothing.

Dorina told her about the television set in the Banker's new house. She said it was the biggest television she'd ever seen and it was colored. Dorina stopped talking about the television set and said to the girl, "What are you doing out here?"

The girl cleared her throat. "My head," she said, her voice scratchy. "Is somewhere else."

Dorina laughed and once again her laugh was much older than that of a ten year old. This woke the girl partially out of her stupor. Her eyes hardened as she looked at Dorina. A pick-up truck on the gravel road beside the field banged loudly as it hit a pothole passing by. Something rattled thunderously in the back of the truck and both girls jumped as if shot. Dorina giggled nervously. The red clay dirt was damp from the storm.

"Torch it," the girl said out of the blue.

"What?" Dorina said.

"The power structure," the girl said. "Burn it down." The girl looked at the sky, then tilted her head back so far Dorina thought for a moment she might fall backward. The girl let out a long sigh. Dorina liked her blouse. Betsy had one just like it. Betsy called it a peasant blouse.

"I polished this ring with baking soda and a toothbrush," Dorina said. "Just like my Mommy does her ring my Daddy got her."

The girl leaned towards Dorina and gently touched Dorina's cheek. "We should go right now–" the girl said, "Back to that banker's house and set it on fire."

Dorina looked curiously at the girl. She had no idea what she was talking about. The girl leaned back on her palms, pushed her face up towards the sun. "You're so young," she sighed. Dorina asked her how old she was. "Sixteen," the girl said.

Dorina tucked her leg under her, brushed wet dirt from her sore knee and thought about what it would be like to be sixteen. She asked the girl if she had a boyfriend.

The girl, her eyes closed, opened them.

"Everyone," she said, then she yelled out, "The whole world is my boyfriend!" Dorina didn't know what to think about this. She rotated the ring around her finger.

"I got one boyfriend." Dorina shrugged. "He ain't really my boyfriend." She was talking about Jacob. She spotted a tattoo on the girl's forearm. It was a blue peace sign about the size of a quarter. She asked the girl if it hurt to get that tattoo put on. "Betsy says you bleed when you get a tattoo."

The girl looked at the tattoo. She looked at it for quite awhile. "I don't remember," she said.

Dorina asked her where her mommy and daddy were; where they lived. She was always asking people this. It was important to her for some reason.

The girl swung her head and locked eyes with Dorina. Her look scared Dorina a little. Not much but a little. The girl looked down at the dirt. "They live in Anywhere, Nebraska," she said. "In a house bigger than the Banker's. They drive a car bigger than the Banker's. They have a bigger television than the Banker's on back order." She returned her gaze to Dorina, who was smiling. Dorina had no idea why she was smiling but she was. The girl was funny. Her eyes blazed as she talked to Dorina. "My father has no mouth and my mother only speaks in Church."

Dorina thought about this. She would think about it for a long time to come. Then she would never think about it again.

The girl asked Dorina where her parents were.

"My Daddy's coming home. He was in Viet Cong." Dorina tried to act older as she spoke, her face growing serious and matter-of-fact. "We're going to Alabama. My Daddy's gonna start a church. I'll sing in the choir." Dorina shrugged. "It'll be all right."

The girl stared intent and yet despondently at Dorina. She stretched out flat upon the lumpy wet freshly plowed earth, put her hands behind her head.

"Everything–" she said. "I mean *everything* will end at the stroke of midnight, December 31st, 1969."

Dorina took the ring off, stuffed it into her front pocket. She got to her feet. She told the girl she had to go.

"Where are you going, Miss America?" the girl asked.

Dorina told her she wasn't Miss America. She told the girl she had to go down to the river and bury her dead baby brother in the river. The girl bolted upright. Dorina asked the girl if she wanted to come.

Yes, she would like to come. She would like to come very

badly. In fact, it sounded like the most interesting thing to do in a long time.

A JOLT

George shut off the gas to the engine of his boat as inspiration struck him as a jolt from an electric chair. Valarie, who was sunbathing at the front of the boat, sat up. She watched as George wrote furiously in his little blue notebook. It made her smile. The passion that moved him to write amazed her. Especially since absolutely no talent was behind this passion. She lit a cigarette and stared at the shore. A farmer drove his red tractor so close to the embankment she feared he might tumble right over the edge. He didn't, though.

The dirt they worked here in southern Illinois was infertile compared to the rich coal-black dirt they worked in the middle of where Valarie was from. She had grown up in the town of Georgetown, Illinois. They say the soil there was ten times as fertile as the soil down here.

George let out an exclamation that startled Valarie. He smiled and nodded. He handed the little notebook to Valarie. She immediately tensed up. Most of George's poetry made her uncomfortable and, frankly, scared her. But she took the notebook anyway and read it.

It was a short poem entitled "A Truckstop Near Death." It was about a waitress and a trucker talking as a pool game went on across the room. It had a great opening:

> Here,
> The crack of the pool balls
> Shakes hands with the drunken thoughts
> Of lonely men riding on bleeding assholes
> In trucks they won't pay off in this century.

Valarie liked the opening. She knew all about how truck

drivers got hemorrhoids. She understood about how much trucks cost to finance also.

Valarie even liked the next stanza:

I sit with a toothless blonde waitress
Who got divorced New Years Eve 1962
And hasn't regretted it but once
Christmas, 1967, when her daughter
asked her if Santa Claus knew
Where her Daddy was.

Valarie even liked the ending.

As a cueball chases a stripe
And knocks in a solid instead.
It rolls dead.
Here in a truckstop near death.

But she thought there was one real clunker in the poem. It was how George described the waitress.

There was a dull sparkle
In her eyes,
Like diamonds left too long
In a nuke plant.

No. This didn't work at all. She told George what she liked about the poem. He smiled and his eyes lit up. Then she read him the real clunker stanza. They both laughed.

Then George tossed the whole notebook into the Wabash, restarted the motor, and upriver they went. Valarie tossed her cigarette into the water and went back to sunbathing.

SOMEWHERE ELSE

"You know, Son," the Game Warden began, his leg up on the front seat of the boat and the shotgun across his knee. "When I was your age my Daddy knocked me across the mouth with the back of his hand so hard I fell right out the boat." He smiled. Several teeth were missing. He brushed a horse fly off the barrel of the gun. Jacob didn't at all like the way the gun pointed at his sleeping grandfather. "I couldn't swim." The Game Warden took a toothpick out his front shirt pocket, put it in his mouth. "I died."

Jacob looked at the Game Warden.

"No, I didn't die, but I could have. I back-talked my Daddy one too many times." He rolled the toothpick to the other side of his mouth. The few teeth he had were stained brown from chewing tobacco, which, between pauses, he would spit the juice of over the side of the boat.

"Now, Son, I'm going to tell you once. Somethin' I never understood when my Daddy said it to me." The Game Warden rolled the toothpick to the other side of his mouth, spit dark brown juice out the other corner. It hit the river and spread across the water like oil. The whole process just about made Jacob sick.

"I want you to get the hell out of here right now." The Game Warden's voice had been firm and matter-of-fact. He looked slowly upriver and then moved his head to look downriver, giving Jacob the time to decide on his own to get the hell out before something awful happened.

Jacob stared at the Game Warden, his heart stopping. He didn't like the gun pointing at his grandfather.

"Where," Jacob began, then he paused. He looked the Game Warden right in the eyes. "Do you want me to go?"

The Game Warden swung his head and glared wildly at the boy, much like his father, no doubt, glared at him before he backhanded him right out of the boat and into the Wabash. The gun reflexively pointed at Jacob now, a finger pressed to the trigger. The toothpick fell out of the Game Warden's mouth.

The Game Warden's expression turned wild and pretty much insane as he glared at the skinny smart-mouthed asshole little kid staring defiantly back at him. But Jacob would not honestly remember it. He wouldn't even remember looking at the Game Warden.

Jacob was doing what perhaps many children do in the face of unpleasant situations. He was thinking about something else.

Jacob was thinking about what he would think about many times in the future during an unpleasant situation or even a boring conversation, really. Throughout his life, Jacob would go back to this place in his memory and hold the memory as reverently and pleasantly as he was doing now, right before the Game Warden planned to shoot him dead.

Jacob was with Dorina at the front of his grandfather's motorboat as they cruised fast up the Wabash River. Dorina was smiling and, at the back of the boat, his hand on the engine's throttle, their grandfather was smiling also. They were all three, at that very moment, having the best time of their life.

A shot rang out.

THE ROCK

The rock that Dorina threw was the biggest rock she could find at her feet. She dug it as fast as she could out of the red clay-dirt there on the hill overlooking the Wabash. The rock she chose was shiny and smooth and gray on one side. But when Dorina picked it up, the other side of the rock was grimy, damp and had several hard-shelled bugs crawling on it. This normally would have made Dorina sick and she would have dropped the rock immediately.

But Dorina had a purpose for the rock. This purpose over-rode all of her feelings of horror and disgust. Later she would even recall how some of those hard-shelled bugs crunched in her palm as she gripped the rock. But she had to hold the disgusting side of the rock because she couldn't get a grip on the shiny side. It was too slick and smooth.

So Dorina got a grip on the rock and heaved it as hard as she could. She heaved it so hard she almost lost her balance and fell off the embankment. But she didn't.

The rock took a long time to sail through the air.

Much later in her life as Dorina sat in her jail cell in Dwight! Dwight! With the television on, she would watch in her head the flight of that rock. The rock would twirl and move seemingly in slow motion in her head. Dorina would watch, as one by one, in slow motion, each little disgusting hard-shell bug would drop off of that rock.

Her memory, her re-living of this event would always end the same way. It was one of those childhood memories that a person would cling to in order sometimes just to put one foot in front of the other and get through the day. Dorina had watched this rock and its path through the air many, many times in her life. And each and every time the rock landed in exactly the same place. Right square between the Game Warden's eyes.

Whether or not Dorina's rock hit the Game Warden square in the forehead was to be a matter of dispute. But not much dispute. After it was all said and done most everyone agreed Dorina's rock arrived simultaneously with three tiny pellets from the General's Remington pump-action twelve-gauge shotgun.

Sober, the General would later agree, the pellets probably would have landed somewhere in the middle of the Wabash. Drunk, he was certain, was why the pellets landed precisely where they should have and did–right between the Game Warden's eyes.

Regardless, most everyone agreed that Jacob and his grandfather had been rescued from death. The Game Warden's shotgun was pointing directly at Jacob and his finger was already pressing against the trigger.

The blast from the Game Warden's gun didn't hit Leonard or Jacob, but it did strike Dorina and sent her flying through the air.

THE FALL

Dorina was shot. Jacob was frozen. He was catatonic there along the riverbank. As Dorina tumbled, a buckshot piercing her left eye and several buckshot piercing her belly and leg, down the riverbank, Jacob sat frozen. He wasn't even sure where he was at the moment. He did know that there were tears in his eyes and he felt his teeth grind hard and silently together, as if he were witnessing the longest fingernail dragging slowly across the hardest of chalkboards.

Then Jacob heard his grandfather's voice. He was yelling. Leonard had awoke from his drunken sleep and jarred sober by the shotgun blasts. Jacob heard his grandfather yelling out his granddaughter's name.

Jacob slowly, as if he had all the time in the world, relaxed. And as he relaxed his vision drew dark. His vision grew very dark. His eyes were open but his vision kept growing darker and darker. His vision didn't stop growing darker until everything went completely black.

But Jacob could still hear other voices yelling out Dorina's name. He even heard someone yell out his name. He tried to move. He couldn't. Then he heard someone crying. Jacob tried to look around. Nothing but black.

Leonard, however, came alive. The shots ringing out did indeed wake him from his drunken stupor and he was up and running. He couldn't believe little Dory had been shot. The sonofabitch. He spun around stumbling and screaming at the Game Warden. But the Game Warden wasn't listening. He lay on his back in his boat, upon Leonard's fish, passed out cold from fright, as there was only three little lead buckshots in his forehead.

Up on the other end of the bluff the General stood, almost proud. He had shot the Game Warden dead, he thought. It was just like when he'd been in Germany in 1944. He had done what he had to do. He hadn't seen the little girl. He didn't know she had even been shot. He just knew he had killed a man.

Now Jacob had his head between his legs, his eyes wide open. He stared between his legs into total blackness.

Behind where Dorina had been, the hippie girl was on her knees sobbing. She kept sobbing and yelling out "Why?" She yelled out that it just didn't make sense. It was an awful and perverse world and nothing made sense. "Why?" she kept wailing. Finally she fell over like a sack of hippie potatoes, still sobbing insanely.

While all this was going on Dorina was in flight. She was tumbling head over heals. One leg going up and an arm bending down as the other arm bent up and her neck springing from side to side as blood spurted everywhere. It may have looked like an almost choreographed tumble down the embankment towards the Wabash.

Later Dorina would recall this fall continually in her dreams. Dorina would split apart during this fall in her dreams sometimes. Other times she would dream that she had rolled up into a tight ball and splashed into the Wabash and just kept rolling and rolling until she sunk into the muddy bottom of the river.

One time Dorina would even dream that she just kept sinking and sinking into the bottom of the river after she'd been shot until she could not breathe. She awoke that time with her black Persian cat sound asleep and purring mechanically between her breasts.

Her favorite dream though of this fall, was of falling off into the sky, her belly leaving her as she soared flying through the air, the shotgun blast that would rob her of an eye liberating her in this dream. It would be her favorite dream of all time.

But Dorina only had this dream once and that was the first night that she would spend in the Dwight Correctional Institution for Women for killing a prominent white lawyer who ran at her naked in a parking lot of a Seven-Eleven.

Now that hippie girl had rolled over on her stomach, still sobbing hysterically and yelling, "Why?" as she pounded her fists theatrically in the dirt. She started kicking her legs also. She looked, on top of that bluff overlooking the Wabash, like some surreal fish out of water.

The blue bundle lay not far from the girl. She had entirely forgotten what was wrapped up inside it.

George was the one who caught Dorina. He stopped the little girl from tumbling into the river. Stunned, he said damn twice as he stared at her bloody eye socket and all the blood that was streaming out of her tiny body. There was blood everywhere. He lay her in the boat and Valarie went right away to fixing her up. Valarie pulled her t-shirt off and made it into a makeshift bandage. She wiped the blood from Dorina's face first. Dorina's good left eye was wide and startled. Valarie forced out a smile and told the little girl that she would be just fine.

"So cold," Dorina said, her little voice hoarse and weak. "My feet are so cold."

This shocked Valarie. She was a nurse. She knew what this meant in a trauma patient. Valarie closed her eyes.

"Oh," George said. He bent down at Dorina's feet and lifted her feet out of his ice chest. He put the lid back on the ice chest, eased her little feet back upon the foam top. "Sorry."

Valarie let out a sigh, gave George a peeved look, then went back to attending to the little girl.

NIETZSCHE

Doc Garrelts smiled pleasantly at the two ladies standing on his patio. "Come on in," he said, his voice gentle and benign. The two ladies appeared to be holding their breath.

Doc Garrelts was dressed in a full three-piece suit, dark blue with black pin-stripes. His tie was black with little dull-white diamonds on it. His white hair was combed back with Vitalis. He looked quite dashing.

"I was hoping I could talk to you about the Lord today. Your Lord." He kept smiling benignly. "And perhaps my Lord too," he added, with more than a hint of sad resignation.

The two ladies looked at each other. They both looked

momentarily toward Heaven. They went on into the upside-down trailer.

"Pardon my mess," Doc Garrelts said. "I'm remodeling." He motioned for them to sit on the sofa. Everything else was either broken or overturned. He asked them if he could get them anything to drink. "Lemonade? A Manhattan?" They both politely declined.

Marsha stared at what looked like a voodoo doll on the floor, or ceiling actually, at her feet. She couldn't look at it long.

Doc Garrelts made himself a Manhattan.

"You know, Ladies," Doc Garrelts said, as he sat down in his rocking chair. "Something like this happens, a storm turns your home upside-down, you say hello, how are you? to death, and all. You re-evaluate everything, you know?"

"God touches you," suggested Marsha.

"Well..." Doc Garrelts said. He shook his head. "You know what Nietzsche said? 'Love for any one thing is barbaric, for it's exercised at the expense of everything else. This includes the love of God.'"

Marsha had no idea who Nietzsche was but this didn't slow her down any. "But God loves you," she insisted.

Doc Garrelts smiled, finished off his Manhattan and sighed deeply. "I lost my wife back in '41."

Both Jehovah's Witnesses gave Doc Garrelts sad and sympathetic looks.

"I found her about an hour later. We were shopping in downtown Chicago."

The looks of sympathy vanished.

"She died a couple years after that, though."

Then Doc Garrelts took out a large machete from the inside of his suit coat. The ladies gasped.

"This killed her." He chuckled. "You know what Nietzsche also said?" He smiled an odd smile. "'There's an impetuosity of goodness that looks like malice.'" He chuckled again. The blade of the machete was large. Doc Garrelts held it up to his face. "But my favorite Nietzsche quote of all is:" He tapped the blade on his cheek.

"'The more abstract the truth you want to teach, the more thoroughly you must seduce the senses to accept it.'"

After this quote Doc Garrelts got to his feet and, with both hands grasping the handle of the machete, he plunged it to the hilt into his bowels. His legs buckled and down he went to his knees. Blood began to ooze upon the ceiling.

Joyce put her hand to her mouth and Marsha's eyes rolled back in her head as she gasped for air.

"Have a good life, Ladies," Doc Garrelts groaned, then he fell forward and seemingly further onto the blade until it poked obscenely out his back.

Both ladies, screaming like mad women, ran out of the trailer.

UNDERPINNING

The only damage Delancey's daughter, Janet, could see done to her trailer was the underpinning. Underpinning was made up of metal strips attached to the bottom of a trailer that stretched all around it and added some permanence to a trailer; as it hid the wheels and seemingly anchored the mobile home to the earth. Janet and her husband had debated about whether to buy underpinning or not. It wasn't cheap and Janet could see no reason to hide the wheels of the trailer or add any semblance of permanency to it whatsoever. She wasn't at all thrilled with living in a trailer anyway.

But her husband had won out and now one side of the underpinning had gotten pealed away by the storm. It made the trailer look like a large can that had been partially opened by a big key. Janet, her hands on her hips, just stared at the ripped-out metal as it flapped some in the breeze. She would surely cut herself if she tried to fix it.

Janet could see the wheels beneath the trailer now and she liked this. It gave her a certain feeling that if she wanted to, she could wheel away, take off for anywhere she wanted to go. She looked around the trailer park. Everyone was out inspecting all the damage that had been done by the storm. There were still quite a few people around Doc Garrelts' upside-down trailer.

Janet looked back at her underpinning. She wanted to rip it all off and hook the trailer up to her Nova and take off. It was her husband's idea, to anchor her here, trap her even more, while he played war games and stuck dollar bills in the panties of off-base strippers. As she guzzled cheap wine, popped mother's little helpers and turned her flesh inside out teaching poetry to rednecks who had asterisks for brain cells. She sighed and banged her head in her hands. She was rapidly becoming a dried-up bitter woman. Something had to change.

Janet looked up at the sky and finding nothing there, looked all around the trailer park. She started some as two ladies ran ranting and raving through the park.

Finally Janet got down on her knees and tried to put the underpinning back in place. It slipped out of her hands and flapped lewdly at her, mockingly even. She cursed and started to rip it out even more but she didn't. She eased back upon her rump. Why oh why couldn't she say ten words to her father? She stared under the trailer at the rust on the rims of the wheels. She should have made her peace with her father long ago. Janet didn't care for this last thought. She grabbed the underpinning with both hands now. By God *he* should have made his peace with *her* long ago. She slammed the underpinning into place, held it there with her knee as she pounded on it. Pounded until her fist and wrist began to hurt. She kept pounding until it stayed in place.

"I hate my father," she said. Janet let her eyes glaze. "Or do I really?"

"You did once," a voice said.

Janet jerked her head around, then seeing who it was let out a gasp. She couldn't believe it. She got to her feet and leaped into the man's arms, wrapped her legs around his waist. He gave her a dip and then a big kiss. They hadn't seen each other in years.

"I heard you were in Vietnam?"

"I was," he said. "I took pictures."

"Pictures?"

"Yep."

She told him he hadn't changed a bit.

He told her she'd gotten even prettier.

Some long forgotten emotion surged through Janet. She gave Daniel Drabeck a longer kiss this time. It surprised him.

TROTLINES

A trotline is a long piece of thin nylon rope that has twenty-five hooks attached proportionally to it. One end of the rope is usually tied to an overhanging tree branch and the other end to an empty Clorox bottle that floats out over the water. The hooks dangle free in the water and are usually baited up with everything from night crawlers to crawdads in anticipation of catching catfish mostly.

Jacob sat in the boat in the middle of the Wabash still blind as Leonard cut the engine on the boat and dropped anchor. They both could still hear the fading sirens of the ambulance that was taking Dorina to the hospital.

Leonard sat in the back of the boat carefully lifting each hook of the trotline out of the water and baiting it, as he talked non-stop. He would reach into a metal bucket filled with grass, remove a crawfish, pull off both pincers, impale the crawfish tail-first upon the hook, and ease it into the warm water. And then he would pull up another hook. Leonard was talking non-stop to keep his mind busy. He talked about how some of the crawfish were already dead. He talked non-stop because if he stopped talking he would cry for his grandchild and he didn't want to do this in front of Jacob.

Jacob had wanted very badly to go in the ambulance with Dorina but he was blind. He was as blind as if he'd stared all day long at the eclipse. He stared forward at total blackness. He had no idea why he was blind. He listened to his grandfather talk once more about that 98-pound catfish. For a moment Jacob wished that he were as deaf as he was blind.

In between the story of the catfish Leonard ripped his

baseball cap off his head, ran his hands through his hair and prayed to the Lord that little Dory would be all right. Then he talked about how it took him almost three hours to clean that catfish.

"Sumbitch still wasn't dead, even after I pounded that spike through his head and ripped every ounce of skin off of it."

Jacob blinked and thought perhaps a thin circle of light was appearing around the blackness. Then his uncle for some reason, came to mind.

Jacob's uncle had been a farmer who went to a doctor and the doctor told him his heart was no good. The doctor told his uncle he had to stop working and, instead, sit in a chair and maybe watch television or listen to the radio the rest of his life. If he did this he might live to be a hundred, the doctor told him.

But his uncle just looked at the doctor. He stared at the doctor as if he were staring at the insides of the most intricate Swiss watch ever made. The Doctor's words made absolutely no sense.

So his uncle went home and went to bed. Then he got up the next morning at four, ate two fried eggs, three pieces of bacon, and three buttermilk biscuits, smoked a pipe full of Prince Albert tobacco, then went and fed the chickens, the pigs, and then the cows, then drove a tractor all afternoon. His uncle did this for a year and a half.

Then one evening when the wind had died and the birds were quiet, as Jacob's uncle sat in a metal chair underneath a Catalpa tree in his front yard, his heart stopped working entirely and he died. His uncle had had no desire to live to be a hundred.

Jacob recalled his uncle there dead underneath that Catalpa tree now as his grandfather talked non-stop to keep from thinking about Dorina.

At that time, blind in the boat, he wasn't quite sure of the connection between his grandfather and his uncle. It was there but he couldn't quite put it all together. More of his vision came back to Jacob. So much so that he was no longer afraid that he would be blind forever.

"She'll be all right," Leonard said, pulling the pincers off a particularly large crawfish. He carefully threaded the crawfish upon the hook until the tip of the hook was well hidden in the rear body of the thing. "That lady's a nurse, you know. A damn good one the way I hear. Hell, everybody in town calls her." Leonard was talking about Valarie. "She came to Nettie's every week and gave her that shot when she had that skin disease." Leonard took a quick sip of beer. "She said Dory'd be all right. But her eye–" Leonard almost broke. He let out a curse and jerked the trotline back up. He stared at a bent hook. "A turtle got hold of that one." He held it up for Jacob to see. "There's more damn turtles in the Wabash this year than I ever seen."

Jacob, his hands folded in his lap at the front of the boat, continued to stare into blackness. His eyes were starting to burn some as more light closed in on the circle of black. Dorina would be okay. She just had to be. Jacob started to pray but then changed his mind. Instead he sat patiently, if not stubbornly, and waited for his vision to return.

His grandfather stood up in the boat and Jacob felt the boat rock and sway. He heard water lap heavy against the side.

"Little Dory gets out of the hospital we're gonna have my big fish fry," Leonard said, his hands in his overalls as he stared out across the water. "A hundred pounds or more. Malcolm'll help me fry it." Leonard spit into the Wabash. Jacob looked towards where his grandfather spoke but only saw his shadow. "She's proud her daddy's coming home." Leonard sniffed loudly and flicked his upper dentures into place with his thumb. "By God we all better be."

Then he looked at his grandson, asked him what the hell was the matter with him.

"Nothing," Jacob said.

SHOPPING

The ambulance was a little crowded. Along with Dorina who was on a stretcher, George and Valarie sat with an elderly lady who was supposed to be a nurse. George looked at the nurse funny.

She wore a gray one-piece uniform and a little white hat. Her expression never changed and she never said a word. George believed she may have died several years ago and nobody told her.

Valarie smiled and patted Dorina's hand and told her she would be fine. Dorina's good eye was wide. She stared at the ceiling of the ambulance. She was all wrapped up in white bandages. Her wide eye went to George.

"Where do people go when they die?" She asked George. Dorina wasn't thinking about herself. She was thinking about her dead baby brother. George looked at Valarie as if he might melt.

"You're not going to die, Honey," Valarie said, patting her hand. Dorina kept staring at George.

"Shopping," George said. The old lady's expression finally changed into a frown. Dorina smiled.

"I want to go shopping," she said.

"No," George said. "Not in Heaven. Everything's overpriced. Plentiful, but overpriced."

Dorina kept smiling. She liked George. Her eye went to Valarie. Dorina liked her too. Then her dead baby brother came to mind. She hoped Jacob would take care of him and bury him right. Tears filled up in her eye and she couldn't stop them.

Valarie leaned closer and asked her if she hurt anywhere.

"Nope," Dorina said. But her eye kept filling up. She had to give her dead baby brother a decent burial.

Valarie patted her forehead with a wet napkin. George had to look away. The old nurse stared out the window at the passing telephone poles and tried to remember what was on television that night, as the ambulance, sirens silent but lights flashing, motored on through the Bottoms.

FAKING IT

Janet put the joint up to her lips and sucked in deeply. Her well-anesthetized lungs took in all the marijuana smoke very well. In fact, they seemed to enjoy it. She held the smoke in her lungs for as long as she could. So long, that the naked body of Daniel Drabek split in two. His head, chest, and even his cock separated and appeared, with muted clarity, on each side of the bedroom. Janet thought she heard herself giggle.

Daniel Drabeck, tourist from Vietnam, came together, leaned over and kissed each of Janet's breasts.

"Ain't that the best dope you ever had?" He said. "I put it in my underwear on the flight back. They don't check out soldier boys anyway." He smiled.

Daniel kissed Janet's belly. "That's the last of it, though. It came from Turkey. They used to sell it by the shoebox for five dollars. Did you say you were married?"

"Yes," Janet replied, her head spinning. She lay back upon the bed. They were in the back bedroom of the trailer.

"I almost got married in Vietnam. I don't know about her though." Daniel leaned back and lay beside Janet. "She used to moan like she'd been shot. She would carry on like I was the greatest lover in the universe. Ah! Ah! Oh! Oh! Yes! Yes! She kept saying, her eyes closed and her body moving. One time when she was carrying on like that I climbed off of her, turned on the light, and lit a cigarette. But she just kept laying there and carrying on. Ah! Ah! Oh! Oh! Yes! Yes! And I wasn't even on top of her anymore." Daniel frowned. "Finally I said something to her and she went 'oh' and stopped." Daniel put the butt of the joint in a roach clip shaped like a crab claw that was attached to a feather. "You think she was faking it?"

This made Janet laugh. Anything would have made Janet laugh at the moment. Daniel started laughing also.

STATISTICS

The antiseptic smells wafting from the Emergency Room struck George head-on and an irrational fear rose in him. These same smells ripped at his nose and practically made him sick one time in high school when he had broke his leg playing football. He sat down in the waiting room.

The only other people in the room was a farmer in overalls who sat beside his pudgy, plain wife. She had on a faded yellow dress that may have fit her several sizes ago. Her white nylons were rolled up in balls around her ankles. Both their faces were a sun and wind-burnt red. They wore the same somber expressions.

"You think Billy will be all right?" The woman said.

"Why yes," the man assured her in a sober tone. "He just had his finger shortened is all. They'll sew it right back on."

George tried not to flinch.

"I'm just glad I found it there beside the combine," the woman said.

The man nodded, then, matter-of-factly, "You might not have if it'a been his pinkie."

George stared a moment at this couple. He stared at their hands folded in their laps. He looked at their unflinching, somber eyes. He would write a poem about them when he got home. George would call the poem "Terrorism in America Today." Valarie came into the Emergency Room. She smiled frailly as she sat beside George. She told him Dorina wasn't as bad as it seemed. She didn't have life-threatening wounds to her body. Valarie crossed her legs, sniffed, and took a tissue from the table.

"She's going to lose her eye, though. The buckshot hit just right."

George put his arm around Valarie. He didn't know what to say. He felt empty. They sat silently for a moment.

Finally, George said, "I want to marry you, Val."

Valarie, still sniffing, tossed a tissue on the table and grabbed a clean one. "What?"

"I said I want to marry you." George, his arm still around Valarie, closed the magazine he had in his lap. He had been reading about the War in *Time* magazine. He looked at Valarie.

"Oh, you do not," Valarie said.

George sighed. He wasn't quite sure why he had asked Valarie to marry him. He didn't regret it, though. He wanted to marry her. He hadn't really thought about it before. He squeezed her shoulder and suddenly wanted very badly to embrace her and ask her again if she would marry him.

Valarie didn't know what to say exactly. George asking her to marry her at this moment seemed extremely strange. She didn't know what to think. For some odd reason she believed he was serious. She blew her nose and grabbed another tissue.

The farm couple listened and stared. An electric clock in a gray metal case on the wall buzzed. It was the only noise in the room.

George thought about why he had asked Valarie to marry him. It might have been his subconscious talking. He wasn't sure. But he had made love to her and then he watched Valarie attend to the little girl and as she ripped off her top and wrapped it around the little girl, he had believed that he had at that moment, fallen hopelessly, unavoidably in love with Valarie. She was a much stronger woman than he was a man, George thought at that moment.

Valarie ripped another tissue from the box. "I forgot to call her mother. I told them at the desk I would." She jumped up and left the waiting room. George and two other sets of eyes followed Valarie out of the room.

George looked at the farm couple and they looked at him. They reminded him of a painting. All they needed was a pitchfork. They kept staring.

They probably thought George was a very strange man for asking a woman to marry him in the waiting room of an emergency room. George stared back at them.

"She has a hot water heater," George said. "Mine's broken." He shrugged. "Any better reason for getting married?"

POP CULTURE

Delancey J. McFadden opened his eyes. He was on his back and had been asleep until something woke him. It had been two screaming Jehovah's Witnesses running all the way to Kingdom Hall. He sat up.

During his nap Delancey had forgotten why he had come to the edge of the trailer park. Forgotten why he had sat upon the stump there by the mailboxes. Delancey had forgotten his daughter entirely.

Instead his observation about houses being built without front porches and how television was responsible for this lingered in his thoughts. He would write this article and thus sleep better at night because he had published and not perished. Delancey looked around. It was sunny and getting warm again. He hated the weather in the Midwest. He took off his glasses and wiped sweat from his brow and it suddenly hit him. He didn't have to worry about publishing anymore. He was retired. He would perish of course, but only one final time.

And then Delancey would go to that place where all academics and critics go. Delancey smiled bitterly. No, not Hell. You have to do something *significantly* bad to go to hell. "Purgatory," he said out loud.

"Why not?" A voice said.

Delancey put his glasses back on.

"Doc," Delancey said finally when he could focus.

Doc Garrelts took an exaggerated step backwards. He was drenched in blood that, as it dried, turned green.

"Why if it ain't Dr. McFadden! How the hell are you?" He shook Delancey's hand vigorously. Delancey looked at all the blood on Doc Garrelts. He asked him what had happened.

"Oh, nothing really." Doc Garrelts sat beside Delancey on the stump. "Just talking philosophy and religion with some folks. It's fun. Hey, I liked that last book of yours. Your best yet, I think. I especially liked Chapter Nine. I thought it was grand the way you put the mini-skirt in the right historical perspective."

Delancey scowled some as he tried to remember his last book. Even though it had only been a year or so ago. "Oh, yes," Delancey remembered. "The critics all said I should have left that chapter out. Said I was reacting to Pop Culture."

Doc Garrelts shrugged. "So what?" he said. "At least you're

reacting." Doc Garrelts pulled off his green blood-stained shirt, wadded it up. "Hell, everybody else is dead in America today. The kids running around, chewing up their food and sticking their tongues out to show everyone." He shook his head. "Hell, in twenty years they'll all be lawyers or accountants, married and too afraid to have their own damn kids." Doc Garrelts had a pained look on his face. "Their parents. They're the dangerous ones, wrapped up and quiet like damn Egyptian mummies."

Delancey smiled. When he had lived around here him and the Doc would sit down at the Cafe and talk for hours. He put his hand on Doc Garrelts' knee, said he was glad to see him. The Doc said it was damn good to see him too, then he got up from the stump.

"You want to come down for a drink? The place is a little messy after the storm but I still make a mean Manhattan."

Delancey slowly got to his feet and as he did so he felt his joints creak. He said it was the best offer he'd had all day. Then he stopped and looked behind him at the stump. Doc Garrelts asked him what was the matter.

Delancey smiled. "Just checking to see if everything got up with me.

Doc Garrelts laughed and slapped Delancey on the back. "Bob Hope, *Road to Utopia.*"

Delancey smiled and nodded as they headed on down through the trailer park.

REGARDLESS

The doll Betsy held meant the most to her. She lay on the bed in the attic with the doll tucked tightly in her belly. She was on her side staring at all her dolls. She mused bitterly about how she had her own real-life doll growing inside of her.

Betsy felt completely alone now. She had no one and there was no one she could turn to and it felt horrible. Everyone who had been close to her was either dead, or in Mary's case, far away in

Chicago. Mary and Ron would most certainly not let her come and live with them now. A hot thick tear oozed down the side of Betsy's face.

Betsy was pregnant and she didn't want to be. It made her absolutely sick to think that anyone would ever find this out.

A certain helplessness mixed with anger caused Betsy to suddenly cry hard now as she lay there on her side. She sat up finally and tossed the doll as hard as she could across the attic. It thudded against the far window and fell upon a coffee can Betsy, as a little girl, had kept her crayons in.

Yet, as quickly as she had started crying Betsy stopped. It was stupid to be so weak. Sitting up, she took a deep breath and decided then and there that she would not cry again because she was pregnant. She was alone but there had to be other people alone right now that did all right.

Her grandfather had told her time and again that she was a hardheaded brat just like her mother, and there was no better time to be proud of that then now.

She got up from the bed and there was a different look on her face now. Betsy decided right then and there that she would do whatever she had to do. In the dirty mirror she fluffed her hair, then decided to tie it back with a red ribbon that hung on one side of the mirror. After she tied her hair back she let out a sigh of disgust as she put her face closer to the mirror and patted her swollen cheeks and eyes. Stupid. Stupid. Stupid.

Then finally, her face close to the mirror, Betsy smiled and the smile was tempered only slightly with sadness.

Betsy Ann Brown was Betsy Ann Brown and she would always be Betsy Ann Brown.

Regardless.

PITCHING WASHERS

The hippies up at the shack all pitched in and helped Leonard get everything ready for the fish fry. They brought down a large rectangular folding table from their shack and they went with the General to his place and hauled back chairs and frying pans and a big cast-iron fish-fryer.

"Now if I can just catch all the fish," Leonard kept saying as he'd light another cigarette and crack open another beer. The sweat was pouring off of him. It was a warm late summer day. But he was only kidding about catching enough fish. In the General's freezer was twice as much fish as they needed and besides, since the Game Warden was laid up and they all said it was self-defense, fishing had never been better.

Just like the fish fry Malcolm and Leonard had every year, the whole town was invited. Not everybody would show up but they were invited every year just the same. Whoever did come usually brought some side dish and Leonard and Malcolm would fry the fish as long as they could and then somebody else would take over. Not much went on besides talk but there was always the washer pitching.

Washer pitching was big along the Wabash. The washers were the kind found in farm machinery- half-inch thick heavy round washers about the size of your palm. The General was in charge of setting up the holes.

The game of pitching washers was very similar to pitching horseshoes. But instead of spikes, coffee cans were put in the ground about the same distance apart as horse-shoe spikes and you tossed four washers into the bottoms of the coffee cans. Some people called washer pitching a poor man's horseshoes but not people along the Wabash. They liked washer pitching better.

He didn't have to but every year the General put new coffee cans into the ground. The hippies all laughed at the General as he pulled the old coffee cans out of the ground and put shiny new ones in their place. They were all new to pitching washers and wanted to see a demonstration.

So Leonard and Malcolm decided to pitch a few and show them. Leonard bent his knees and held the washer up to peer through the hole of the washer for a second. Then he swung his arm back and under-handed, pitched the washer towards the coffee can buried in the ground. The washer remained flat as it flew through the air, moving only slightly like some flying saucer. Eyes went wide as the washer plopped solid right dead into the buried coffee can. Leonard smiling only slightly then went through the same motion and let the next washer fly. It hit just in front of the hole and stopped right on the lip of the coffee can. He threw two more washers and one landed right smack dab into the hole and the other washer sailed right on past the hole.

"Good shooting," Malcolm said, as he stuck his cigar stub in his mouth, then he got ready to let his first washer fly. His motion was a little different. Everybody had their own way of pitching washers. Malcolm brought his hand back behind his back and snapped his wrist before letting the washer go. The flight of the General's washer was way different than Leonard's had been. The washer twirled end over end as it flew through the air.

It landed square in the hole on top of Leonard's two washers. The hippies spontaneously clapped. It looked so easy. Then the General pitched two more washers into the hole and his last washer struck Leonard's washer that was on the lip of the hole and it flew away. Leonard cursed and slapped his knee. His two ringers were cancelled out by Malcolm's and Malcolm's third ringer was worth three points. Malcolm also got a point for landing a washer closest to the hole. Damn, Leonard thought.

The hippies who had earlier been shaking their heads and laughing at this stupid game now all wanted a chance at playing.

Leonard and Malcolm went and sat down as the hippies all took turns tossing the washers. Most tosses fell about halfway or went way past the hole. They didn't even come near making a ringer.

It was an awful humid day and the Wabash was quite low now. The sky was gray and overcast. A brief shower wouldn't hurt a thing, Leonard remarked.

Lately when Leonard and Malcolm sat together they didn't talk much. Leonard's little granddaughter was still in the hospital and they said she lost her eye. Malcolm was rather pensive now and always said the same thing when him and Leonard sat alone.

"I just wish I'd killed that sumbitch."

Leonard agreed and then they got up and headed down to Malcolm's boat. It was time to run his nets.

Shortly they were out in the boat. A few chilly raindrops struck them and thudded hard against the side of the boat. Leonard looked up at the sky. The clouds weren't heavy enough for a storm.

As they headed on upriver they heard a collective yell as one of the hippies, after moving in about halfway between the coffee cans, finally put a washer in the hole. They both watched as the hippies whooped and hollered at this accomplishment. Leonard and Malcolm looked at each other and said nothing. There were fish to catch.

ST. LOUIS

In the attic Dorina had her eyelid of her good eye turned inside out as she stared at her new black eye patch in the full-length mirror. Betsy was in a corner of the attic in a rocking chair. She held a doll and was quietly singing to it. Jacob lay on the bed and stared at the ceiling.

Dorina's eye didn't hurt anymore. Her eye socket used to hurt but no more. It felt good even. It itched and Dorina's mother said this meant it was healing. Dorina popped her eyelid back to normal. She stared into the mirror. She decided she liked her new eye patch. It scared her at first but now she liked it. No one else Dorina knew had an eye patch so this made her like nobody else and Dorina liked this.

She rolled her good eye slowly around and around and looked all over the attic. They kept telling her she couldn't see as well with only one eye but Dorina didn't believe it. They told Dorina she had to be careful on bicycles and walking down streets because she couldn't see as much with one eye as she could with two eyes.

"I can see better than I did before," she said. Jacob heard her. He had been thinking about when he was blind for a day. He hadn't told anyone about it. He hoped it would never happen again.

"I can," Dorina insisted.

Jacob went back to looking at the ceiling. He watched swirling, lazy dust reflect off sunlight. Nothing was as it had been before and he didn't feel good about it. Betsy had a baby growing inside of her and cried all the time it seemed like and Dorina only had one eye.

It was turning out to be the worst summer of his life. The creak of the rocking chair stopped. Jacob sat up and looked at Betsy. She looked serious.

"I'm going to St. Louis tomorrow with that nurse who lives in the trailer park." Betsy said. She said she couldn't remember her name.

"Valarie," Dorina said with a smile.

Betsy did not smile. "We'll only be there about an hour. Then we'll come right back home." Betsy paused. "Then I'll stay at her house over night."

Dorina started asking a stream of questions. Why was she going? Why stay only an hour? Could her and Jacob go? And why couldn't they go up in that Arch?

"Please, please, please," Dorina kept begging.

Betsy stared in front of her. She had a look on her face that Jacob had never seen before. She didn't really seem upset. But somehow Betsy seemed more than upset. Betsy said she didn't care who went with her. Then, beginning to rock again, Betsy said she didn't care if the whole town came with her.

THE BIG ONE

Delancey J. McFadden went home that day after a couple Manhattans with Doc Garrelts and began slamming upon his typewriter like he had not done in over thirty years.

Inspired partially by what he considered a brilliant idea and mostly by the words of the man he respected more than any of his peers, Delancey rolled a piece of paper into the typewriter and took off.

"We must all put that exclamation point there at the end of our lives," Doc Garrelts had said, as he leaned upon the handle of a green-stained hard rubber machete. "No question marks, no ellipses, and definitely no last nail-in-the-coffin periods. Exclaim!" And that's what Delancey had been inspired to do. Exclaim!

So pushing everyone and everything out of his mind, as he had done for the better part of his life, Delancey walked home at a quick pace and sat down and began to type.

He typed for hours it seemed like. Energized and revitalized eloquence punctuated his prose like Chinese fireworks (The Fourth of July analogy isn't a good one. Delancey had been a long-time Communist).

Working at a hell-bent pace, Delancey plowed into an essay that rang with observations and declarations that codified and hyperbolized and chastised the American spirit for castrating the American home of its most vital and essential element: The front porch.

The front porch was the symbol, Delancey wrote, of America's power to empathize with nature and neighbors and the rest of the universe, for God's sake. He wrote on and on.

Then Delancey put still another piece of white paper into the typewriter and played his mildly arthritic fingers upon the ivory keys as he took off like an academic racehorse to chastise the American Dream. The American Dream, as it plowed into the seventh decade of the century, had become an opiated nightmare that was causing Americans to drop everything and stare gap-mouthed and dead at the greatest evil to strike humanity since the atom bomb. It wasn't just a coincidence that houses were being built without front porches.

Delancey paused for a moment and stared intently at the typewriter. Then finally he slammed out the word that was the greatest evil, the one major reason that front porches were no longer needed; the one major reason Americans were heading straight to hell in a helium balloon: Television! Yes, television. His fingers began to fly again.

Sometimes it was like his mind and fingers seemed no longer a part of him and were creating on their own. Delancey even thought that once he got up and went to the bathroom and, as he stood over the porcelain stool, he swore he could still hear his typewriter going.

And he kept at it. Eight pages, then ten, then before he knew it, twenty pages. He paused only a few times to marvel at prose he had not seen coming from his fingers in forty years. He smiled and was proud. He continued on well into the night.

It was one of those rare sittings, Delancey was certain, where a first draft, except for a few minor mechanical things, was all that would be needed. And how did he end this essay to end all essays? Of course! With an exclamation point!

Finally, satiated and exhausted, Delancey leaned back in his chair, the paper at last finished. Tears welled up in his eyes as several tired old goose bumps floated across his body. Delancey had done once again what he felt he had long since been unable to do. And it was good. He knew it. He would leave this world raging and attacking the empty and callous American Dream. Leave an essay that encapsulated all that he had spent a lifetime trying to explore in his writings. It might be the greatest essay he had ever written. Delancey sighed and relaxed. Then something caught his eye.

Leaning against the doorway into the den was his daughter, Janet, her arms crossed and a cigarette dangling between her fingers. Janet looked all around the empty den. She had just finished looking all around the empty and dead house.

"Damn, Dad," she said, drawing hard on the cigarette, her face showing disgust. "You have to at least get a television in this place."

Delancey had the big one.

A KARMA DAY

George stood tense and vibrating by the mailboxes this morning. It was a Karma day, he just knew it. George had over twenty-five poems in circulation and today would be the day that one of them, at *least* one of them, would cause someone out there to acknowledge his existence. It's all anyone strives for really: Acknowledgement of their existence.

George lit another cigarette and finished off the last of his third pot of coffee and began to twiddle his fingers upon a corrugated tin mailbox. The mailman was on his way. He heard that familiar squeak of breaks on the tan '64 Ford. George swallowed hard.

Valarie would not marry him. It had been totally ignorant to ask her to marry him. And eventually he would have to tell Valarie that he was the one who impregnated that teenager she was taking to St. Louis. He looked up at the sky as a wave of sad embarrassment swept through him. He planned to give Betsy the two hundred dollars as soon as he could get it.

Perhaps it was in the mailman's hands at this very moment. Perhaps fame was riding in a tan '64 Ford Falcon that had bad breaks and a bearded long-haired postal worker behind the wheel.

Perhaps George would never again post a single rejection slip upon his bathroom wall. He would be famous shortly. Then he could practically shit on a piece of paper and someone would still buy it. George smiled. He would also take fame wonderfully; this he knew. In interviews he would tell mini-skirted media madonnas how easily writing came to him. He would tell of all his influences but also voice why they all fell short of what he was striving for in his poetry.

George would also, regardless of its relevance, open up his carpeted utility room and show them the biggest fucking water heater ever made.

He was smiling and his eyes were glazed as he watched the mailman pull his car up to the trailer park mailboxes.

ABRAHAM LINCOLN

The rest park had a big granite rock on the lawn that had an embedded plaque with a bronze face of Abraham Lincoln on it.

Dorina ran her fingers over his face and beard. The rest park was on Interstate 64 heading towards St. Louis. After much pleading, Betsy had said that Jacob and Dorina could go with her and Valarie to St. Louis.

All the way Dorina kept looking in the rearview mirror at her eye patch and babbling on and on about everything. Most of her babble was about her Daddy coming home. One time she stopped babbling and asked Jacob where her dead baby brother was. She had forgotten all about her dead baby brother and now wondered if Jacob knew what happened to him after she got hurt. Jacob about died. Luckily he and Dorina were in the backseat and Valarie and Betsy were in the front seat talking about something else. They hadn't heard Dorina. He whispered in Dorina's ear to first, shut up, and then that he had put the blue bundle under their Grandfather's shack. This satisfied Dorina. She would bury him when they got back from St. Louis.

Then Dorina loudly asked if they could go up in the Arch. Valarie and Betsy both stopped talking. They heard her this time. "No," they said in unison.

At the rest park near the restrooms two girls in flowery blouses and brown suede vests and huge faded bell-bottom blue jeans passed a corncob pipe between them. One of them wore an Indian-beaded headband. What they were smoking was the sweetest smoke that had ever drifted into Jacob's nose. They both flashed him the peace sign as he walked by. Embarrassed he put his head down and walked through the glass doors and on into the restroom.

Dorina sat down beside the two girls on the concrete sidewalk in front of the new brick rest park. "I ain't got an eye," she said as she stared at the corncob pipe the girls were passing between them.

"Woe," one of the girls said. "That's awful."

Dorina shrugged. "No, it ain't." She tucked her ankles under her bottom. "My mommy says smoking makes your lungs black." One of the girls reached over and very gently brushed Dorina's hair out of her face. Then she said very seriously and with considerable conviction, "There's nothing wrong with being black." The other girl very slowly nodded in agreement. Dorina's brow furrowed. She was too young to understand the logic of the sixties.

Jacob walked out the back way of the rest park so he wouldn't have to pass those girls again. There were young freshly planted trees not much taller than him and picnic tables in the back of the rest park. Right beside the trees and picnic tables were new black iron grills set in cement. A rabbit, chewing furiously on something, sat immobile under one of the picnic tables. He waved his arm at it and tried to scare it. It didn't move. Then he was startled. Leaning against the brick wall stood Betsy.

Her arms were crossed and her head rested back against the brick. She had been crying. She had stopped though. Jacob asked her if she was all right.

"Shut up," she said, her voice hardly loud enough to hear. Jacob didn't know what to say. He hurt inside for Betsy. He wished that he could do something to make everything better. He bit down hard on his bottom lip. Sudden desperate emotion rose in Jacob like a small tidal wave. Jacob felt a compulsion to say something, anything to make everything better for Betsy.

"I think–" He looked out at the rabbit and the picnic tables and the grills. He shrugged. "It'll be–" He just didn't have anything worth saying. Then he blurted out, "I love you!"

The earth stopped. His voice had been so loud that he had startled the rabbit and it bounded off. Jacob felt himself slowly melting into the concrete he stood on. He had never said such a thing to a girl before. Betsy's reaction would be etched into his memory all through his life. Her painful expression did not change. She kept staring straight in front of her.

"Grow up," she said.

DEATH DANCE OF FATHER

"Hey, George," the mailman said as he got out of his car, his hands full of mail. "How goes it?"

"Shitty," George said. "I want fame, Frank. Unadulterated, undiluted, asymptotic fame."

The mailman laughed. "Maybe it's your lucky day, George," and in his enthusiasm to find the piece of mail George had been waiting for, the mailman dropped most the mail he held.

George stared down at the pile on the ground and his eyes froze on one particular letter. It was that familiar shade of off-white. George reached down, picked it up, and reflexively held it up into the sunlight. This time he saw something else besides the standard outline of a rejection slip.

George exulted. There was not only a letter, but a wholly unfamiliar green outline inside the envelope. There was a check inside.

"**CHRIST ALMIGHTY SON OF A BITCH!**" George shouted. "A check from the fucking *Atlantic Monthly!*" George didn't hear what the mailman said to him. He was off and running, his arms outstretched. "I made it! I fucking made it!" Halfway through the trailer park George stopped dead in his tracks. He walked in a circle all around, nodding cockily and smiling. "I'm there," he said. "I'm there." He took off running again, waving the envelope like a crazy person.

The old lady who lived across from George sat on her wooden porch reading the newspaper. George alarmed her when he ran up to her, told her he was famous now and gave her a big kiss. Then he was off again, ranting all the way up the large mound of dirt at the other end of the trailer park. The mound had been put there by the builders of the trailer park years ago. It was now covered with grass and weeds except for a bike trail that went to the top of it. George ran up the trail.

Atop the mound George exulted once more. "**MY APOGEE!**" He was out of breath. He sat down hard upon the mound. At the bottom of the other side of the mound two annoyed kids on bicycles stared up at him. They rode bicycles with banana seats and hi-rise handlebars.

George closed his eyes and ran the envelope across his nose. It smelled like nothing. He cautiously turned the letter over and traced his fingers over the embossed return address of *The Atlantic Monthly*. A long-anticipated feeling rose in George. In his hands at this very moment was precisely what he had dreamed of for so long. In his hands at this very moment was a culmination of years of sweat and pain and angst (five years, in fact. George had wanted to be a science-fiction writer before that).

As he basked in the glory of his success there atop the mound, George didn't see the mailman walking towards him waving a postcard. George instead tore open the envelope finally and looked first at the check. $250.00. "Water heater," he said. Then, "Well, first Betsy, I guess." His voice was resigned now; almost quiet even.

Then George began to read the acceptance letter. He proudly scanned it first, picking out the words *pleased, impressed* and *stylized*.

Then his mouth fell away from his face. The poem they had accepted of his was called "The Death Dance of Father." George couldn't recall ever writing this poem. He thought he had sent them "Dancers from Another Planet." His eyes finally went to whom the letter was addressed to. Janet Kittell, Lot 15, Wilson Trailer Park. "No," George said.

He looked up at the sky. There couldn't be another goddamn poet in the whole goddamn county, let alone one in the same fucking trailer park in southern Illinois. The mailman was at the bottom of the mound now waving the postcard.

"You got something from *Grass Clippings and Whole Earth Words*, George." The mailman smiled. "Sounds like a pretty wild press, my man. You're famous." The mailman looked at the postcard. "And you get two free copies, to boot. Ain't that something? Wow."

George, his bowels falling out his ankles, could only smile.

REVELATION EARTH

Valarie gave the two girls from the rest park a ride. One sat in front and the other sat between Jacob and Dorina in the back. Dorina had to sit by the window. She didn't want to miss the Arch.

"We're going to Colorado," the girl in front said. Her name was Connie. "To a place called Revelation Earth or...Birth."

"Something like that," the one in the backseat said. Her name was Becky. She smiled and eyed Jacob but he didn't notice. He was staring out the window and still burning up inside from what he had said to Betsy.

"Revelation Earth," Connie in front said. "No, maybe it was Birth."

"Birth!" the girl in back said. "I'm sure because it's a place for girls who are going to have babies. A commune." The girl in the back opened up the leather pouch she carried and removed a compact. She tapped a pimple on her chin, as she looked at herself in the tiny mirror. "Connie's going to have a baby." Betsy perked up.

Connie shrugged. "I'm three months." She pushed the cigarette lighter in. When it popped out her and Valarie both lit cigarettes. "I found out about the place from my sister. She lives in Denver."

"It sounds cool," The girl in back said, snapping the compact shut. "They have gardens and animals and musicians and artists."

"All you have to be to get in is pregnant," Connie said. Dorina, drawing stick people in the dust of the car window, asked how long it was before she could see the Arch.

Valarie asked about the father.

Connie shrugged. "I didn't tell him." Valarie looked at the girl in the backseat in the rearview mirror, asked her how she was going to get in.

"I plan to be pregnant before I get there," the girl said with a smile. "I know this guy in Kansas City."

Valarie said they better be careful about this place and then

Connie took out a flyer. She unfolded it and read, "Revelation Birth. Billingsly, Colorado. Funded by the Scarlet Women of the New World." Connie turned the flyer over. "It even says you can get your diploma and take college classes if you want to. It gets money from colleges and stuff." Betsy took a keen interest in the flyer. She asked if she could see it.

A big semi-truck roared by and this scared Dorina. She huddled into the lap of the girl.

Jacob, still wrapped up in his own embarrassment, continued to stare out at the passing telephone poles and underpasses.

BRAKE LININGS

The loud rap at the door startled Janet. She sat on the floor next to the sofa beneath her front window. She held a three-quarter empty bottle of red wine. She sat in a ball with her knees pulled up.

"It's open!" She said as loudly as she could muster. She heard the knob go back and forth, then back and forth again. "No, it's not." Janet took another swig of the wine. "The key's under the mat."

Outside the window at the door George rolled his eyes and thought bitterly, "*Atlantic Monthly* poet puts her key under the mat. Creative little thing, isn't she?" He unlocked the door and walked in.

All George could see upon entering was mostly darkness. All the curtains had been pulled and the television was off. He didn't know at first where the voice was coming from. Then his eyes focused and he saw her sitting on the floor. He asked her if she was okay. Janet, shaking and looking weak, held out an unlit cigarette. George found his lighter and bent over to light the cigarette for her. She looked like hell in the flash of the lighter. Her eyes were puffy and her face was incredibly pale. But her legs poking out of her shorts still looked great, George noted.

"I have some good news for you," George said. He sat on the edge of the sofa. "You got a check from the *Atlantic Monthly*."

Janet didn't even blink. She was staring up at a picture of her mother and father on the far wall. It was too dark to see them but she stared at the picture anyway. She asked George if he got along with his parents. George gave the question some thought.

"Oh, I don't know. Okay, I guess. Better now that they live in Arizona. They kind of think I'm some sort of an aberration. My brother works for the railroad and my sisters have nice middle-class families. I read and write poetry and can't find a decent job. My dad's a retired mechanic." George wrung his hands together and continued to talk. "I thought about suicide when I was fifteen." George puffed hard on his cigarette. "I told my Dad this." George paused. "He couldn't think of a damn thing to say to me." George chuckled. "He told me to go change the brake linings on our Buick."

Even though it hurt, Janet smiled. She passed the wine bottle to George. He took a big drink, handed it back to her. He asked her about her parents.

"They're dead," she said. They sat silently for a moment. Then Janet continued. "My father was a history professor. If I would have went to him about suicide he would have handed me Camus' *The Stranger* and told me to read about what *real* suffering was." George laughed this time.

Janet tapped ashes onto the threadbare carpet. "I got the last word in, though."

George looked at Janet and expected her to add something. She didn't. "How's that?" He asked.

"I killed him," Janet said.

George was taken aback. He didn't know what to say. He shrugged, took the bottle back from Janet. "I'll drink to that," he said, and immediately regretted saying it.

THE ARCH

Valarie told Dorina not to hang out the window but Dorina couldn't help it. She pointed and shrieked. The Arch loomed over the mighty Mississippi River like a gargantuan metal rainbow.

Dorina kept saying over and over again that she wanted to go up in it and everyone else, as they peered at the Arch, said something or other to the effect that they had no desire to go up in it. The Arch stretched high above the other buildings in downtown St. Louis.

Jacob stared at the river. He was awed by the size of the Mississippi. It was surely twice the size of the Wabash. Maybe three times as wide. As they went over the bridge Jacob stared at a riverboat moored to the Missouri side of the river. Down from the riverboat huge barges piled high with coal floated in the middle of the river. A tugboat, only a fraction of the size of the barges, pushed the barges from behind. Finally, the baseball stadium came into view. It looked like a great big flying saucer. That and the Arch and the other tall buildings made St. Louis look, through Jacob's eyes, like some futuristic city out of a DC comic book. He forgot his embarrassment for a moment and just soaked in the wonderment of the city of St. Louis. Dorina couldn't contain herself. The city of St. Louis and the mighty Mississippi was just too much for her. She had her head stuck out of the car window and was laughing and singing.

Then suddenly Dorina stopped laughing and singing. They were almost across the river and into Missouri when her eye fell upon a beat-up pickup truck that had three children in the back. They stared back at Dorina. Dorina eased herself back into the car but her eye remained glued to the children in the back of the pickup truck. Finally it roared on by. Dorina grew strangely quiet.

It was the very first time in her life that Dorina had ever seen real black people. She rubbed her hand over her arm and stared down at that arm that was exactly the same color as the inside of a Milky Way candy bar. Her eye went back to the Arch again but this time without the same excitement. Dorina stopped looking at the buildings entirely now. She wasn't even impressed by the stadium.

For some reason Dorina, quiet now, stuck her head back out the window and kept looking for more black people.

SHAKESPEARE

George convinced Janet that they needed a little music at least. The record-player sat under the television on the bottom of the metal stand. He rummaged through the small stack of albums and all he could find were Beatles records mostly. George hated the Beatles. Then he came across the Who. "Wow," he said, taking the record from its sleeve. He decided to keep the volume down, though. Her voice not more than a whisper, Janet told George where he could find another bottle of wine. George went and got it. He stretched out on the floor beside her. His head began to bob to the beat of *The Magic Bus*.

"I think your poem's great," he said. Janet could barely muster a smile. She eased one bare foot out and touched his shoulder.

"My father didn't even know I wrote poetry."

"That's sad." George took a sip of wine. "But not that sad. Hell, most people think poetry sucks anyway. You write great, though." Staring up her outstretched leg, George caught the slightest hint of pink silk panties peeking out of her cut-offs. The woman had class.

"No one knows I write poetry, really."

"I do," George said. He took a big drink of the wine this time. "Hell, everybody I know knows I write poetry." He shrugged. "I tell them all the time."

This made Janet laugh and she had a sweet laugh, like a hummingbird sneezing. George ran his hand along her calf. It was as smooth and soft as a baby's bottom.

"Oh, my," he said. Then, "The expense of spirit in the waste of shame—"

"Is lust in action," Janet said, completing the sonnet. George tried to remember more of it but he couldn't.

"It's not really about sex, you know," Janet said.

George thought about it, then said, "The opening line's enough for me." Janet laughed again as she pulled her leg back and sat up straighter.

"So how long have you been a poet?" she asked.

"I'm not a poet really. I try to be but I don't get it right much. I'm like a lot of people in America today, in love with the notion of being a poet."

"Oh, don't say that. There's worse things to be in love with."

"War," George said. Janet agreed. Then she asked George what kind of poetry he wrote. He bolted upright, dug deep into his back pocket.

"I always carry my three best poems with me." The poems were crumpled up and folded tightly together. George very carefully unfolded them. This simply delighted Janet. When he got them unfolded he smoothed them out on the carpet, then shrugged.

"Um–" he put his palm up. "You want me to read them to you or, like–do you want to just read them?"

Janet felt like weeping.

"Go ahead," she said.

A WOMAN'S RIGHT

Dorina did not move from the window of the building for a solid hour. They were on the twelfth story of an old building in downtown St. Louis. Jacob and her were in the hallway. The place smelled funny. There was a matching vinyl couch and chair at the end of the hallway that had metal and wood arms and yellow cushions that had been smashed flat with age. Jacob occasionally flipped the metal lid back and forth on an upright ashtray next to the chair he sat in. The noise rang hollow in the hallway. The ashtray was stuffed with cigarette butts and candy wrappers. He was worried about Betsy.

The two girls they had picked up left as soon as Valarie parked the car. They were on their way to Colorado.

Dorina sat with her knees on the hardwood floor and her elbows resting in the windowsill. The city enthralled her. Her eye scanned everything, every hint of movement she locked onto. Occasionally she told Jacob to come look but he was no longer interested in the city. From Betsy and Valarie's conversation he had figured out what Betsy was having done and it made him sick and nervous.

An elderly lady had greeted them at room 1204 and she hadn't been friendly at all. She didn't like Jacob and Dorina being there and had practically yelled at them to stay in the hallway and be quiet.

A helicopter swooped over the city and Dorina let out a yell and ran to Jacob. She had never seen a helicopter before. She slowly went back to the window and watched the helicopter fly high above the Arch, which peeked up over one of the old buildings across the street. Dorina watched a black lady hang a white sheet over the metal staircase outside her apartment. Two small black children hung out the window and watched their mommy. There were black people all over the place. Dorina couldn't believe it. Before today she hadn't been certain that black people ever really existed. She finally realized for certain that her Daddy existed. That he was coming home and that he was truly as black as coal. All the black people she saw were as black as coal.

Dorina was startled by the squeal of brakes and then horns honking. Two black boys about her age had dashed across the street in front of a large grain truck. The white driver stuck his head out the driver's window and yelled and shook his fist at the boys. Both boys stuck their middle fingers up at the driver, then dashed down an alley. Dorina covered her smile with her hand.

"My Daddy's coming home," she said in almost a whisper as she rocked her elbows on the windowsill and tapped her toes against the wall.

Jacob, as he nervously flipped through a beat-up *National Geographic*, kept one eye on the door Betsy had gone through an hour ago. The door opened shortly.

The sun was setting behind them as Valarie drove them all home. Jacob sat in the front seat and Dorina and Betsy were in the back. Betsy was sleeping with her head on a pillow in Dorina's lap.

Dorina rubbed Betsy's head and sang quietly along with the radio. The setting sun and the empty sky cast a red tint upon the corn and bean fields they passed.

"Do you know what Betsy did?" Valarie asked Jacob.

Jacob stopped staring out the window, turned to look at Valarie. "I think so," he said.

Valarie turned the radio down. "She's awful young," she said. Then after a long pause, "But it's a woman's right."

Jacob looked back out the window. They passed a combine as it devoured several rows of corn at a time. Speaking low so as not to wake Betsy, Dorina said she bet her Daddy was at home at this very second. Valarie smiled and said she hoped so.

FIREFLIES

It was dark out when they all got back from St. Louis but Dorina had never been afraid of the dark. Dorina was chasing fireflies. They were thick tonight. Their little yellow flashes were everywhere. Dorina caught one, let it crawl over her hand and then she shook it off. She stood on the concrete in front of the fire station. She twirled around and did a dance. She didn't want to go inside yet. St. Louis had left her too excited to think. She decided that when she grew up she wanted to move there. It wouldn't be that far from her grandfather and Jacob. She could visit all the time and they could visit her. She bet Jacob would live there, too.

She caught a firefly with one hand and then another firefly with her other hand. She held her hands together and let both little flashing bugs fly away. One time Jacob and her put grass inside a glass jar and caught a whole jar full of fireflies but they all died and Dorina didn't want to do that again. Dorina froze. Her mother was calling out her name. She ran towards home.

Dorina sang quietly and waved at fireflies as she half-ran and half-skipped towards the house. Her mother was on the front porch. She thought she could see Jacob sitting in the dark on his front porch too, but she wasn't sure. She yelled out his name but he wasn't there. Then she stopped running and stared.

Ambling out on the porch was a man a full head taller than her mother. Dorina stopped. In the dull yellow porch light Dorina could not see the man's face but she knew this man was not any man that she had seen on her mother's porch before. She watched the man drape his arm around her mother's shoulder and then her mother wrap her arm around his waist. Dorina watched them exchange a kiss on the lips.

Dorina closed her eye and prayed and said thanks to God.

Her Daddy was home. Taking a deep breath and shivering slightly, Dorina, her head held high, walked slowly towards the porch.

TOMATOES

Jacob stared out his bedroom window at the silhouette of a cat stretched taunt on a trashcan. He lay in the darkness of his bedroom too hot to sleep. His mind buzzed with fuzzy, disjointed thoughts. His bed was against the wall almost level with the open window. He rested his chin on his hard feather pillow. He wanted very badly to be with Betsy, to have her curled around him like she had been that one morning by accident. She had been so tired when they came home from St. Louis. And weak. He helped Betsy into the nurse's trailer and she was as limp as damp toast. Jacob momentarily clamped his eyes shut. He prayed to God that Betsy would be okay and return to her old self again as soon as possible.

Jacob stared out the window at the night-blackened beefsteak tomatoes ripe and bending the vines in the backyard garden almost to the ground. He would have to pick all the ripe ones tomorrow. It was one of his jobs.

Jacob, as he lay there terribly sad for Betsy, wasn't quite sure whether or not he believed in God. God should have been nicer to Betsy. God should have been nicer to Dorina. If there was anything that bugged Jacob more about the God he had been taught to love out of fear, it was God's random impoliteness.

The cat pounced finally upon a mouse. It tossed the mouse around in its mouth, then let it drop. The back was broken on the mouse and all it could do was wiggle around upon the broken concrete leading to the trashcan. From where Jacob lay, the mouse looked no bigger than a bug. The cat watched the mouse wiggle awhile, then batted it around a few times, snatched it back up in its jaws, and marched off arrogantly into the darkness. Jacob watched the whole procedure with a detached fascination.

His thoughts were still intense and wrapped completely around Betsy. She had to be all right. Jacob had to help make her all right as best he could and let her know somehow how he felt about her. Or maybe he should never say another word to her ever again. He slumped back upon the bed, sweating and uncomfortable, his erection in his underpants more painful now than pleasurable.

Jacob stared awhile at the ceiling and let his thoughts melt into the various shades of blackness until finally he was sleeping.

THE BEST DAYS

The fish fry was going strong now. A bearded young man in overalls and cowboy boots played a guitar. Leonard eased the first fiddler catfish into the metal vat of molten lard. He took a step back from the fryer. It looked like a beautiful day for a fish fry.

Out on the bluff overlooking the Wabash sat the General. He stared into and through the river as he sipped corn liquor.

A girl from the shack now stood beside Leonard. She stared into the bubbling brown grease. Leonard rolled a cigarette and lit up.

"Will I like catfish?"

Leonard blew smoke, said, "There ain't a person on this planet won't like catfish. At least the way I fry it."

The girl wrinkled up her nose. "My mother used to fix salmon patties every Friday." She pulled a purple and metal smoking pipe from her front jeans pocket. She ran her pinkie inside it to clean it out. "I used to drop acid right before dinnertime." She looked at Leonard. "I tried to eat the crystal one night."

Leonard reached over and nudged the catfish around in the hot grease with a thick stick. "Probably taste better than that damn salmon patty. I was in the hospital one time and had one. It had little round bones in it. Nurse said you could eat those bones. My ass. I ain't eatin' no fish bones."

The girl smiled. "Do you believe in love?" She asked.

His eyes froze for a moment upon the girl. *Here we go again*, Leonard thought, as he eased some more catfish into the fryer. He asked the girl if she would go get him that big platter over there on the table. That was where the catfish were dipped in egg and then lightly rolled in cornmeal before they went into the fryer. The girl turned around and marched after the platter.

There had been a brief shower earlier but now it had cleared up. The rain left a cool breeze behind and this offset the late August heat nicely. Leonard looked up at the sky and thought that these were the best days of the year. He nudged the catfish around in the fryer. They were beginning to float to the top and this meant they were about done. Leonard was cooking the bigger pieces first as they would stay hot longer. Then the tastier, smaller pieces would go in. He caught a whiff of the potatoes and onions that were frying in a big cast-iron skillet over the fire.

The kids from the shack had fallen in love with washer pitching. One of them put a washer on top of her head and tried to balance it there. Another sat on his knees and very carefully wiped away the leaves and dirt around the lip of the coffee can buried in the ground.

On the bluff the General once again, as he tapped on the lid of the corn liquor, squinted his eyes and pointed the shotgun at the Game Warden. When he pulled the trigger this time the General felt the percussion as pressure in his ears. His eyelids heavy, Malcolm thought he heard someone call out his name. He looked up. It was only the wind and the rush of the Wabash River.

Leonard explained to the girl the art of frying fish. "It floats to the top when it's done and you have to take it out at the right time or it gets tough."

Something caught Leonard's eye. He looked up and there his wife, Nettie, stood. He nearly had a heart attack. By God, he hadn't seen her all summer.

Nettie wore brown plaid polyester pants and a clean, freshly pressed white shirt. One of Leonard's shirts. Her short, curly steel-gray hair was, as it always was, slicked back with Vitalis. Leonard was so tickled to see his wife he couldn't bring himself to say a damn thing.

Nettie almost smiled but she didn't. She asked curtly who was watching the potatoes and did he salt them before he put them on? Leonard didn't say anything. He wasn't expected to. He loved this stout old woman.

The girl watched it all. She watched Nettie, carrying a metal cake pan, storm past Leonard on her way to the potatoes. The girl saw Leonard and what his eyes looked like.

Her question answered, the girl turned and went to join the others in pitching washers.

THE END OF SUMMER

It was the end of summer and a little brown was creeping into the green of the leaves on the trees along the Wabash River. It was the end of summer in the year of our Lord 1969 and if the world was indeed incandescent with all the wrong kinds of excitement, you couldn't tell it by looking at this small Illinois town that took root and aged along the Wabash River. Two grain trucks were backed up at the elevator. Both drivers sat on the hood of their trucks smoking cigarettes and staring across the road and down along the river. An old lady flapped a rug out a window and then paused to stare at the river. Two children threw rocks off a boat dock. Across the river on the Indiana side and through a sparse row of trees, a man on a tractor turned soil up in a field in preparation for planting next Spring. Two turtles sat on a tree branch sticking out over the river, their heads not moving. Several people came out of their houses after listening to the radio and stared and pointed at smoke billowing up in the West. It was the only hint that in the year of our Lord 1969 that America was fucked up. It was the burning of the Old Main Building on the campus of the college that was near to this small town. Students were rioting and police were pounding heads and everyone was raging as the oldest building on the campus was in flames. History would say that the building had been set on fire by a janitor smoking in a closet, but as the flames ravaged the building and students and establishment alike finally gathered together to put the flames out, everyone was convinced that the fire raged as hyperbole to the times.

Times that caused people to lose respect for each other and America's established way of doing things. Times that pleasantly inverted everyone's perspective. Times that made people say Hell, No! To War and Hallelujah! To rebellion. Times that made people ignore the Future and instead concentrate on the indignations of the Now. It was a wonderful time, really. When people believed in *something*, regardless of how volatile and crazy that belief might be.

But it was just a phase, however. A phase that didn't affect this small town much, or any small town for that matter. The following year brown would replace green in the trees and the grain trucks would still back up at the elevator and the old lady would shake the dust out of her rugs and pause once again to stare at the unspoken magic of the Wabash River. And life would go on.

But somewhere else there was a party going on. Over thirty people gathered at Leonard Down's camp along the Wabash River. Some pitched washers and others walked on the Ferryboat and some even fished. But most just stood around talking and eating catfish. It was the highlight of Leonard's life, this summer-ending fish fry. He was so drunk that someone else had to fry the catfish, but that didn't matter. A lot of people were getting drunk. Many of them were dancing as Doc Garrelts played "In the Mood" on a pearly white Steinway piano on the back of a flatbed truck. Leonard was laughing and staggering around and trying to get his wife, Nettie, to dance. He reminded her that he could still do the Charleston. He stumbled trying to show her. She went back to cutting up more potatoes.

George and Valarie sat down by the river. They were talking about love and all its possibilities. They both wringed their hands as they talked. George told her he was the one who got Betsy pregnant. Valarie said she knew. George froze. She did? Yes, she did.

"Women talk more than men, George," Valarie said.

And? George asked, mentally preparing for some heavy-duty repercussions. Valarie didn't look at him.

"You can swallow something horrible and it can either kill you or you can somehow pass it and move on." After Valarie said this George started talking nervously. He said it was an accident. He wouldn't do that kind of thing again. He tried to say everything and anything that would rectify the situation.

"I was drunk, I mean come on. Men are as faithful as their opportunities in that state."

Valarie had been doing all right with his confession up to that point. George tried to rectify this also. He didn't do very good. He gave up. He gave out a long exasperated sigh.

"I fucking love you though, Val. More than... more than.... Poetry, for Christ's sake."

Valarie looked at him out of the corners of her eyes. She had never heard his voice so weak, so sweet. Maybe she loved him too. She crossed her legs, stared out across the river.

"I don't know about marriage though, George." Valarie tossed a cigarette butt into the water. "I've been burnt once. You're younger than me. I'm past child-bearing years–"

"No, you're not," George said. He shrugged. "So what if you have a Mongoloid? They're happy kids." Valarie shut her eyes. Valarie didn't want to laugh, but she did anyway.

Down aways from them but not quite out of hearing distance Jacob sat watching his rod and reel. He was using night crawlers for bait. He wasn't having much luck, though. He wanted to crawl into a hole and die. Betsy was going to Chicago. She would not return. Dorina's father had come to take her away also. Twelve was a horrible age. He reeled in his line and adjusted the night crawler on the hook and tried tossing it more upstream. Then the music stopped. Everyone stopped talking. Somehow, Jacob knew why. He bolted up the riverbank.

At the top of the riverbank Jacob froze like all the other people at the fish fry and stared at the man in the middle of the road.

Dorina's father was a tall, thin black man with hair cropped short. He wore a brown suit with a thin brown tie and a perfectly pressed white shirt. His shoes were brown and white wing tips. Both Dorina and her father stood in the middle of the dirt road right beside Leonard's camp. Everyone had stopped doing whatever they were doing. Dorina stood beside her father clutching his hand and holding her chin as high as she could. She wore her best yellow dress and shiny black patent leather shoes. New shoes her father had bought her. The only one at the party moving was Leonard and that was because he was too drunk to stand still. Finally, he staggered towards Dorina and her father.

White Dwight!
I turn my collar up and stare at a black ribbon of barbed-wire bent atop a tall metal fence. Dorina is inside. Fifteen years later and traveled all this way and now standing outside the Dwight Correctional Institution for Women as something between rain and snow drops out of the sky. A cold midwestern wind slices through everything.

There is a scary emptiness inside me as I watch someone in a uniform pace lazily in a tower. Dorina spent time in this place. But Dorina is alive and where there's life there's hope, perhaps. I stare up at the gray sky.

CHARLES B. BROWN

Slowly extending his trembling wrinkled tar-stained hand, his face a mix of revulsion, sadness, and maybe even a little simple awe, Dorina's grandfather said to her father, "Welcome to the Wabash, young man." Then, "Leonard Lee Downs."

Dorina's father took her grandfather's hand, shook it strongly. He was surprised at how frail it felt. "Charles B. Brown," he said. "I've heard a lot about you on the way here, Mr. Downs."

Doc Garrelts began to play the piano again, some old lazy blues number this time and this unfroze everyone. They started the party again. Washers started flying and talk continued.

Leonard led Charles over to a chair and offered him a beer, which he took. They sat down. Dorina was ecstatic. She ran and leaped on Jacob's back and told him her daddy was home and he had to meet him.

"Get off!" He said, embarrassed. He didn't want to meet her daddy. Jacob hated to admit it, but Dorina's daddy meant she would be leaving him, too. The worst summer of his entire life continued on in full-force. Still unable to contain her excitement, Dorina hugged Jacob tightly and kissed the back of his head. Totally embarrassed and afraid someone saw her do this, Jacob pushed her off.

She stumbled laughing and started to jump on him again but then she stopped.

"My baby brother," Dorina said.

NOWHERE NEAR THE SEA OF CORTEZ

Jacob had put her blue bundle right under Leonard's shack. Then he had forgotten about it. Dorina went and got it. She would do what she had planned to do–bury her dead baby brother in the Wabash River.

Bundle in hand, Dorina walked by where her father and grandfather sat. She stopped. They were talking and her grandfather was getting loud. Someone had gotten her father a plate of fish, which he devoured steadily; pausing only to laugh and nod at what Leonard was talking about. Her daddy shoveled in potatoes and cole slaw, bit into a piece of fried catfish and laughed as Leonard talked about fishing on the Wabash. Leonard waved his arms and ashes fell from his cigarette.

"Now I'll tell you this, young man," Leonard pointed a finger at Dorina's father. "They say there ain't never been a catfish caught out of that river weigh over sixty pound. By God, they're wrong." Dorina went and sat on an overturned metal milk crate beside her grandfather. She put the blue bundle in her lap. She had heard this story so many times. She knew every version her grandfather told by heart. She looked at her father, and then at her grandfather. Dorina could only beam. She couldn't believe how they were getting along. Her daddy laughed at the things her grandfather said and she swore it sounded just like her laugh.

Jacob felt like dying during it all, as he stood off to the side calling out Dorina's name. He was almost in tears. There was a dead baby wrapped in that blue blanket. He wanted to knock himself silly for not taking care of it before now.

"I caught it on a fifty pound test trotline." Leonard continued. "That night about three in the morning I went out and put fresh crawdads on every hook." He paused to cough and roll another cigarette. He opened another beer.

"I like to fish," Charles B. Brown nodded, wiped cole slaw off his bottom lip. "When I was stationed in San Diego. We'd go down to the Sea of Cortez."

"I'll tell you something else," Leonard said. "Back in '26 I watched my own daddy pull a forty-eight pounder out of a net." Leonard's speech was slowing and his eyes drooped. Dorina knew what this meant. She began to worry. "That sumbitch was a big fish but I swear on that little girl's life there I caught a flathead cat every bit twice the size of that one my own daddy caught." Dorina looked at her grandfather. She had seen that look in his eyes before. She looked at her father. He stared at his food. She wanted her father to listen more. It upset her grandfather when people didn't listen to his stories. Listen!

Charles picked a tiny catfish bone out of his mouth, flicked it on the ground. "I ain't done much river fishing. We lived in the city. Now down there in California—"

"I'll tell you something else—" Leonard's voice boomed. Dorina stared anxiously down at the ground and tapped her feet hard in the clay dirt, her teeth gritted and her face in turmoil. "I fought that damn fish for half a day." Leonard held out his palms. "You could see bone where I'd had hold of that trotline fightin' that damn fish." Leonard knocked over the beer at his feet, drew hard on his cigarette, reached down and fumbled with the overturned beer. "I bled like a stuck hog."

Nettie walked up with another plate of fried fish. Dorina's father politely told the old woman thank you but that he was full and couldn't eat another bite. "It was mighty good," he added with a broad and warm smile.

Still staring down at the dirt and fidgeting, Dorina said under her breath to her father, "Listen!" She wanted everything to go right. She didn't want her grandfather getting upset and mad at her daddy. Jacob, at the moment, had his eyes closed and his forehead resting against the bark of a tree.

Leonard mumbled something, got his drunken thoughts back together. He stared intently at the black man. "There ain't never been a fish caught any bigger than the one I caught that day."

Charles B. Brown paused to stare at this old drunken white man. Then he let out an uncontrollably loud and booming laugh of his own. His laugh continued. Then he caught himself. He wiped his hands on a paper towel and emptied his beer. "Maybe not around here, Mr. Downs. But this ain't nowhere near the sea of Cortez."

Leonard's eyes turned a different color.

"They have ocean catfish three times that size. I seen one hauled in that weighed in at over three hundred pounds. One day we stood on a dock and watched them haul in a twelve hundred pound ocean perch." He nodded. "That's what they weighed it in at. I swear it. I watched them." Dorina's daddy laughed again. He looked at his daughter. "I get back from my next tour of 'Nam, Dory, we'll go there."

Dorina was in tears now, her face frozen towards the ground, and her blue bundle tight against her chest. She mumbled something. She didn't want to look at her grandfather. She didn't want to look at her father either.

Finally Dorina lifted her heavy head upwards.

Leonard had strained to swivel his head so hard that veins popped out on his neck like snakes. He put his burnt-orange and bloodshot eyes right up to Dorina's one good eye. His look frightened Dorina. She hadn't seen this look on her grandfather's face before. And for the first time in her life she could smell his foul breath.

Slowly, and with a malicious kind of deliberateness, Leonard spoke. "Nigger talk," he said.

Dorina and I swam naked one final time beneath a small wooden bridge crossing a creek that eventually winds into the Wabash River. We had played under it many times in our childhood. It was 1975.

This time I lift her up onto a slanting concrete slab beneath that bridge as she laughs and runs her hands through my hair. One palm on cool concrete and another gently cupping a warm lean buttock, I kiss her shoulder, as she keeps laughing, guides me inside. We copulate so freely there under that bridge in the Bottoms, celebrating perhaps a return to puberty, the death of our grandfather, the end of the Vietnam era.

We do it twice actually. Three times, I think. We try a fourth time upon hard-packed clay dirt down by the water but we are both too sore. Naked we ease our feet into the clear, slow moving water, lay back.

Under that bridge back in 1975 after our Grandfather's funeral we put our clothes back on and get back into the car and drive fast through the Bottoms along the Wabash River. The water never looked so blue and vital. The windows are rolled down and dust flies up thick everywhere but we don't care. Dorina rests her head in my lap and her brown feet stick out the window. She still has a bite of a Milky Way candy bar left. She offers it to me. I don't want it. I pull the car up beside a bluff overlooking the Wabash. The wind blows hard but it is hot and sunny. Singing, Dorina gets on top of the hood of the car. I climb up beside her and she laces her arm through mine and hugs me tight as we stare down into the river. There was never a better moment in our lives.

That was the last I would see of Dorina for a long time.

Fifteen years later she walks towards me in a prison. Her hair is cut short and her eyes look a little older but she is as beautiful as she ever was. She smiles and it is the same smile I remember. Without a word we embrace.

THE BURIAL

It wasn't an intentional reaction. Dorina had not planned to do what she did. But when Leonard Downs said what he said, Dorina lost control. She grabbed the blue bundle and without thinking, swung it full-force into the face of her grandfather. Startled, he went flying backwards. The bundle went with him.

Then everyone quickly gathered around and stared horrified and amazed at the old man on his back, and the partly powdered and partly mushy remains of a dead baby wrapped in a blue blanket plastered across his face. Not a single one could think to say a word.

Dorina stood like an upright rag doll, her solitary eye wide and unflinching. Everyone, at first, looked at the gruesome sight on the ground, watched Leonard gasp for breath, then their eyes all went to Dorina.

Without thinking, Dorina got down on her knees and carefully put the remains back into the blanket and wrapped as much of it as she could up tightly. Dorina wiped her hands on her new dress and, holding the blue bundle, she got to her feet. She stared only at Jacob. Leonard stayed on the ground on his back; his eyes wide and mouth gaped open as he gasped for breath. He looked like a fish out of water. Jacob stared down at his grandfather, and for the first time in his life, hated him.

Dorina, very close to crying but absolutely refusing to, said to Jacob that she wanted to bury her dead baby brother in the water like she saw on television. With her free hand she straightened out the wrinkles in her dress.

Jacob glared angrily at everyone as Dorina spoke. Not a single one of them better be laughing at her. "That's what we're gonna do then," Jacob said. Still glaring at everyone, he put his arm around Dorina. They started towards the river.

Everyone got out of their way. All the people at Leonard's party gathered around and watched these two children and the remains of a dead baby go down the riverbank and climb into the General's boat. No one said a word as Jacob tried once, then twice to jerk the engine to life. Not a word was uttered as the boat sputtered, coughed, and finally came to life. Jacob let the boat drift away from the bank and then turned the handle on the motor. The boat headed upriver.

Everybody stood and watched as the two children and the dead baby vanished shortly around a bend in the Wabash River.

It was a solemn thing to bury her dead baby brother. I had to say a few words about it going to Heaven and Dorina cried and cried but then when we both tied the anchor around the little body and eased first the blue bundle and then the anchor into the water we both felt a strange kind of release. We hugged each other a little while.

Then I pull-started the engine. It fired right off this time. Full throttle, I sent the boat flying through the middle of the Wabash River.

The front end of the boat rose, and Dorina, sitting in front, clutched the metal seat and looked back at me, her hair flying crazy in the wind, her free hand dangling over the side to feel the warm white foam flying up at her. Dorina let out a thrilled laugh. I smiled and then let out a laugh of my own and we both sat back and enjoyed the ride.

DONUTS AT 9:35

It was chilly this morning so Leonard had a pretty good fire going. He stoked it and then sat down and rubbed his hands together. Malcolm showed up with a white box full of donuts. He sat down beside Leonard. He opened the box of donuts.

"Damn, it was some kind of summer, wasn't it, Leonard."

"Hell it was," Leonard said. He washed his first bite of donut down with a beer.

Malcolm shook his head. "Pretty awful thing that dead baby and how you pissed little Dory off and all."

Leonard sniffed loudly, glanced at Malcolm. "What's so goddamn funny about it all?"

"Well, goddamn it, Leonard. It ain't particularly funny or anything but you know what Nettie always says-it's always better to laugh about it then it is to cry."

Malcolm was trying not to smile. Leonard didn't think it was a damn bit funny. But the donuts were good. He told Malcolm they were the best damn donuts he ever had. Malcolm said there was a new donut shop in town.

"Leonard, what time is it?"

Leonard looked at his watch. "9:35."

"What say we have donuts at 9:35 every morning until one of us drops dead."

Leonard looked at Malcolm. He was nodding and staring into the fire.

"Well, all right, Malcolm," Leonard said, as he was thinking Malcolm was getting as crazy as he was anymore.

"Deal then," Malcolm said. "Donuts at 9:35."

Leonard shrugged and pulled out his smoke sack. Donuts at 9:35.

CORRALES COMMUNITY LIBRARY

COR51555

HAR Harris, Jim.
     Nowhere near the Se
     of Cortez /